*To Dav
with me
your support and
endorsement.
Tony*

Childhood, Boyhood, Youth

Childhood, Boyhood, Youth

Tony Warner

The Book Guild Ltd

First published in Great Britain in 2023 by
The Book Guild Ltd
Unit E2 Airfield Business Park,
Harrison Road, Market Harborough,
Leicestershire. LE16 7UL
Tel: 0116 2792299
www.bookguild.co.uk
Email: info@bookguild.co.uk
Twitter: @bookguild

Copyright © 2023 Tony Warner

The right of Tony Warner to be identified as the author of this work has been asserted by them in accordance with the Copyright, Design and Patents Act 1988.

All rights reserved. No part of this publication may be reproduced, transmitted, or stored in a retrieval system, in any form or by any means, without permission in writing from the publisher, nor be otherwise circulated in any form of binding or cover other than that in which it is published and without a similar condition being imposed on the subsequent purchaser.

This work is entirely fictitious and bears no resemblance to any persons living or dead.

Typeset in 11pt Minion Pro

Printed on FSC accredited paper
Printed and bound in Great Britain by 4edge Limited

ISBN 978 1915853 219

British Library Cataloguing in Publication Data.
A catalogue record for this book is available from the British Library.

For Laura Kirman

"Happy, happy, never-returning time of childhood! How can we help loving and dwelling upon its recollections? They cheer and elevate the soul, and become to one a source of higher joys."
(Leo Tolstoy)

Childhood

Wednesday

She must be the woman from the Social. No-one round here dresses like this. Matching knitted skirt and top. The sort with bobbles in it. Mam will know what it's called. Pale blue, show the dirt in a minute. Bet she doesn't bother using the bus, scuffing her bum on the same seats as the likes of us. Runs around in a motor. Proper leather shoes, all shone up. 'Sensible' shoes, not Saturday-night shoes with matchstick heels or the waterproofs the lasses from the factory wear. And a hat. Not a scarf like Mam puts on when she's had her hair washed and waved but a funny pill-box thing. In matching blue, of course.

I suppose she's quite old, nearly thirty probably. A light pink lipstick, so soft it's only because I'm looking close I can see it at all. Nothing on her eyes, which are dark brown with no wrinkles round them. Mam's mascara gets clogged in hers when she doesn't take it off properly. Black hair wrapped round her head like a helmet. Not sparing on the hairspray, this one.

She smiles. Obediently, I smile back.

'Is your mother or father in?' she asks.

'Mam's here, miss. I'll just get her for you.' She hesitates, probably expecting I'd let her straight in. Mam wouldn't like that. Only police get away with pushing their way in. Doorstep for everybody else.

Childhood, Boyhood, Youth

Dad is out, down the bookies or off drinking with his mates. Looking for a job, we'll tell the woman from the Social. Always let them know you are trying so they don't stop your dole. Mam is the same. The kitchen is bare, no dirty leftover dishes here. The parlour, too, is ready, cleared of ash trays and teacups. 'Creating a good impression,' Mam calls it. 'Always create a good impression,' she says. 'Keeps the bastards off your back. Don't let them know what you're thinking or what you're doing. Keep your business to yourself; the busybodies will try and get it out of you. What they don't know won't harm them; what they do know can cause you no end of trouble.'

Mam comes downstairs in full rig: dedicated housekeeper dress and slippers, slightly stained pinnie. 'I'm sorry,' she says, 'just cleaning the toilet upstairs. How might I be of assistance?' This in her telephone voice, where she puts on the posh, uses phrases she has heard on the radio, never drops her aitches.

The lady shows a cardboard slip with the Council's insignia at the top, identifying her as Miss Smith or something from the Social Services department. 'May I come in a minute?' she asks.

'If you must,' says Mam. Takes her into the parlour, to my surprise. Even the police get no further than the kitchen. Sits her in the best chair, the one with all the springs intact, plonks me on the sofa, sits herself down next to me. 'How may I help you?' she asks.

At school they say I'm not very clever. Sums and spelling wash over me as I daydream on the back row. But I'm sharp; you just ask Dad or Mam. I know when something's out of the ordinary. Mam is giving this woman the full treatment and not because of her smart blue suit. She's a danger. Mam is protecting us, or herself. She twists her hands around the edge of her pinnie, gazes past the woman's head and out the window. I know what she's thinking: 'Should have opened the curtains, but the windows are so dirty.'

Miss Blue Suit wrinkles her nose. The air is stuffy in here, never clear of the odour of tobacco smoke and dirty socks. Bravely,

Wednesday

she forces out another smile, pushes on in her determined best council official manner. 'I would like to talk to your son, if you don't mind?' she says.

'Only when I'm here with him,' says Mam. She knows the score. Children cannot be questioned by police or officials without the presence of a parent. Well, that's what she says and none of them have ever queried it. This one has been briefed, knows what to expect. Nods her agreement.

'How are you, Daniel?' she begins.

'I'm not Daniel, I'm Danny,' I say. 'Everyone calls me Danny.'

'Fine, Danny. I'm Miss Harris. We haven't met before. I'm your new welfare officer. Do you know what a welfare officer is, Danny?'

I nod. It means another busybody trying to take me away. 'Hello,' I say.

'How are you, Danny? Getting enough to eat, sleeping well? Settling back in with your family?'

'I've been back here over a year, miss. It's wonderful. Far better than the children's home. Dad can be bossy when he's in a bad mood, like when he's spent all day looking for work and not found anything. Our Harry snores and keeps me awake sometimes. If I push him, he stops. Then there are the other kids in the street to play with. We get out and kick a ball about between the flats sometimes. Gerry Pettit, he kicked the ball so hard last week it went right through Mrs Thompson's window. And…'

Yes, I know I said not to let on our business. I'm not talking business; I'm talking wet flannel. None of it takes her where she wants to go. Some excitable, polite kid rattling away, not a care in the world. Why would she want to take such a happy boy away from his loving family?

'Why are you not at school today, Danny?'

'I've not been well,' I say. 'Mam sent the school a note. Something I ate, maybe. Harry had a bit of it as well, though not as bad as me. Did you get it, miss? I had the runs for days.'

'Do you like school, Danny?'

'Not much. But I leave there in September. Then I won't have to wear that horrible school blazer.'

'Yes, I'm sorry about that,' says Mam. 'It's really too small for him but I can't afford another with only a few months to go. Harry can have it once Danny moves up.'

A long silence. Miss Harris is writing on a form attached to a clipboard. While she does so I reflect on my clothes. Mam keeps them clean but they're either two sizes too large ('you will grow into them') or two sizes too small ('Harry can have them when I can afford a replacement'). Harry complains he never has any new clothes, only my old cast-offs. Not that any of our clothes are new, all bought from a second-hand stall on the market. Mam's the only one who has new clothes. 'A business expense,' she says. Great one for business is Mam.

'Do you get many visitors here?' Miss Harris asks.

I know what she's after. Mam continues staring out the window. 'Mrs Thompson came round the other day,' I say. 'Thought it were me what kicked the ball through her window. Told her it were Gerry Pettit. She went on something rotten, claimed Gerry had said it were me. Ask anyone, I said to her, all the lads will tell you.' Anyway, Gerry would never split on me. Wouldn't dare.

She sighs. 'I mean grown-ups, of an evening, or at weekends,' she says.

'Not while we are up,' I say. 'Harry and me, we're in bed by eight at the latest. Never hear a thing.'

Mam shifts a trifle closer, puts a hand on my arm. 'I'm sure Miss Harris doesn't want to hear all the details of your doings, Danny. She wants to make sure you and Harry are comfortable, properly fed. Tell her what you had for breakfast this morning.'

'Toast and strawberry jam!' I say with enthusiasm. The first proper breakfast in three days. 'And milk,' I say. Milk which wasn't on the turn, either. Maybe Mam had known Miss Blue Suit was coming. 'Was I naughty having the jam?' I ask. 'Mam says I should only have dry bread today, settle my stomach.' I jiffle to imply that matters might be stirring once again down below.

'I've got some nice cod in for supper,' Mam breaks in. 'We may have to leave it until tomorrow, if it doesn't go off.'

'I shouldn't worry, Mrs Morley. Some boiled fish is excellent for invalids.'

Normally Mam would give her hell for taking the piss like that. Today she smiles an executioner's smile, takes a firm hold on her pinnie. 'Very kind of you to say so,' she says. 'I trust you are happy as to how you have found us? As you can see, Danny is well fed and well clothed as well as being properly brought up. Not in any physical or moral danger, as you can see. No reason for him and Harry not to stay here where they are loved and looked after. I'd like our Salanne back as well.'

'Returning your daughter doesn't depend upon me, I'm afraid. As long as the police continue their objections our hands are tied, as I'm sure you know. They don't regard this house as a safe environment for a young woman.' Mam sniffs. 'However, I can reassure you there are no obvious grounds for taking the boys into care again. Danny shows no sign of deprivation, apart from being a little small for his age.'

'I've lost a lot of weight while I've had the—'

'That's enough, Daniel.' I know it is time to shut up once Mam starts calling me Daniel. 'Closing the deal', she calls this. You'd think she has been on a college course with all the jargon she uses. Used to sell cars before she married Dad and had us kids. Couldn't go back. No-one buys British cars anymore, all Japanese now.

'As I say, a little small for his age, though bright and attentive enough. The case conference is next week and I will certainly recommend the status quo continues.' She certainly has been to college, foreign words and all. 'Moreover, I don't believe a monthly visit is strictly necessary any longer. Quarterly will be quite sufficient.'

Childhood, Boyhood, Youth

'If you could give me a little notice next time,' says Mam, 'so I can get the house ship-shape for you, not the mess it is this time.' Bollocks. Our house has never been this clean since they brought me and Harry back. One of her mates had dropped her the word, which explains the strawberry jam and the spotless kitchen.

Miss Blue Suit smiles agreement, considerably more relaxed than when she arrived. Offers to shake Mam's hand. Mam refuses, rubs her hands together. 'As I say, I've been cleaning the upstairs toilet. Had a good wash before I came down, but you never know.' Puts on her best downtrodden housewife look, grabs at her pinnie once again.

She shows the woman from the Social to the door. 'A pleasure to meet you,' she says.

'Thank you very much for your time. And thank you too, Danny.' Away she trots, her neat little car parked up the road. Walks round it to check the bodywork. Not completely wet behind the ears.

'Off to see the Moffatts,' observes Mam. 'Won't have such an easy time there. Didi will feed her tea out of cracked cups she hasn't bothered to wash up. No blue suit's going to stand up to Didi's kitchen. On good days she might say "yes" and "no". More like it'll be "effing this" and "effing that", all in the heavy Glasgow she puts on when she's in a bad mood. Young Gary will be a cheeky little sod, like always.'

'That's why he's excluded, Mam,' I say. 'Swore at the headmaster something rotten and pulled the hair of one of the dinner ladies. We all laughed, it was such fun. Why do we have to be so nice? Can't we have fun like Gary, give the snooty woman from the Social the what-for?'

'A bad return on the investment,' says Mam. 'Not worth the candle. Exactly what Dad did when they took you away. Got their backs up something terrible. Smarm them is the way, make them think you know your place. Take her. She thinks you are a

Wednesday

polite and charming boy, not the rotten little sod you are really. Even thinks you're off school because of your stomach instead of twagging it because you can't be bothered to go. Give her a mouthful and you'll have the truancy over here in a shot. You don't want to go back to the Home, do you?'

A difficult question. The Home had its good points. Plenty of food, and regular. Warm clothes in winter. No drunks, no fights, no noisy parties at weekends. What more could I want? Then there was the staff. Good, most of them, except for that vicious bastard, Bradley, always ready with a fist or a cane. And the other boys. Get three or four together and they were on the lookout for someone small like me to take it out on. Me, I took no shit, nearly bit one's hand off. Took a beating but they didn't bother me after that. One of the staff talked about hanging a sign around my neck: 'This boy bites.' He thought it was funny; I never understood why.

No time to think. I was always looking after Harry. Three years younger than me, even smaller built. Crying out for a hard nut to have a go at him. Couple of them got him round the back of the gardener's hut one time. Stubbed out their cigarettes on the back of his neck until he looked like a scabby dog. Told him he shouldn't tell anyone or he'd get the same treatment again; over his bare arse this time. Harry never told no-one. Except his big brother, that is. Tell big brother everything. Apple crumble and hot custard for supper next day. Very wobbly, the dining-room floor. Tripped on it, lobbed the lot down chief thug's neck. 'Not my fault, sir. See, the lino's ripped up there. I didn't see it. Of course I'll apologise to him, promise it won't happen again.' Funny, he ended with the same bandage around his neck as Harry had around his.

Then there was school every day without fail. No excuses, no sick leave. Compulsory baths on Sundays, church once a month. Busybodies all the time. 'What do you feel about this? Are you adjusting to your new home? Do you love your father? How do you feel about going home?' At first I'd say 'don't know' or 'don't care' until Mam started coming over to see us again, began my education, taught me to be polite. Got me and Harry out of prison. Now I can go where I like, stay off school, throw stones at the police, as long as I don't get caught.

That's what pisses Mam off, us getting caught. She went proper barmy over the bike. Some kid had left it chained to the bike sheds at the back of the big school. Or thought he had chained it up. The chain was there and it was certainly locked, only it didn't pass round the iron work of the shed. Careless of him. 'Nice bike,' I thought. 'Too good to be hanging around here to be knocked off.' So, I took it. Went for a ride round the estate. Lovely bike. Took some time to understand how the gears worked, but she flew like a bird once I'd sorted them out. Rode off as far as the park, zooming round the tarmac walkways. Nearly ran over the parkie who was trying to stop me.

I know now what I should've done. Should've dumped it in the bushes and walked home, innocence all over my face. Not what I actually did, took it home and left it in the back garden. Police at the door within a couple of hours. 'I thought it were dumped, Officer. It were there in the park, not locked up or nothing. I need a bike, so I brought it home.' Not worth their while to push it further, taking a ten-year-old to court doesn't look good, but they gave me hell and shouted at Mam and Dad into the bargain.

'Stupid little prat, bringing the cops round here,' shouted Mam when they had left. Gave me a good hiding. No supper or nothing else for a couple of days. Had the scars on me back for weeks. A lesson learned: don't get caught. Not like the feller across the road, but I'll tell you about him later.

'You stop daydreaming and get out from under my feet. Get the dogs fed, then bugger off. Your father will be home soon. I don't want him to see you until after school time. And it's school for you tomorrow, young man. It's Thursday; you know Thursday's a busy day.'

Wednesday

So it is. I quite like Thursdays, love the hustle and bustle, Mam all dressed up, Dad in a good mood for a change. A quiet night, no fuss and nonsense afterwards. For now, I have to feed the dogs. I hate those bloody dogs. Noisy, smelly, neither use nor ornament. Scabby old things, tongues hanging out, teeth long and yellow, always looking to have your hand off while you're not paying attention. Nearly got our Harry one time, started throwing him about like a rag doll until Dad set about them with his baseball bat. They've not done nothing like it since but I know they're always on the lookout; I can see it in their eyes. As long as I give them food I'm their best friend. One day I'll forget or have none to give and they'll be on me. Dad keeps them to scare the punters. 'No trouble while the wolves are loose,' he says.

The yard smells of piss and shit. Dad's supposed to clear it up and hose it down at the weekend. Usually he forgets or can't be bothered so it sits under a covering of flies until he stirs himself at last or gets me and Harry to do it. I'm not washing down today. Fill up the feeding bowls with scraps, splash water into the bucket. Then I'm off to see if Gerry is back from school yet.

'What did you say to that woman from the Social?' I ask him when he appears, one lapel ripped from his blazer after a game of British Bulldog in the playground.

'Didn't tell her nothing. If she got it from anywhere it was that old bag Ma Thompson. You know I wouldn't tell on you.'

'Not if you know what's good for you,' I think, putting an arm round his shoulders. Quite a difficult feat, since he's about six inches taller than me. No heavier, built like a stick insect. Superb for the school football team. Stick the ball in the air and Gerry will head it in. Forget his feet. He's totally uncoordinated, can't kick a ball for toffee. The pair of us annoy the hell out of the headmaster. The head thinks I'm too small to play in the team but he has to include me because I can lob over the ball at the height Gerry likes it. Goal every time. Play the ball on the ground into the box and Gerry makes a right pig's ear of it, just like he did when he broke Ma Thompson's window. He either picks both of us or neither. If he does that he loses his entire strike force.

'What did the Social want, anyway?' he asks. 'You've not been nicking bikes again, have you?'

'Nothing. Checking up on Mam. Looking for an excuse to send us back off to the home. Mam put on her telephone voice and sent her packing. Got any sweets?'

'Nar, old man's on the club again. Bread and dripping all week.'

'We could go shopping.'

'Not local. They know us there, never let us out of sight. How about nipping over to Barnswood? There's new people in the shop there. You look smart enough and I can carry my blazer. They'll think we're from Barnswood Junior, take no notice of us.'

'What if we get caught?'

'We won't. You know the drill. Leg it out the shop. You go left, I go right. By the time they decide which one of us to chase we'll be long gone. That always works.'

'Nearly didn't last time.'

'That's because it was local. They was watching us like hawks. Come on.'

Barnswood is an estate like ours but the people there are different. 'Aspiring,' says Mam. That means they are trying to be posh. Nearly all of them have jobs: working as builders or decorators with the Council, looking after the old folk in the care home, cleaning at the hospital. Working in offices, some of them, too proud to get their hands dirty. There are motorbikes in the back gardens, even one or two cars in the street. The local paper doesn't like that, council tenants being able to afford cars.

So there's money in Barnswood, not like the Chatham Estate. In the middle, round a small green, stands a group of shops. A chippie, of course, and a bookies as well as a small grocery, a bicycle repair shop and one of those newsagents which sells absolutely everything. As well as counters on each side there is an

Wednesday

island down the middle displaying newspapers, magazines and comics. Gerry and I thumb through the latest copies of the *Beano* and *Dandy*.

'Over there,' whispers Gerry. One counter has a display of sweets stacked in a diagonal rise of trays. Little signs on the back of each tray give the price 'four for a penny' or 'four ounces for sixpence'. A woman in a green smock and sporting three chins guards them like her kids would starve if any of them were to go missing.

A man in blue overalls strolls in, lolls against the counter on the other side. 'Ten Woodbines, please, missus,' he calls across the shop. The guardian woman waddles across, squeezes behind the counter, turns her back to lift down a packet of cigarettes from the shelf. Gerry and I push our comics back under our shirts, rush round to fill pockets with sweets, hurry out the shop while the man in the overalls is counting out his payment.

'Pity we couldn't grab any fags,' I say as we slink away. 'Save some for ourselves, sell the rest at school.'

'I could give some to my old man, put him in a better mood.'

'Nothing will do that with mine,' I say. 'Not unless he's had a good day on the horses.'

'Then him and my old man will drink it all away down the pub.' We shrug. At last the world is beginning to make sense. Some behaviour is predictable, even if the motivation for it remains obscure.

'Let's go down the den,' suggests Gerry. 'Too early to go home. We can sit and read our comics.'

I'm more interested in eating the sweets we swiped from the shop. Tea tonight will be no better than Gerry's bread and dripping, despite what Mam said about a nice piece of cod. The nearest Harry and me will come to cod will be when we fetch it back from the chippy for Dad's tea. Could be we'll get a bag of scraps to share between us or nick the odd chip out of the wrapper on the way home.

The den isn't up to much. When the Council bought the land for the estate they saved a bit between the new church and the taller flats as a play area. Some said it should be a football pitch, others a proper playground with swings and the like. In the end there was no money so now it sits three feet high in grass with a thick hawthorn hedge along one side. Me and Gerry have pulled out some of the low branches, woven them into a kind of roof. We can crawl in and hide, be on our own with no-one watching us.

The roof isn't up to much either, except in the summer when it keeps us cool on the few hot days. Most of the time round here it either pisses it down with rain or pulls in a dull drizzle off the North Sea. If we dodge the main drips, we can be comfortable enough for a while. Today's overcast with heavy cloud so we sit and browse through the comics at our leisure. I can't decide whether I like Lord Snooty or Desperate Dan best. Half-heartedly I pick at a brown liquorice allsort, pretending it is a slice of cow pie.

'Mrs Reeve says we have the big tests next week,' says Gerry to break the silence.

Mrs Reeve is our class teacher. Usually the fourth-year classes have a man teacher but Mrs Reeve is the headmaster's wife so no-one dare cheek her or play about. All the teachers use the cane. Often you can tell their heart isn't in it, swatting at you like a cow brushing away at a fly. Not Mr Reeve. He enjoys it, throws the full force of his arm into every blow. Pull your hand away and he'll give you an extra one, twice as hard. So no-one plays up Mrs Reeve. Except Gary Moffatt. He's been excluded, sure enough, but we think the exclusion's only so he can recover from the beating he got. Reeve really set about him, hit him everywhere, even if the education people say a child under eleven can only be caned on the hand.

'What's the point?' I ask. 'None of us is going to pass. Have you any idea what's in them tests?'

Wednesday

'Not a clue,' says Gerry. 'They're something to do with codes, like they done in the war. You know, getting into German secret messages and things.'

'Don't see the point of cracking German codes. We're not at war anymore. Supposed to be friends, aren't we?'

'My old man says never to trust a Kraut, so I suppose we have to be prepared for the next war. Just as long as they don't have the tests on a Friday.'

Friday is our best day. The top class spends all Friday morning doing practice tests. On Monday morning their class seating is changed to reflect the order in which the kids finish in the tests. Half the class are scrambling to get a better place; the other half have given up and barely bother to write anything on their papers.

Us in the B stream, we have no truck with stupid code-breaking. Instead of doing tests, we go out and play football on the playing field. Real football with a marked-out pitch and proper goals, not like the scratch games in the park with our blazers for goals and the parkie trying to chase us away. Me and Gerry want to be footballers when we grow up, play for Town in the league. The paper says some of the players earn as much as twenty pounds a week. Mam says she sees then out nights drinking till two or three in the morning in the posher clubs. Sounds good to me: twenty pounds a week and as much beer as you can drink. Not that I like beer, but you have to drink a lot of beer if you are going to be a real man.

I'd rather be out playing football or squatting here in our den than doing stupid tests or sitting in a dark office playing around with codes. As long as the tests are not on a Friday I suppose I'll turn up, if only to stop Mrs Reeve getting cross. Better than sitting reciting our times tables or painting stupid pictures of birds and rabbits.

'Getting dark,' says Gerry. 'We need to be off home.'

'Where's the plastic bag? Hope no tramp has pinched it.' We fumble around in the undergrowth for the shop bag we keep our valuables in. Not especially valuable; things like toy soldiers we have found, or old comics. Real valuables we keep at home, the den is too public and open to others for them. Our comics can go in there; too incriminating to take home. Mam would never believe I paid for mine and Gerry's mam would throw his in the bin. Doesn't approve of reading, Gerry's mam.

There is a police car outside our door when I get home.

'Where the hell have you been?' shouts Mam.

'Down the park, playing footie,' I say, summing up the situation immediately. Dad is there, hanging around. He usually does a runner when the police come in sight so he's not bothered on his own account. Mam's been at home all day. So she can't have done nothing, and Harry's sitting at the kitchen table as if butter wouldn't melt in his mouth. Which only leaves me.

'Which park?' asks one of the cops, a big burly lump with a red face criss-crossed with blue veins like one of those diagrams of the network you see at railway stations.

'People's Park,' I say, picking on the one furthest from Barnswood.

'Been there all day?' He thrusts his chin forward, barely preventing himself from poking me in the chest with his forefinger.

'Nar,' I say. 'Weren't feeling too good this morning. Then the lady from the Social came over. Ask her, if you want. Then I got bored and went off down the park.'

'What have you got in your pockets?' asks his mate, a long streak of lightning with a nose you could cut cheese with and a chin made from a paving slab.

'Nothing,' I say. 'Wanna look?'

'Yes,' he says. 'Turn 'em out.'

Dad looks at Mam, a bit worried. Mam has her blank face on, the one she always wears when the cops are around. 'Know nothing, say nothing' is her motto as far as the cops are concerned.

I empty my pockets onto the kitchen table, pull out the lining to show there is nothing left. A piece of old chewing gum wrapped

Wednesday

in newspaper; a pocketknife with the bottle opener missing and one blade broken in half; a handkerchief, been there since I had a cold last month; two cigarette cards (Bobbie Charlton and Martin Peters); and a threepenny bit.

'Where's the sweets?' asks the network diagram.

'Where's your comic?' demands knife nose.

'Not got no comic, can't afford 'em. Not got no sweets, bad for me upset stomach.' Dad almost smiles. Mam's face relaxes a fraction.

'You been over to Barnswood?' the skinny one asks.

'Don't go there,' I say. 'Not for the likes of me. Too posh. They'd call you lot as soon as look at the likes of me.'

'Which is exactly what they did,' he says. 'Especially after you nicked the sweets and the comics from the shop.'

'Never been in no shop,' I say. 'Never been in Barnswood. Been down the park, playing footie.'

Now, if it were a murder they'd be asking who I played with, what was the score, where all the other lads live. But they're not going to do that for a few sweets and a couple of comics, then end up spending three hours hanging around in the juvenile court or writing stuff up for care proceedings.

'You watch out for this lad, missus,' says the pudgy one to Mam. 'I've got my eye on him. One step out of line and I'll have him in the lock-up. He's a bad lot, like all you round here. You watch your step. We know all about you. Record as long as me arm.'

'I'm a reformed character, Officer,' says Mam blandly. 'Fully accepted my responsibilities as a wife and mother. You ask the lady from the Social. Clean house, well-fed, well-spoken children. No reason for you to come here persecuting us whatever.' She smiles as she says this, or at least her lips open slightly and her mouth gets wider.

She's still smiling when she bursts back into the kitchen, having seen the cops off in their new squad car. 'Well done, our

Danny,' she says. 'A right chip off the old block. No cheek, nice and polite. Fancy some beans on toast?'

I shrug. 'Not really,' I say.

'All those clats you've been eating,' says Mam. 'Must've shovelled them sweets down in double-quick time. Suppose you stashed the comic away in that den of yours. Very sensible. Don't bring the evidence home. Your father could do with some of your sense.'

'I didn't have time to move it on,' Dad says grumpily. 'And Norman didn't have anywhere to put it at his place. Nothing came of it. A year's probation; next to nothing. Come on, our lass, don't spoil things. I've had a good day; you've got rid of the nosey parker from the Social and Danny boy has shown off the cops. The fleet will be in again tomorrow. Settle the kids down and we can go out tonight and celebrate.'

Mam is always ready to celebrate. By law Harry and I are too young to be left on our own, but who's looking? We can sit up and play cards all night, sneak back into bed when we hear them coming home, squiffy from the pub.

There is a harsh smell. Harry's toast is burning. Mam snatches it off the grill, scrapes the burnt bits into the sink, washes them down with a squirt of cold water. His beans are burnt as well. 'Only at the bottom of the pan,' she says, scraping them over his toast. I've never said a bad word about our mam and never will, but I have to admit she's the worst cook on the estate, maybe in the whole world.

Thursday

Harry gets me up early. Mam and Dad are still in bed, sleeping it off. Harry is going through a goody-goody phase. 'Mam said you had to be sure and go to school today. She said the woman from the Social will check up. If you're not there she'll be back asking more questions.' I know he's making sense, but it is snug and warm in bed.

'Dad will give us shit if we're still here when he gets up.' Sickening having a little brother who is always right. They were out late last night, well after we had got fed up with the cards and gone to bed. Means they'll both have a hangover when they finally pitch out.

I moan and groan but crawl out of bed nevertheless, throw on yesterday's underwear, pull out the school uniform from the floor where I threw it last night. Together we creep downstairs. Last night's washing-up is still on the table, together with a half-finished packet of sliced bread. I toast a slice each for me and Harry, palest brown, just the way he likes it. There's some marge in the tub but it looks like the jam has all gone. As has most of the milk. Enough for a couple of cups of tea for Mam and Dad. No way we're going to touch that.

There's a light drizzle, but there always is, so we don't bother with our coats. School's about as far away as possible and still the nearest one. Nobody thought about building a new primary school when they planned the estate. There's the big school, of course, just round the corner from us, which caters for both our estate and the new bungalows further out along the main road. Doddery old folk there, too old to have kids our age. Our school is on an estate over a mile away, some of it built after the war, the rest old terraces from when the area was a separate village. The school was nice and new when I first came here five years ago, but it's beginning to look run-down now, the plaster flaking off the walls, the metal window frames rusting under the paint. Still, the heating works in winter and the doors keep out the draughts.

For a change we're not late, lots of kids milling about in the playground, screaming and shouting, letting off steam before we have to sit quiet and well-behaved for the rest of the day. One of the young teachers comes out and rings the hand bell for us to line up. I know he's young because he still has a spotty face with yellow pimples. Not as many as when he started back in September but still enough for the boys in his class to call him 'Blob'. The bell's also being rung in the girls' school next door. I don't understand why we have separate boys' and girls' schools in the juniors and a mixed school in the seniors. Perhaps it's a way of getting us to marry one another.

Harry lines up with the other lads in 2C, talking to another boy who lives a couple of streets away from us. This lad's a bit simple and Mam says he should really be at a special school. I don't like Harry talking to him. People might think Harry's a bit simple as well. I push myself into the 4B line, a few from the front. Most of the other boys don't understand, but I have it all worked out. Only the goody-goodies line up first or sit in the front row in class where the teacher can see whatever they're doing. The naughty lads sit at the back. That is stupid. Even 'Blob' knows to watch out for trouble on the back row, which he patrols regularly. Old hands like Mrs Reeve spend most of their time there, ruler in hand, ready to give some layabout the 'what-for' if he's slacking or

Thursday

causing a nuisance. Stay in the middle, part of the dull grey mass, is the secret; neither too conspicuous nor too obviously about to cause trouble.

We file in, change our outdoor shoes for plimsolls, stuff the shoes into the wire mesh cubicles, hang coats on the pegs with our names on them. There's no rush to be first in the classroom. The slower we are the shorter the day will be. I find a seat in the middle, towards the window. Since we do no tests in this class there's no ranking by test results, seating is purely a matter of personal choice and what group you belong to. Usually I sit with the sports lads, though I could sit with the heavy gang if I wished. The heavy gang are stupid, always getting caught for something they've done. What's the point of getting caught all the time? The idea is to do what you like and get away with it. Like I don't cheek the teachers, even the 'Blob', who wouldn't know what to do if I did. I'm not good; I'm not bad; I'm unnoticeable.

We do sums. I don't mind sums, they make sense. You have half a crown, if you spend four pence, sums tell you how much you will have left, two and tuppence. Better than art. Why bother drawing something? Why not just take a photograph? Or English? So you can write a letter applying for a job, Mrs Reeve says. Not the sort of job I'm likely to get. Just turn up on the docks or at a building site and ask. That's what Dad does, when he can be bothered. I can write my name. That's enough. And all these silly stories! Don't see the point.

Later, Mrs Reeve has some old man in to talk about fishing. Not the boring stuff, sitting by a river in the cold drowning worms, but the real thing. He's talking about being caught in storms off Iceland and trying to gut cod when the boat is pitching about all over the place.

'Do you eat fish all the time?' Frankie asks.

The old man laughs. Laughing wrinkles his forehead into half a dozen lines, which fight valiantly to find a lodging in the tiny space between his eyebrows and his hair line. His hair is black and

Childhood, Boyhood, Youth

wavy as if he's brought the ocean with him. 'Sometimes we don't eat at all,' he says. 'If there's a gale blowing we daren't keep the stove going in case the rocking of the boat sets the ship alight. Where would we be then? In the middle of the Atlantic in a howling gale with the ship in flames beneath us. In good weather we're too busy fishing to bother about what we eat. We take whatever the cook cares to throw at us. If we don't like it, we throw it overboard. If he serves up rubbish too often we throw him overboard as well.'

He plonks a bag on the table, proceeds to grope about in it for various items he has brought with him: a cork float, a yard of netting and, most exciting for us, a villainous-looking filleting knife, sharpened to a stiletto after years of use. 'I can fillet four cod in a minute with one of these,' he tells us. In a choreographed move Mrs Reeve hands him an old exercise book covered all over with coloured scribbles. Holding it out in front of him the old man effortlessly draws the knife through it from top to bottom, allowing the severed half to fall to the floor.

'You have heard about the Gurkhas who keep their kukris so sharp they can cut off a man's head with them? A filleter can do the same with his knife if he keeps it in good condition.' We are impressed. All of us have little enemies whose heads might roll in the dust if we were brave enough and had a sharp-enough weapon.

'Isn't it dangerous?' I ask. 'Filleting fish while the boat is rocking about in a storm?'

'We don't fillet in that sort of weather; we leave it until the seas are calm, often on the way home. The dangerous part is lowering and pulling in the nets.' He grabs a lump of chalk and draws the outline of a trawler on the blackboard. 'There is the seabed,' he says, 'where the plaice live and the cod and haddock in the middle. If you just throw the nets overboard they tangle up or get caught on the seabed, so there are great flat boards called otter boards on either side to keep the net open and stop it snagging. They are this big.' He throws his arms apart like the policeman

Thursday

holding back the spectators at the football, the sleeves of his shirt flopping down at either end.

'Aren't they heavy?' asks Frankie.

'Very heavy, as much as a strong man can manage. You have to be especially careful pulling them on board. Sometimes they get caught up in the nets, then free themselves unexpectedly. If you're not watching they can do you no end of damage.' In a theatrical gesture he pulls back the sleeve on his left arm, revealing an irregularly scarred stump.

'Got caught between the transom and the otter board. Smashed me hand to pieces. We were well out by Iceland, in the middle of our best trawl for weeks. Skipper kept us out for days. By the time we got back in port the hand was a right mess: bones sticking out, skin peeling off, pus all over. Not sufficient good bone to try to knit together, they said at the hospital, so they simply took it off. Must say, I was glad to be rid of it. No more pain after that.'

The whole class is sitting with their mouths open. This is what school should be like, we think: blood, gore and otter boards. I tell Harry all about it on our way home, dwelling with relish on the scars at the end of the amputated stump. 'That's where all the bits of splintered bone were poking out,' I tell him, not that the fisherman had said anything of the kind. 'But they landed all the fish,' I continue, 'brought home a top wage.'

A wage of any sort's an alien concept for both of us. Income in our family is irregular and a matter for dispute between Mam and Dad. 'I make it and you spend it,' Mam always says to him. They seem to feel this is a normal state of affairs but I'm aware we are an exception. Men round here either work or take money off the Social. The women stay at home and look after the kids, using whatever cash they're handed on a Friday night. Mrs Parker is another exception. All the women joke about it. Fred Parker steps in the door Friday night, she grabs him, seizes the pay packet out of his hands. Later he gets his pocket money, enough for a couple of drinks with his mates on Saturday night, but no more. A tanner a day for a cup of tea at work to go with his fish-paste sandwiches.

'Poor bugger,' says Mam. 'Fancy living like that.' At the same time, she envies Mrs Parker, who has both a refrigerator and a washing machine, while we have neither. What I know, but Dad doesn't, is that Mam is squirreling away a pound or so at a time to buy herself a fridge. Not on the never-never so it can be called back the moment Dad drinks away the instalments, but outright, ours to keep. Me, I want a washing machine. What's the point of having a fridge when most of the time we have nothing to put in it? There's washing to be done every day. Mam puts it in a big corrugated metal tub full of soapy water. After school I have to posh it, using a long handle fixed to what looks like one of the three-legged stools you see in the fairy stories in the books at school. I posh and posh until there is a dirty foam on top of the water and sweat's running down my back. Then I pull each garment out with a set of wooden tongs and put it in a bucket. Sometimes they sit in the bucket for days, until Dad complains he has no clean underpants or Harry has to have a shirt for school.

Mam keeps a mangle in the back yard, a sheet of plastic over the top to stop the birds crapping on it. Once upon a time it was dark green with the maker's name in bold red letters. Now the paint's peeling, leaving more rust red than red lettering. Neither me nor Harry is allowed to use the mangle. 'You'll get your fingers trapped,' Mam says. 'Then I'll have all the bother of taking you to the hospital and explaining to the Social I didn't do it on purpose.' This is something Dad keeps threatening to do when we get out of order, stuff our fingers in the mangle. After the talk at school today I view the rollers of the mangle with greater respect.

Today being Thursday, Mam is ironing with the radio on. Apart from *Family Favourites* on a Sunday we don't listen to the radio much. Thursday is an exception, a day when both Mam and Dad pay it close attention. Not the BBC or Radio Luxembourg (of which I have heard talk but never managed to find at the much

Thursday

advertised 208) but an obscure place on the dial permanently marked with a scratch from the scissors. On this wavelength we can pick up the radio conversations from the trawlers as they negotiate the channels in the estuary, asking for docking rights or organising a gang of lumpers to help unload the catch.

A good skipper will always aim to dock on the first tide on a Thursday. That way all his fish will be lumped, filleted, sold and on the fish trains to London and the Midlands for the next day, Friday being the day when there is greatest demand. Thursday night the fleet will be in port, the fishermen flush with their pay and determined to make a night of it. This is Mam's busiest night and what pays the rent on our house.

Sometimes the fleet is held up so they miss the tide. Mam doesn't bother to go out and we have less food than usual the next week and Dad's in a foul mood even when he's drunk. Storms are to blame usually, the Atlantic storms which leave the boats hove-to facing the waves, forced to wait until the winds die down. Even now when all the boats have modern Perkins diesel engines there are natural forces which have to be obeyed. 'What cannot be cured, must be endured,' Mam says.

Not this afternoon. The voices on the radio are cheerful, asking for docking berths, exchanging banter with the docks office, fixing the number of lumpers they require, chatting about which pubs or clubs the crew's going to visit first. This is prime information as far as Mam's concerned. If she can be in the Lamb or the Victoria when fishermen arrive flush with cash burning a hole in their pockets she can clean up on the competition, make her pile before moving on to working the clubs after closing time. Getting in early means there is no dragging back, all the work done quietly in side alleys or the dozens of cheap pay-by-the-hour doss houses around the docks.

I'm not supposed to know about any of this, but I have ears and eyes. Mam and Dad can be quite gobby when they've had a few, and we kids talk. The women round here who are on the game talk to one another, or about one another. Naturally we spread what we hear within our tight little circle, monitoring what our parents get up to and what they say about one another. From them I know Mam is seen as something of a star. Always well made-up, a flashy dresser, regularly makes more money than anyone else.

Mam doesn't like to talk about her work very much, but she tries to give me lessons in life from which I can infer how she operates. 'Be polite,' she says. 'No-one likes anyone who is too sassy or full of himself. We all like people who are pleasant company, not some loud smart-ass who won't let you get a word in edgeways. People, especially men, like to talk about themselves, tell you how smart they are. By the time they've finished doing that and they've had a few drinks you're their best friend who is only doing business with you because you are such a wonderful person.' Mam undersells herself. She's utterly beautiful, as I constantly tell her. Who could possibly resist her charms?

Harry and I grab some cheese from the cupboard, hack off a couple of lumps of bread. Mam complains when we do this, says it makes the loaf impossible to cut. Why should she care? I'm the one who will be making the toast tomorrow. Mam's upstairs having a bath. When she comes down she'll be smelling like a perfume shop, her hair piled on top of her head like a steaming cow pat. I love to watch at this point as she teases it into a candy-floss tower which sways as she walks. Odd wisps are twirled around her fingers, tucked into the mass until it looks like a trawler's funnel. At last she takes two cans of stuff which smell of petrol and sprays it on her hair. Gradually, the smell dies down. Once it's disappeared completely she takes a little cut-glass bottle and sprays perfume over the top.

Now the family can have a proper supper. Bread and cheese can only go so far. On Thursdays we always have mashed potato. With pork sausages today. Dad says it's to line his stomach so he can drink more. Why he wants to drink more beer than normal

Thursday

I cannot understand. He needs to stay sober in case one of the customers gets upset, he says. He needs to protect Mam from bad people.

After tea I wash up. Other days Mam does the washing-up, or it gets left in the sink. Thursdays, there is always the chance of a certain amount of dragging back; unusual, the fishermen concentrating on drinking as much as possible before going back to sea on Sunday or Monday. Harry dries, absolutely meticulous to wipe away every drop and drip like the devoted goody-goody he is.

I wash as quickly as possible so I can watch Mam putting on her make-up. We went to the circus once. Most of the clowns wore make-up but the chief clowns had plastic masks, held at the back by tightly strung elastic. Mam does not wear make-up, she wears a mask. First she puts on some cream, then covers it with stuff she calls 'foundation' which changes her from brown to cream. Over the top she rubs in red paint from a tube, thinning it over so she looks like an early spring apple. Using a little brush, she adds black stuff to her eyelashes. Some of her friends glue on artificial ones, but Mam's dismissive of this as if it's some form of cheating. She uses the black stuff on her eyebrows too, though not as much, before pulling out a tray of paints to work in above her eyes. I love this, watching her being clever, thinning down greens or yellows in preparation for the lipstick of the day.

Lipstick's one of her joys. Dad says she spends too much on it. Mam says it's an essential business expense. Last Christmas I stole three different containers of it from the department store in town. It was easy. Whoever expects a ten-year-old boy to be stealing lipstick? Tonight she plumps for a brilliant orange, which goes with the pink on her cheeks and her eyeshadow. Absolutely beautiful!

I don't care for her dress very much. A light silver with a low neckline, a slightly flared skirt and a long slit up each side showing the tops of her stockings. 'The stocking tops are too much,' I tell her. 'They are not sophisticated. Trying too hard.'

Childhood, Boyhood, Youth

'It's Thursday night,' she replies. 'Everyone's out on the town. One likes to be noticed. The stocking tops are my unique selling proposition.' I have no idea what this means but Mam knows what she's doing.

Dad also dresses in his uniform. Great thick working boots in case someone needs a good kicking. Sensible work trousers, clean and tidy with no stains, acceptable in any pub or club. A white tee shirt, fitting closely over his belly, showing off the tattoos on his arms, still muscly from his long-ago stint of national service and compulsory physical exercise. A dog-tooth jacket over the top in black and beige. Mam says he uses the jacket as a warning signal. When trouble's brewing he takes it off, flexes his arms, making the tattoos ripple. Nine times out of ten the other feller will back off. If he doesn't Dad gets in first, wrapping a bottle round his skull. Saw him do that once, when an Icelander was outside on the street threatening to call the police. The man went out like a light, blood streaming from a gash over his eye. His mates had to carry him into a taxi, ferry him to hospital.

Before we were taken away Mam used to tuck us into bed, lock the doors and leave us. One night a nosey neighbour called the police, who found Harry and me all alone and without a scrap of food in the house. That's when the Social got involved and we were sent to the Home. First off when we came back she got Grandma to babysit. Grandma made us go to bed by seven in the evening, even if it was bright summer sunshine outside and there was no school the next day. Finally, I got fed up and refused to go upstairs or get undressed. Grandma tried to drag me by the arm but I was having none of it, wriggled away, shouted and swore. She wasn't going to take that from any little brat, had a real go at me. In the end I pulled her off me by her hair, not that there's much of it, and she stormed away in a huff, refusing to set foot in the house ever again. So, that's why Mam has to leave us on our own when she goes out, hoping the neighbours won't get too nosey or the police and the Social start asking questions.

Thursday

Harry snuggles down in his bed, telling me a story which sounds like Red Riding Hood. Even before the wicked wolf turns up he's fast asleep, his lips still moving, making muttering sounds. I'm still fully dressed under the covers. Throwing them off, I tiptoe downstairs, unlock the back door. One thing Grandma always insisted on was that we could get out of the house in case of a fire. Given the chance, I'd lock the house up with Harry inside and take the key with me but I've thought about what Grandma said. Looking after Harry is a pain in the bum, but I wouldn't want him burnt to death.

Wiggie, Francis Wiggleton, lives in the next street. We get together sometimes and make ships out of aluminium milk bottle tops. You can weld them together with wax and rig them with paper or strips of card. Wiggie and I take them to school, float them in the puddles in the playground, fight out pretend battles or have races when there is a decent breeze blowing, which is more days than not.

Mrs Wiggleton's in the kitchen, bent over her washing machine, a smart twin-tub affair she got on HP. She needs it, with six kids. Every time I come over she's washing or ironing. They have a contraption in their kitchen, wooden railings fixed to a rope and pulley. She hangs the wet clothes on it and uses the rope to pull it up to the ceiling out of the way. Sometimes she forgets to wring them out first, so they drip onto you as you walk underneath.

Wiggie's one of the sporty ones at school. Already he has thick legs without what Grandma calls 'puppy fat'. All his muscles are in his legs so he's useless at ball games and not coordinated enough to make a footballer. But hell, is he fast. He can outrun anybody in the school and came second in our age group in the county sports last year. Wiggie is blond with a touch of ginger in his hair, which is rare around here among all us black-haired types. His two sisters are the same, which accounts for them being reckoned among the young beauties on the estate. Neither of them is as beautiful as our mam.

We try out a new model for our boats. Mrs Reeve has been going on all week about the Greeks and the Romans who had long boats with three banks of oars, called triremes. If we cut the bottle tops with scissors we can glue three or four of them together, then build up the sides with clippings from torn tops. While Wiggie's mam is concentrating on her washing we try them out in the kitchen sink. 'It's no good,' says Wiggie. 'They keep toppling over, even without the sails attached.' I remember something the old fisherman told us. A trawler is far more stable on the way home with a hold full of fish than it is on the way out, when it skips and bobbles about. 'What it needs is ballast,' I say. 'Ballast will keep it steady, weigh it down in the water.'

We try out various solutions, including marbles (too large) and grass stalks (too light) before settling on tiny stones from the back garden, which can be adjusted fore and aft as well as for depth. Wiggie stands at one end of the sink, pushing the boat while I stand at the other pushing at back. There is a car outside. No-one here owns a car. A bicycle or a motorbike even, but not a car. Any car must be a taxi.

Wiggie's dad bursts in through the back door.

'Hello, ducks,' he says to Mrs W. 'Hello, kids.' He unlaces his kit bag and dumps the dirty clothes inside onto the kitchen floor. 'Get them done for me, ducks. We are back out Sunday. Francis, stop messing about in the sink and run me a bath. Get me suit out for me while you are up there. I'll find a shirt later.' In a second he's gone, stripping off a top layer of clothes as he goes. The taxi is outside, engine running.

Well, the fleet must be in. I need to get home in case Mam drags someone back or they decide to throw a party. First I have to help Wiggie clear up, scrape the wax off the surfaces, throw away the bits of bottle tops we didn't use, scrunch up our failures and put them in the bin.

The taxi is still outside, engine running.

Mr W appears at a rush, his hair still wet from the bath, in full fisherman's shore rig. Bright blue suit with black velvet collar on the jacket, string tie held together with a metal toggle in the shape of a longhorn cow, brilliant white shirt, winkle-picker shoes. All ready for a night out which might extend itself into Sunday morning, in time for him to pick up his kit bag full of clean clothes and off to sea again.

Mam would never put up with a life like this, even for a refrigerator or a washing machine, but a lot of the women do. Dad might fancy the three-day drinking sessions but you can't see him sticking the intervening three weeks at sea.

Me neither. I'd rather play football.

Friday

Harry and I creep out the house like two frightened mice. Good or bad, last night will have exhausted the pair of them. Looks like it was good this week. There are two hessian bags on the table, the sort known around here as basses. Sea water's dripping through them, making twin stains on the kitchen floor. Something's moving in the sink. Four ocean crabs, their claws tied shut, are trying their best to crawl out and find somewhere to hide. Harry pokes at one, which raises its ineffectual claws in protest. Unless Mam and Dad sell them on we will have an excellent supper tonight.

    Our anticipation will have to suffice, because there is nothing laid out for breakfast. Yesterday's bread has all been eaten and the half inch of milk left in the bottle has separated into two smelly layers. Anyway, it's better to go hungry than risk waking them up this early in the morning. My football boots are under the stairs, still thick with mud from last week, wrapped in my shorts and shirt, which are at least dry. An unexpected blessing; last week they were soaking wet.

    On the walk to school Harry tells me a story. He's always telling stories, is Harry. This one is about a little boy lost on the seashore who comes upon a mermaid. The mermaid looks after him, takes him out to sea, where he grows a tail and learns to talk

Friday

to the fishes. Eventually a fisherman catches him in his net and takes him back to shore. The fisherman turns out to be the boy's father. The father's delighted to find his long-lost son but put out at having a child with a tail. Instead of taking him home the father lets him stay in his boat. Of course the boy can't go to school or play with any other boys, so he spends his time talking to the fishes. His father wants him to show him where the best fishing places are, but how can the boy betray his friends? There are nice fish and nasty fish. The boy's fish friends tell him where the nasty fishes live so that he can guide his father to them. Now the father becomes rich and is delighted with his son, who eventually marries a mermaid and lives happily ever after.

I am very worried about Harry. Perhaps he's deranged, suitable only for the new special school for backward children?

For a change my class lines up outside the school with no pushing or shoving, marches into the locker area in perfect order. Changing shoes takes half the normal time and Mrs Reeve speeds through her register without having to record any absences. There's assembly, which is a pain. We older boys act as police, keeping the youngsters in order, moving them along like soldiers under training. Even Mr Reeve cooperates, picking a hymn with only three verses and the shortest Bible reading he can manage before warning the whole school to be on its best behaviour next week because there will be important examinations in the school hall.

We burst out in complete disorder, charging off towards the changing rooms, throwing on our football kit, milling around in a mad circle in one of the goal areas. Mr Reeve's usually in charge of football, but today he's making arrangements for the exams next week, so the Blob's in charge. He picks out two captains at random: me and Frank Harrison; possibly because we are the smallest lads in the class. He probably thinks no-one will pick us for their team, so he's trying to be fair. It's true about Frank, but not about me. I immediately pick Gerry for my team. 'It's not fair, sir,' comes a chorus from the rest of the class. 'They are the two best players. If they are in the same team, the others don't stand a chance.'

Usually a teacher would ignore anything we tell him, knowing we are trying to pull a fast one, but this time the Blob realises his pupils might actually be telling him the truth.

'Very well,' he says. 'Let's go back to the beginning. Harrison, you have first pick.' Naturally Frank chooses Gerry, while I'm left with the only one in the class who is tall and brave enough to make a competent goalkeeper. Halfway through the first half the drizzle turns to steady rain. We don't care, being used to playing in the rain. At this point Mr Reeve would blow his whistle for half time and cut the second half down to ten minutes, leaving his wife to deal with forty annoyed and recalcitrant youngsters. The Blob is made of sterner stuff, gives us a full hour. Perhaps like us he would rather be out here than cooped up in a stuffy classroom.

There are no showers in the changing rooms. Forty of us mill around three wash basins, trying to wash off as much dirt as possible from faces and knees. Only the two goalkeepers get priority. Even Frank and I, as the two captains, are left fighting our way through the crowd. The remainder of the morning is quiet reading time. An hour of football is sufficient to quell the most frantic of ten-year-olds. Several of the lads in the class have trouble with reading. They are tired and sit staring at the pictures until lunch time.

I leaf through a book on deep-sea fishing left on a desk from yesterday's talk. Most of it I already know, but at the back is something strange, a selection of recipes for things I have never heard of. What on earth is 'crab bisque'? Or a 'fricassée of haddock'?

I put my hand up. Mrs Reeve's taken aback. For Danny Morley to ask a question in class is unheard of.

'Yes, Daniel.'

'Please, Mrs Reeve, may I take this book home with me this evening? I've read it through once but it's so interesting I'd love to

Friday

read it again. And there are a few things in it I don't understand which I need to ask my dad about.'

Mrs Reeve has met my dad. She's well aware that there are few things anyone but the police would bother asking him. Nevertheless, this is a breakthrough, a chance not to be missed. 'Of course, Daniel. Please look after it and bring it back in good condition on Monday morning.'

On the way home I'm bursting to tell Harry of my discovery but he's full of a story his class teacher read to them at the end of the day about two children lost in a wood. What is it with Harry and getting lost? Is he pining for the Home, or frightened he'll be taken back there?

D's in the kitchen, boiling a huge pan of water. He drops in the crabs, one by one. Waits until it stops struggling, studies the inert body with all the concentration he devotes to the racing pages of the *Daily Mirror*. Finally fishes the crab out using the wooden tongs Mam keeps for pulling her washing out of the poshing tub. Another one follows, watched with relish by Harry and me. We listen to the futile scrabble of claws on the side of the pan.

'Cook them too long and the flesh turns to mush,' Dad tells us. 'Don't cook them long enough and all you get is sloppy string. Let them cool down before tearing the legs off. Now the first one is cool, wrap it in newspaper and leave it in the shade outside where the cats can't get at it. We'll have it for early supper tomorrow. You, Daniel, put this one in the bass and take it to your gran. And no backchat, you hear me?'

I quite like Grandma, as long as she isn't looking after me and fussing over whether I've had a wash or brushed my hair. 'Can I come too?' Harry begs. Why not? Grandma always gives Harry sweets when she sees him and she can hardly give him some and not me, can she?

Grandma lives in one of the new flats round the corner. They've put her on the ground floor because of her age. 'I'm not that old,' she says, 'but in ten years' time when you have kids of your own you won't want to be dragging them up six flights of stairs to visit your poor gran, will you?' I'm still in short pants and she has me married off with a house full of squalling brats already. All the old women round here are the same. 'Get married, have children,' is what they tell us. Not necessarily in that order. Half the girls catch a man that way, according to Gran. 'Get a bun in the oven, shame the Council into giving them somewhere to live, grab some poor unsuspecting feller and live off him.'

I know Mam did exactly the same, got knocked up by Dad when she was barely seventeen. 'Marry in haste, repent at leisure,' is what Grandma says when I remind her of it. According to her every girl in town is trying to capture a man, every man is trying to get into their knickers before doing a runner. Who would want to get into my gran's knickers, even when she was younger? Maybe one day I will understand this sex thing.

Gran wears boots and thick knitted socks with coloured designs on them. Her skirts all look the same: some flannel material in black or brown which might once have had a pattern, now faded and covered with old grease marks which never disappear however often they're washed. On her good days she wears see-through blouses in a variety of bright colours. They barely fit, the buttons popping open to reveal her pink corset beneath. Most times it doesn't matter because she always wears charcoal-coloured cardigans closely fastened by whichever buttons remain.

'Come and pull the hairs out of my corset,' she orders, putting a bag of sweets on the table and unbuttoning the top of her blouse. I reach down her back, squeezing a hand beneath the pink elastic, reaching as far down as I can. Both of us know this is a fiction. Gran has barely enough hair to cover the dandruff on her head, none to spare to carelessly drop away and find its way under the tight-fitting underwear. She needs a good scratch is what it is, the corset irritating her rolls of fat in places where she can't reach herself. Only old women have corsets nowadays, Mam says. Roll-ons are the thing, with a pretty brassiere. Mam doesn't bother: suspender belt and stockings when she goes out, just knickers when she doesn't.

The road outside is busy, a lorry hooting its horn. 'The coal man,' says Gran. 'Danny, go and tell him I want two bags. I'll pay him next week when I get my widows' pension.' The coal man isn't sure, he's heard this tale too often, but if he doesn't give tick round here he'll lose most of his custom. If I met him in the street in his best clothes I'd never recognise him, so covered is he by coal dust. As tall as Dad but much skinnier. You'd expect a coal humper to have shoulders like a weight-lifter, wouldn't you? Especially in these flats where he has to carry sacks up to the top floor, then dump them down the coal chute each flat has on the communal landing. Perhaps he's happy to give Grandma tick because she's on the ground floor and he doesn't have to climb the stairs.

'Good boy,' says Gran when I get back in, heralded by the sound of coals plummeting into her coal bunker. 'Diddly-de-dum' rings a bell outside. No coal man; this is Ada's Ices. Real ice cream straight from a metal tub. Mam doesn't like us having Ada's Ices. She says you don't know how hygienic they are. Harry and me don't care. We stare expectantly at Gran. She fetches two glasses from her cupboard. 'Two scoops each,' she says. 'No more.' Her purse magically appears from under the cushion on her armchair. Hiding its contents from us she carefully counts out a few coppers, the exact money to the penny.

We rush out into the street, not bothering to look out for traffic, a rarity in this part of town. Ada's isn't sold from a motorised van but from a tricycle with a large box on the front which holds the metal canister of ice cream. Vanilla or vanilla is the choice, though you can have it either as a wafer or a cornet. Harry and I go for the third option: scoops of ice cream into our own glasses, topped off by extra wafers. Like this we get four wafers instead of only two. Back at Grandma's we stir the hard white balls into a smooth consistency. Ada, if there is such a person, leaves the odd lump in her ice cream and freezes it rock solid to survive the old-fashioned mode of transport allowed to her sales force. As long as I can remember the sales force has been the same old man with a droopy moustache and eyebrows like a pair of demented spiders. On the sea front you can now buy the new version which stands up in peaks and tastes of absolutely nothing. Ada's may be lumpy and unhygienic but the taste is delicious.

Gran watches us enviously. 'I'm a martyr to me stomach,' she tells us. 'Anything fat or creamy upsets it something rotten. It was the war what done it. No butter, almost no meat, or what there was strictly for the kids. Stomach turns over at the sight of anything stronger than a carrot or a slice of bread. Always ready for some nice fish or a well-cooked crab, though. Your dad may be a layabout and a pimp, but he knows how to cook a crab, I'll give him that.'

I seize the opportunity. 'Grandma, what's a crab bisque?'

Grandma looks like she's got her fingers caught in Mam's mangle. 'Wherever did you get a word like that from?' Worrying. She only asks me that when I bring up a new swear word I've picked up in the playground at school or playing football with the older boys in the park.

'At school,' I say. 'I found it in a book. And haddock fricassée as well. If they're nice I could make one of them for Mam and Dad.'

'Haven't made either of them for years,' says Gran. 'The bisque is a quaint old thing my mam used to make when we were skint back in the twenties. Simple stuff. Boil up your crab shells, get all the goodness out of them, throw in onions and carrots. Don't forget to take the shells out first. Warm it up with a couple of bay leaves and that frilly weed that grows on the bomb sites. I knew a Frenchman once, when your granddad was still in the forces after the war.' Grandma smiles, then pretends she hasn't. 'He used to do it with garlic. Hard to get garlic nowadays, not since the onion sellers packed it in.'

Friday

'It's a soup, then, Grandma?'

'You could say that. It's posh nowadays, but back then it was what you had when there was nothing else. Always plenty of crab bones available round here, even at the worst of times. Now, a fricassée, that's something else. Look, I'll show you, since you've brought me this nice new crab. Come on into the kitchen.'

Gran's kitchen has cupboards all round the edge, which leaves only enough room for one person. Where she used to live by the docks the kitchen was part of the living room and her cooker was a blackened old open fire with metal mini-cupboards on either side for keeping the food warm. There was always a huge kettle perched on top of one or the other, gently steaming day and night to make an instant pot of tea for whoever dropped in. Now she has a white gas cooker with a grill at eye level so she doesn't need to bend down to see if her morning toast is ready.

To keep out the way I sit on one of the cupboards while she gets her ingredients ready: oil, flour, a huge onion, two celery sticks, a wrinkled carrot and a white knobbly thing about half the size of a cricket ball. 'Garlic,' she says. 'Got it at the new Paki shop in town for half price. Can't imagine he sells much, even if he's open day and night. He won't last long.' She breaks a piece off, skins it carefully, hands it to me. 'Take a sniff of that.'

'Urgh!' I say. 'It smells like my willy when I haven't washed it properly.'

'Then you should wash more often. This is garlic. Be careful with it. A little bit increases the taste, too much and it completely takes over. Crush it, like this.' She flattens it with the blade of an old blunt knife. 'Do you remember how to make a roux?'

Of course I do, Grandma has shown me many times. What she calls basic cooking: make a roux and you've a nice thick base for anything you wish, cheap and filling. I stir the pan while she cuts her vegetables before adding them one by one, leaving the garlic until last. She adds water to the mixture. 'Slowly,' she says, looking at me severely. I just poured it into one of her meals once, producing great lumps of coagulated flour which had to be lifted out one by one.

Harry huddles over a deep plate in the living room, engrossed in one of his favourite occupations: tearing the legs off the crab and breaking them into segments. He lifts the flap off the underbelly before breaking into the main body. Slowly he allows his head to drift forward until he looks like the mad professor in the *Beano*. He uses Grandma's silver spoon which she keeps in her best sugar bowl to scrape out the flesh onto one of her saucers.

'Bring the crab over here, young Harry,' Grandma orders, keeping an eye on me, making sure I'm still stirring the pot, from which she ladles out a good helping into a smaller pan. 'That's for me,' she says. 'I'll add my crab when I serve it. Daniel, do you remember how to cook rice?'

'Yes,' I answer doubtfully.

'Make sure it's tender this time. I nearly broke my new falsies on it when you did it last week. Just one cup full. Easy enough for the four of you. Right, mind you don't spill the pan on your way home. Off you pop. And here are a few sweets to keep you going until supper time.'

Friday night is never as busy as Thursday. Last night the fleet was flush with cash. Tonight they'll be more careful how they spend their money, trying to make it last over the weekend until shipping out again on Monday or Tuesday. Many are still drunk or hungover, grumpy as bears until the second or third pint, when they can get into the swing of things again. Mam is still in her curlers. Dad's sitting at the kitchen table, bottle of beer in hand, breaking open one of the crabs. 'Come help me at this, little Harry. Your fingers is smaller than mine, you can get round the edges better.'

Harry nudges in so close you'd think he was going to dig out the meat with his nose. 'Our Daniel's got something special for you, Dad,' he says. 'he made it over at Grandma's. She says it's a cassie.'

Friday

'Fricassée,' Mam and I correct together. 'My mother used to make it a lot when we were young. She'd make it with anything that came along: bit of smoked haddock, a dozen prawns in their shells. Rock eel, even. Right tasty.'

Dad doesn't look impressed. He digs out the white meat from one of the claws with one of Mam's hair clips. 'Can't beat a good plate of whelks,' he says. 'None of this fancy rubbish. Good down-to-earth stuff. Even you can't go wrong with proper English food.'

I look at Mam. She doesn't seem convinced by Dad's argument or by his attempt at flattery either. We all know Mam's so useless in the kitchen she got thrown out of Home Economics in her second year at school. The teachers thought she was playing about and taking the piss, when in fact she was plain totally useless. I saw her trying to make baked beans on toast once. Put the tin in a pan of boiling water, then set about making the toast. Got so engrossed in reading *Woman's Own* the toast caught fire. By the time she had put it out and thrown the charred ashes in the dustbin the pan had boiled dry. The tin of beans exploded, scattering beans all over the walls and ceiling, completely wrecking the pan. She hadn't even thought to put a hole in the top of the can. And she made me clear up the whole lot, as if it was my fault! We were scraping bits of dried beans from cupboards and off the sink for days afterwards.

Which is why Mam lets me have the run of the kitchen, though so far that's only got as far as making her a pot of tea and a cheese sandwich or unwrapping the fish and chips and piling them onto their plates. Now and then she takes me shopping. 'Buy some potatoes,' she will say, or, 'Them tomatoes look good.' Meanwhile I slip interesting things into the shopping bag or into my pockets if they are small enough and look expensive. Ruined me school blazer once when I crammed in a pack of liver, bursting the bag so the blood ran everywhere. Mam was furious, but she still ate the liver.

'I need to get my clothes out for tonight,' she says at last. 'Danny will get the tea ready. Charlie, feed the dogs for us, love. We don't want them howling the neighbourhood down on us or disturbing the kids when they are in bed.'

Dad ambles off, grumbling. 'It's the bloody boys' turn,' he mumbles. 'Spend too much time with that old cow of a grandmother, that's their problem.'

Bloody idle, that's his problem. Never does anything around the house. Mr Reeve says we should honour our father and our mother. He can't have a father like mine. At least it leaves me on my own in the kitchen. On the last shopping trip with Mam I bought some rice. Not the sloppy stuff in tins, the real thing in a packet, like Grandma buys from the Paki shop. She's shown me how to cook it, in boiling water with a good pinch of salt. Stir it from time to time to stop it sticking to the bottom. Grandma strains it off in a colander but we haven't got one, so I use the lid of the pan instead, scrape up the bits that escape into the sink with my hand and push them in the pan. Back on the stove, cook it as long as I dare before it burns and sticks to the bottom.

Two big platefuls and two small platefuls. Ladle the fricassée over the top with crab meat mixed into each, the white bits for Dad and Mam, the brown for Harry and me. We also get the leg pieces, together with a hair pin each. 'Supper's ready!' I shout up the stairs, then again out the back door.

'Looks very nice, Danny,' says Mam as she sits down but I can see she's worried. Harry sticks a finger in his, licks it, pulls off a piece of crab meat from the top. We all wait for Dad to come in from the dogs and settle down at the table.

At last he pushes open the back door, takes his time rinsing his hands in the sink under the cold tap. 'Bloody dogs,' he says. 'Fleas all over. Send the boys out to sprinkle them with powder after supper. What's this, then?' He eyes his plate with suspicion.

'A crab fricassée, Dad,' I tell him. 'I got the recipe out of a book at school.'

Friday

'Never anything good ever came out of book learning. Specially for the likes of us.' He picks at the crab meat with his fork, sniffs before putting it in his mouth. 'Smells funny,' he says. 'Sure it's not off?'

'It's the one you cooked today, Dad.'

'Still smells funny. And what's this underneath? Rice, bloody rice! Rice is for pudding with milk and jam. Don't you know nothing?' He scrapes the mixture off the top, pushes it aside.

'That's pudding rice, Dad. This is long grain rice. It's what they eat in India and China and other places.'

'Fucking foreigners. Don't you go telling me what fucking foreigners eat. This is England, this is. We eat proper food here. No messing about serving puddings for a meal. If you want rice, there's a tin of Ambrosia in the cupboard. Use that.'

'But it doesn't go with the crab, Dad.'

'Too fucking true it don't. Let's see what the rest of this muck is.' Aggressively he shovels a large spoonful into his mouth. We watch as he swills it around, swallows. Spits the whole mouthful back onto his plate. 'What sort of shit have you put in here? Tastes like garbage, all bitter like it's full of thistles. You've gone and spoiled a nice bit of crab. I've spent all day slaving over them crabs and you ruin them in five minutes. I'm not eating this muck. Which are you trying to do: poison me or starve me to death?'

'Something different, Dad. Grandma gave me some garlic special, like, to help flavour the dish the way it says in the recipe.'

'Might have known that old witch would be behind it somewhere. Vicious old cow. Never serves up a decent meal when we go there. Always foreign muck. That's what comes of spending the war fucking Frenchies.'

'Not her fault, Dad,' I say. 'I only used what's in the recipe. It can't be foreign if it's in the book at school, can it?'

'Don't you backchat me, you little brat!'

Next thing I know I'm flat on me back on the kitchen floor, head in Mam's lap, blood gushing from my nose as she tries to wipe it away with a wet tea towel. Harry's curled up in the corner, sobbing so hard I think his head will burst. Dad's dinner plate, broken into four pieces, lies upside down on the floor, rice and sauce oozing out round the edges. Of Dad himself there is nothing to be seen.

'Gone off down the chippy,' says Mam. 'Danny, sit up, wrap the tea towel round your nose. Harry, stop that bawling. Bring me the coal shovel, the wide blue one with the short wooden handle.'

Reluctantly Harry eases himself to his feet, shuffles out to the coal bunker. Returns, still sniffling, with the shovel. 'Put it there,' Mam orders, indicating the edge of Dad's abandoned meal. 'Give it a push.' Mam lends her weight to the far end of the mess, manoeuvring most of it onto the shovel. The rest she scoops up with a spoon. Takes the shovel full out of the back door and dumps it in the bin.

'That will teach you not to talk back to your dad,' she says as she returns. 'You'll have a right shiner in the morning. Anyone asks, tell them you got it playing football. Now, get the washing-up done, you two. I need to get dressed and off to work.'

Saturday

My eye's nearly closed and there's a constant throbbing behind the left cheekbone. Mam and Dad aren't up yet; they always sleep late on Saturday after two days of hard work. There's a dirty plate in the sink. Mam must've finished off the last of the fricassée. There are two empty beer cans on the kitchen table, which I throw in the rubbish. Why can't he throw away his own beer cans? Usually I make Harry beans on toast for breakfast on Saturdays. 'Not today,' he says, 'not after all that rice and crab. I'm still stuffed.'

'Did you like it?'

'Well, I ate it.' As much as I can expect from a seven-year-old who can hardly read and goes around telling weird stories to anyone who'll listen, and to himself when he has no other audience. Harry can be a fussy eater, so I suppose his empty plate last night was something of a compliment.

The cupboard is unusually full. Thursday must've been a wonderful night for business. Toast, jam and milk for us, making sure we leave plenty for Mam and Dad. 'Let's go down the Willows,' I say. 'See if we can find some sticklebacks.'

Harry's delighted; he loves paddling in the water and chasing the ducks. We don't go there very often because Mam is frightened we'll drown ourselves. I tell her the river isn't deep enough to drown anyone. 'All you need is four inches of water,' she says.

'They told me that when I was in hospital giving birth to Salanne. Don't put her in the bath, they told me. Wipe her over with a cloth or wash her in the sink. Baths are dangerous for babies. And drowning's not the only reason you shouldn't go to the Willows on your own. There are lots of funny men over there, always on the lookout for pretty young boys like you.'

In which case I'm perfectly safe. Whatever else people say about me, 'pretty' isn't one of them, especially now I only have one eye.

The joke about the town is that it's exactly like Rome: built on seven hills. Well, not hills exactly, seven mudflats. Mrs Reeve says that when the Vikings were raiding Britain they moored up in the middle of the estuary for safety, putting up temporary shelters on one of the mud banks to keep out the wind and the rain. Temporary tends to become permanent, she says, and the settlement spread to other parts of the estuary. Then she started getting difficult, talking about isostatic readjustment and changing sea levels, which raised the land a few feet higher so we became part of the mainland, a soggy marsh intersected by dozens of small streams. Most of them are now underground, built over by modern housing estates like ours. Only the Willows remains, a thick, meandering dribble, just large enough to be called a stream.

Because it's the last one and because the area has a bad reputation it acts like a magnet to all us kids. We flock to it in summer, rigging up trapeze swings. If you hold on to the trapeze and make a run the trapeze will take you across the water. On hot days you let go and plunge into the cold below. Not the weather to take a risk like that today. Besides, I have to keep an eye on Harry before he gets lost or drowns himself by accident. He wants to wander off and explore some bushes but I grab his arm and pull him along. 'Listen,' I say. 'Can you hear that mewing sound?'

'Could be a kitten,' he says. 'She's got herself lost and her mother doesn't know where she's gone. The mother is searching far and wide for her, crying all the time. But the kitten can't hear her and is sitting under a bush crying. Then two little boys come along and rescue her. They tuck her up inside their shirts and carry her home with them to feed her on bread soaked in milk. She's so happy she does not want to go back to her mother but lives with the two boys for ever and ever.'

I shrug. Typical Harry. We look around. The sound seems to be coming from a part of the riverbank which has been reinforced with a sheet of corrugated iron to stop it flooding the nearby fields. 'In there,' says Harry. 'Dan, you pull back the metal and I'll reach down and pull out the kitten. My hands are smaller than yours and I can get into tiny spaces. Use your hanky, in case the iron's sharp.'

I tug and tug but nothing moves. 'Use a stick,' Harry suggests. 'You can poke it down the edge and force it open.'

Sticks are at a premium on a marsh. The area may be called the Willows but the willows themselves are long gone. I hunt around for anything I can find. An old cricket stump, maybe, or a stick some huge dog has left behind. The search takes me in wider and wider circles. At last I come upon two old chairs someone has dumped to get rid of them, the padding falling all over the place, like Mam's hair when she has forgotten to put her rollers in after a bath. One of them has its legs splayed out in every direction, like the chairs in the comic where Billy Bunter has sat on it and it's collapsed under his weight. I stand on the seat, tug at one of the legs which gives way with a sudden crack, leaving me laying on my back in a stand of nettles.

Never mind, I've had worse and at least I now have my weapon. Time to get back to Harry.

Who isn't there.

'Harry,' I shout. 'Harry, where are you?' Mam will play hell with me if he's got lost. When little boys get lost they have to call out the police and the police are the last people Mam wants to have anything to do with.

I wander further along the riverbank. 'Harry,' I shout, 'Harry, we have to go home. Come on.' There's some movement in a big clump of bushes further along. A dog, maybe, or some of the bigger boys. A man's hand grasps a thick stem, hauls himself out. Not properly dressed for a riverbank. Polished black shoes, smart tan trousers with a crease down the middle of each leg, a white shirt and dark blue tie done in what Grandma calls a Windsor knot, much fatter than the one we all use for our school ties. His hair is black and wavy, beginning to go grey around the edges. There's a packet of wine gums in his free hand.

'Have you seen our Harry, mister?' I ask.

He looks frightened. Maybe it is my black eye or the chair leg in my hand; he thinks I'm a thief or a murderer. Whatever it is he turns away, walks off as fast as he can, almost breaking into a run. 'Danny,' says a voice, 'over here, near the water.'

Harry's crouched on a miniature beach where a huge bush dips its head into the stream. 'What the hell are you doing there?' I ask him roughly, still panicking about what Mam will say when she finds out I lost him.

'The man said he knew a good place where there are lots of fish. But there weren't any fish, so he said it didn't matter and gave me some wine gums instead. Then he put his hand up my shorts. I didn't like that and tried to run away but the bank is so steep and he kept pulling me back. Said what a pretty little boy I am and wouldn't I like to do him a favour. Then you came along and he rushed off. Took his wine gums with him.'

'You can't tell anyone about this,' I say. 'If you do you will have to admit to Mam that you wandered away and got yourself into trouble. Just tell her about the kitten. Say we couldn't rescue it to bring home. Think what would have happened if you'd turned up with a kitten! Soon as he got in a bad mood Dad would have fed it to the dogs. Remember what Grandma told us: least said, soonest mended.'

'All right. Can we drop in to Grandma's on the way home, then?'

'I thought you wanted to come to the football?'

'No, I can't see over the barrier properly and Grandma always bakes cakes on a Saturday for when her friends come round tomorrow.'

'You are Billy Bunter and I am Roy of the Rovers. Race you back, fatty.'

So we race off back to the estate. Of course, I let Harry win, to make sure he owes me a favour. I drop him off at Grandma's, leaving him on the doorstep so she can't see the state of my face. She's daft enough to call the Social, which would put the cat among the pigeons. Even if she didn't, she'd kick up stink at home and I'd end up with another leathering.

Just after the war, Town were in the semi-final of the cup and in the First Division. Now they are in League Three (north) and fighting for promotion. None of the old gaffers believe in any brighter future, just relieved there is no system of relegation to a lower league. A local businessman runs the club and he's tight with his money. 'I didn't get where I am today by pouring money down the drain,' he says. The whisper among the men making their way to the ground is that he got ahead by a combination of low pay, bribery and shoddy workmanship. We kids don't care, as long as he lets us into the popular end of the ground for free.

The other running joke is that we're the only club in the league which never plays at home, the ground being technically outside the town limits. Whichever council is responsible, neither has ever improved the road up to the main stand or enforced planning and safety regulations. Both stands have a roof of sorts, corrugated asbestos sheets left over from building emergency housing after the war, but the popular end is open to the wind and the rain which sweeps in from the North Sea. I've never been to an away game but the adults say this is the most unwelcoming stadium in the whole of the football league. No way we'll get back into the first division with facilities like these.

I'm there with Gerry, hanging around outside waiting for someone to drop his programme or offer to buy us a hotdog.

Someone did once and we've been on the lookout for him ever since. Instead of our one-time benefactor another figure catches my eye. Tan trousers, white shirt, blue tie, all now topped by mackintosh and a black and white scarf hanging down loosely. I set off after him, fired by the idea I can shame him into a couple of hot dogs and two lemonades. He's too quick for me. One glance over his shoulder, his face turns white and he forces his way through the crowd to a doorway marked 'Directors and Players Only'.

'Who was that, just went into the players' entrance?' I ask a bent old feller in a cloth cap.

'Don't you know?' The old man coughs without removing the cigarette from his mouth. 'That's Burnham, owns the big department store in town. Shifty bugger, he is. They're all shifty on the board, him especially. A nice young lad like you needs to keep out of his way if rumours are true.'

Much to his surprise I thank him excitedly, even call him 'sir'. Can't imagine anyone has called him that since the day he was born. The police, perhaps when he was arrested for drunk and disorderly, like they did once with Dad.

Gerry wants to know what it's all about, but I'm saying nothing. He doesn't tell me his family business. If I tell him I'm following a feller handing out wine gums he'll want some as well.

Disappointed in our hunt for free food we drift into the ground just in time for kick-off. I've played in better games at school. Both sides seem to feel they can win by booting the ball straight down the pitch in the hope the opposition goalkeeper will make a mistake. Gerry and I spend most of our time running around the half-empty stand, playing catch between woollen trouser legs. Our only moment of distraction comes when the opposing centre-forward goes up for a high ball. Town's defender knows a trick worth two of his. Goes up at the same time, elbows pumping as if to gain extra height. Catches the opposing player smack in the left eye. 'He'll have an even better shiner in the

Saturday

morning than you, my lad.' One of the home spectators grins at me. In the end, one more boring nil-nil draw.

After six by the time I get home. Thursday or Friday Mam would be primped and primed, ready to set about her business, but not tonight. She hates Saturday nights. 'Amateur hour,' she says. 'Drunken lasses giving it away free or trying their chances for a few quid behind the pub. Middle-aged men out with their wives for a bit of a knees-up, young lads on the pull with hardly a shilling between them. Waste of time. Your dad spends more money over the bar than I make in the night. Better off staying at home and having a jolly family night in.' We all know she doesn't mean it. Staying in of a Saturday night is a sign of old age and decrepitude, she says in one of her more sullen moods. Everyone goes out on Saturday night, even if it's to loll about smoking outside the chippy.

Me and Harry don't get to go out, of course. Or at least I don't. Harry stays out all night playing Newmarket or pontoon for sweets with Grandma. She's fierce at pontoon; there is no question here of her letting Harry win. He still gets his sweets but she's clear they are a consolation prize, not the real thing. Then she will make him eggy bread for breakfast on Sunday morning while all I get at home is dry bread and no butter.

Mam is in respectable gear tonight, skirt down to her ankles but tight as a snake's skin around the bum. White satin blouse, loose enough to show a bit of cleavage when she bends forward, transparent enough to show off the lacy black bra beneath. Her stilettoes are no higher than any of the lasses round here wear to go out dancing on a Saturday. Dad sports a proper jacket with a white shirt and mauve tie. Not dockland tonight, then, but one of the respectable pubs in the centre of town. Aiming at the businessman market now the fleet has almost run out of money. 'Nothing like a bored businessman on the razzle,' says Mam. 'Bored stiff with his job, marooned in a strange town, worrying about what his wife is getting up to while he's away. Might as well have as much fun as he can, put all he spends down as travelling expenses. Wouldn't be surprised if one didn't turn round and ask me for a tax receipt!' Mam splutters with laughter. Dad's probably had a good day on the horses.

'Do you know a man called Burnham?' I ask her. 'Dresses smart, expensive shoes, face like a rat's arse.'

'How often have I told you not to use gutter language like that? Looks like he's just shat himself?' She giggles. Dad must have had a tenner on a ten-to-one shot. 'The sort of feller you and Harry need to keep away from. Likes nice young boys. Men, too. Only his mates at the masons keep him out the nick. Why do you ask? Has he been trying to touch you up? I'll have his bollocks off with a filleting knife if he has.'

'No, Mam. I saw him at the football today, going into the players' entrance. Except he looks too old to be one of the players. Doesn't look like he'd be happy getting his knees dirty.'

'He gets other bits dirty enough.' Another giggle. 'Suppose he's on the board at the football club. Gets into the games for free, spends the time supping whiskey and spending the money the club should be using on new players. Never had a good one since they sold Raich Carter, your dad says. Here, hold this compact while I put me make-up on. What do you think to this colour?'

'Very nice,' I say. 'Very respectable light red, not like your Friday-night super neon.'

'Different advertising for different clientele,' says Mam, her nose in the air, a film star on her way to an audition.

I watch her and Dad walk off down the street arm in arm to catch the bus into town like a couple of lovers out for a stroll, Dad throwing back his shoulders in pride at having such a beautiful woman on his arm, Mam twitching her bum just a little bit to express her satisfaction with how lovely she is.

Sunday

Earliest start of the week. Six thirty on the dot. Glad the days are getting longer and the mornings lighter. Sunday's the only time I am allowed into Kirkwood's newsagents unsupervised, ready to pick up my bag of papers from the counter. His children and grandchildren are already out there, fanning out across the surrounding estates dropping off weekly magazines, comics and the *News of the World*, or 'news of the screws', as we all call it.

Officially I am too young to be employed, even on a paper round, just like most of Kirkwood's grandchildren. The story is they are merely helping their parents, who happen to give them their week's pocket money at lunch time today. I started like that last November in the middle of the annual flu epidemic. Half the Kirkwood family were sick in bed. Alex, John Kirkwood's son, who is in the top class in my year, asked if I would give him a hand because he had to do his uncle's round as well. So we did both rounds together and split the money. Not a lot, half a crown each plus any of last week's comics left unsold. In the end they forget I was merely temporary and let me stay on.

Delivering newspapers is easy work, merely shoving them through letter boxes. My round is part of the council estate, where all of them are regular standard size and horizontal. No-one here takes more than one paper and perhaps a magazine or two. The front gardens are short so you don't waste too much time from one house to the next. Most people are happy for you to take a shortcut across the front of the two houses without going down one entrance then back up the next.

You can tell the posh houses. They have all sorts of shapes and sizes for letter boxes, often tiny vertical things with super-strong springs and draught excluders. People who live here take the new multi-part papers with colour magazines and extra supplements. The houses have huge front gardens with high hedges or fences between them and the house next door. Woe betide any postman or delivery boy who's spotted taking a shortcut through a hole in the hedge or over a drooping barrier of chicken wire.

We're not trusted with these houses because they often leave payment out in an envelope behind the milk bottles. Kirkwood thinks we'll pocket the money and claim the customer has not paid. He's dead right. The other thing we are not allowed to do is sell cigarettes. Neither is Kirkwood, if truth be told, except in the shop. Only the adults carry Woodbines or Park Drives, which they sell either in the full packet of ten or by the two or three. Newspapers are on credit; cigarettes are purely a cash deal. They're also a source of blackmail. Don't pay your paper bill and you get no cigarettes. Wake up on a Sunday morning with a raging hangover and desperate for a fag and the guy on the doorstep refuses to sell you any until you settle your bill. What do you do? Wouldn't work with us kids, of course, so we are kept out of that side of the business.

The other good thing about working on Sunday morning, besides the money, is keeping out of the way of Mam and Dad. Nothing about Saturday nights is satisfactory. Plenty of custom and Mam is tired out after three nights in a row. A bad night and Dad will have drunk too much. He'll be horribly hungover and Mam will be furious he has ploughed so much money across the bar. Harry and me will catch the crap whichever way it goes, so Harry is hiding his head at Grandma's and I'm out on the street pushing soggy newspapers through letter boxes. Only a couple more streets, then I can whip back to Kirkwood's to pick up my money before collecting Harry.

Gran's collected as much of the family around her as she can manage this Sunday. There's Muriel's husband Jersey, stranded here after the war, complaining how he can never go back home. Harry's sitting at the dining-room table when I get there, supping a glass of milk while Jersey thumbs through the *Sunday Express*. 'World's going to rack and ruin,' he says. 'Bloody Russians do anything they like. I'm off to America before they come over here.' Complaints about the Russians are all I ever hear from Jersey, delivered in his thick foreign accent.

Dad always refers to Jersey as Grandma's fancy-man. 'Nothing of the sort,' says Grandma. 'I am far too old for him. He's quite happy with his Muriel. She looks after him well enough. Like he looks after me from time to time when there are things around the house I can't manage. He's not escaping from Muriel, it's those stroppy kids of his he can't stand.'

Grandma is right. Jersey's two boys are three or four years older than me, always in trouble, continually excluded from school as well as being excluded from Kirkwood's newsagents because they keep trying to steal the cigarettes they sell to the other kids. Neither of them has been properly taught by Jersey and Muriel. 'Don't get caught' has never made sense to them. At home they're right terrors, haring around the place, jumping on and off the furniture, nicking money out of Muriel's purse, drinking Jersey's beer so he's always looking for new hiding places. I think Grandma keeps some for him in one of her kitchen cupboards.

At school Mrs Reeve tells us that Jersey is a part of the United Kingdom. 'It is down here,' she says, indicating a collection of tiny islands next to a peninsular on the map. 'Right next to France, a leftover from the days when the English kings ruled from Calais to Bordeaux.' From her tone of voice, we understand this was a good time and she regrets it having passed.

I once asked Jersey if he was really from Jersey or from one of the other Channel Islands. After all, he does have a foreign accent. He laughed so much I thought he was going to burst. Grandma had to hit him on the back and push another cup of tea in front of him before he stopped. 'I'm not from the Channel Islands at all,' he said once he had recovered himself.

'Where are you from, then?' I asked. 'You are not from here. Are you American? South African? Australian?'

'What do they teach you at school? English schools, all they care about is English kings and queens. Anything the other side of the Channel might as well be in outer space for all the attention you pay it. Let me tell you.' He bent his two fingers on his right hand backwards until they cracked and I thought they were about to fall off like the absent two must have done at some time. 'When I was young, I lived in a country called Poland. Then it was occupied by the Germans and I had to run away and fight for the English. When we'd beaten the Germans I wanted to go back to my village in Poland. But my village wasn't in Poland anymore; it was in Russia.'

'How did the Russians move a whole village?' I asked.

'Moving a whole village is very difficult. All they had to do was move the border. Moving the border is easy if you have enough soldiers and an atomic bomb.' I have visions of thousands of soldiers picking up a border, something which looks like a huge run of cable, and walking with it from one village to the next. Why they also needed an atomic bomb, I do not understand.

'Every time I read the newspaper,' Jersey continued, 'I can see the border getting nearer and the Russians coming closer. They already have half of Germany. In two minutes they can swallow up the rest and be in Calais within an hour. Then where would we be? In America I will be safe.'

Grandma turns up her eyes. She has heard all this before, since the day Jersey married Muriel. According to Grandma, Jersey's two sons are my cousins even if Muriel is not Mam's proper sister. 'She's her half-sister,' she once told me. 'I was two months pregnant with her when I married your grandfather. Neither of us knew at the time. Neither did the other feller or he wouldn't have run off and left me. Maybe. So your mam and Muriel have the same mum but different fathers. Makes no difference; men are unreliable creatures at the best of times. One day Muriel will turn around and Jersey will have disappeared to America without a word, leave her with the kids. Let's hope he waits until they can fend for themselves.'

'Can we go now?' asks Harry. He's not bored, he's hungry.

Grandma has her Sunday bag packed. Every Saturday lunch time Mam slips her a few quid for some shopping before Dad can get his hands on it. After the newspaper round on Sunday I collect it from her to take home alongside one of Grandma's apple pies. She makes three: one for us, one for Muriel and one for herself and whoever else might drop in. 'A leftover from the war,' says Jersey. 'Apples were free in the winter. All you had to do was pick them off the ground and you had enough pie for a week. A couple of rabbits from a friendly farmer or a cod smuggled off the docks and there was the family fed.'

Today there is a fat chicken in the bag alongside a dozen deformed and muddy potatoes and a bunch of wrinkled carrots. No cabbage, thank God. I hate cabbage. Mam boils it for three hours until it looks like mushy baby food and tastes of absolutely nothing. I don't have time to cook it today; Dad will be crawling up the wall by the time it's ready.

All the men round here expect their wives to set to and make a lovely Sunday lunch. Not a bit of it, not our mam. I'm not going to let her loose on a chicken or even another can of beans. If anyone's going to cook Sunday lunch in our house, it's going to be me. If the Social knew, they would go spare, especially if they saw me sharpen up our only decent knife for Harry to use peeling the potatoes. I trust him. He does a good job, the potato inches from his nose as he turns it across the knife rather than the other way round.

When she cooks chicken Grandma slips bits of garlic under the skin. No point in cooking like that with Dad around. I take a chance and rub it all over with salt before dumping it onto the baking pan and covering it with lard. The pan still has traces of whatever we had last Sunday which hasn't been properly scraped away. Never mind, it all adds to the flavour. Harry hasn't yet finished the potatoes so I can't put them in with the chicken. I'll boil them up, put them in the oven for the last half-hour or so, which means I can use the same pan for the carrots. I can cook them first and heat them up later. Dad insists on soft carrots and doesn't like to wait. He's already getting restless, listening to *Family Favourites* on the radio and complaining at how late dinner is. I've not told him he's got over an hour more before he can eat.

Today's Sunday lunch is the highlight of the weekend for me. Not so much the eating, but the cooking. Everyone leaves me alone. Mam because she knows she'll only get in the way and mess things up, Dad because he thinks it's women's work and nothing to do with him. Calls me 'a little pansy', especially when I put on Mam's pinnie to stop the fat spraying all over me clothes. Doesn't stop him wolfing it down when it's ready, picking out the best bits. 'Why is a roast chicken like a suntanned woman?' he asks for the umpteenth time. 'Because the white bits are the tastiest.' And he laughs again at his own old joke.

By three the chicken is only just cooked so we don't sit down until nearly half past. Dad is especially grumpy but a great lump off the breast and a bottle of beer cheers him up no end. Harry attacks the meal as if it's the last of the week, which it might be if business doesn't go according to plan or the horses run too slowly. Grandma's apple pie goes down a treat. Apple pie demands custard but Grandma hasn't bought any milk. Last time I tried to make custard it all came up in uncooked lumps. Anything which is a powder defeats me. 'You'll learn in time,' Grandma told me. Even if she's right, it's safest not to do my learning with Dad sitting there waiting to be served.

Sunday

Now comes decision time. Since no-one else is going to do it, do I boil up a kettle and do the washing-up or skive off in the hope that Mam will pile the dishes in the sink? If she puts them out of sight Dad won't notice, just doze off in his chair with another bottle of Hewitt's best bitter. The sun decides me, shining sharply through the parting in the curtains.

'Just off out, Mam,' I shout as I grab my coat and disappear through the back door. She says something in return which I pretend not to hear.

Kirkwood's newsagent is still open, one of the daughters-in-law in sole charge at this quietest part of the week. 'I suppose you want Alex.' She pokes her head round the connecting door and screams up the stairs, keeping an eye on me as she does so. There is no way she's going to let a reprobate like me have the run of the shop. 'Wait for him outside,' she says. She'd do that even if it was pissing it down with rain or three feet deep in snow.

Out on the pavement I can hear Alex thundering down the stairs. 'Come on,' he says, bouncing a football with his left hand. Alex is cranky about learning to do everything equally well with both hands and both feet. 'The other player will work out which is your soft side,' he says. 'Then he'll take you on that side every time.' Alex is the centre-half in the school team. Like me and Gerry he aims to make the Town team and has been studying carefully at all the home matches. Apart from being able to pass the ball onto a sixpence at pace he also knows how to leap for the ball with elbows flying in the general direction of the opposing centre-forward's face.

Because he's in the top class the teachers think he's a nice lad. A nice lad who lifts the nails from the studs on his boots so he can scrape them down the shins of anyone who gets too close. In short, he's a thug, much happier with us lot from the B stream than the swots in A. Like many here his father is not around. Despite lacking a dad he's still 'respectable' since his mother works as a clippie on the buses and only has a man round from time to time.

Childhood, Boyhood, Youth

'Mam says if I go to the grammar school I can have a new bike,' he tells me, 'so I suppose I'd better turn up for the tests next week.'

'No point in me bothering,' I say. 'I wouldn't get a new bike even if they made me a skipper of a trawler.'

'My mam says no son of hers is going to work on the boats.'

'My mam says the same. Far too dangerous, she says. People get injured or drowned. Suppose you'll work in an office.'

'Not if I can help it. I'm going to join the army and become a general. Here's Gerry's. Let's dig him out. With three of us we can get in some passing practice.'

'Nar,' says Gerry. 'Passing practice is for the girls. Let's dig out some of the other lads, play three or four a side. I'll go round Gary's. Alex knows Frank Harrison's place. I know he's only a titch but he's the only one who'll go in goal.'

'And I'll turf out Wiggie. His mum don't care how late he stays out as long as he comes home reasonably clean.'

Mrs Wiggleton is washing up from lunch. Wiggie stands by clutching a tea towel, ragged round the edges, with which he gives the plates a cursory wipe before stacking them in their appropriate places. His eyes light up.

'Don't you dare leave this house until you've finished wiping up,' orders Mrs W. 'I've still got your dad's kit to pack; he's off soon.'

'But he's still in bed, Mam. There's no hurry.' Wiggie puts on the face he would adopt if he were told the world's going to end in five minutes.

'You do as you are told, young man. Can't you hear him wandering about upstairs, looking for his work socks or something? Get those pans wiped and put away. Be here when I get back.' I take a seat at the kitchen table, happy to see someone else washing and wiping up for a change. Sounds of argument from upstairs. Socks, shirt or pullover have gone missing. Wiggie takes even less care of his duties than before, aiming to get all out of sight before his mum reappears.

60

Sunday

Which she soon does, weighed down by a kit bag, stained interesting patterns by long exposure to sea, salt and sun. She places it carefully in the centre of the sitting room, stands over it like a guardsman on duty. Mr W scoots downstairs, a man with a mission. Last time I saw him he was in his best fisherman-on-the-razzle gear. Today it's work boots, heavy-duty trousers, faded plaid shirt and black padded waterproof.

'Here, our lass,' he says to Mrs W. 'Lend us a few coppers for the bus. I'm a bit short. I'll pay you back when we land.'

'You ought to bloody look after your money, not booze it all away. I've a good mind to make you walk. Serve you right.'

'Ah, come on, love, it's only a few coppers. If I walk I'll miss the boat completely. Then they'll have me up again as a "disobedient fisherman". Cost us fifty quid last time. Took me months to pay it off.'

'Took me months, you mean. All me child allowance and more into the bargain. Next time you're home from sea I'll do what Maureen Parker does and take your pay packet off you before you can blow the lot. Here's two bob. Enough there for a bus ride to the docks and back again instead of wasting money on a taxi. Now, get your ugly face out of my house.' She thrusts the kit bag into his arms, throws her own around his neck and gives him a long, lingering kiss. Wiggie and I look at one another. Shrug. Hurtle out of the door before either of his parents can notice.

On the way to the park we pass the nearby bus stop. Half a dozen men stand around chatting, three days' stubble on their faces, kit bags sagging at their feet. The young ones look vaguely excited, the older ones bored and resigned. Tide is nearly up and the fleet is getting ready to sail.

Monday

'Aw, Mam. Can't I stay in bed? It's siling it down with rain outside and all I've got at school today are those silly tests. No point in me going.'

Mam is in an old black dress which looks like a rusty drainpipe. She wears it on her non-working days when she sits around the house smoking too much or making some sort of effort to clean the kitchen or do last week's washing. Black doesn't show the dirt, she says, so it's a perfect colour for a busy housewife. A hard-working woman needs clothes she can slop around in, forget the make-up and the sheer nylons. I hate her in this dress. It makes her look plain and ordinary when I know she's the most beautiful woman on the whole estate. She has her hair tied up in a brilliant purple scarf, which adds much-needed colour to the dreary morning.

'You get yourself up and dressed. I'm not having you and Harry under me feet all day. There's work to be done, bedclothes to be washed. Maisie Kirkwood has her lad off to school already, to make sure he's in time for the exams. The most important ones in his life, she says. Had herself put on late shift out of turn so she can be around in the morning for him, give him a good breakfast, set him up for the day. If it's good enough for Maisie Kirkwood, it's good enough for me. Up you get. There's bread and hot milk on the table. Oh, shit!'

Mam exits at speed. I know what's happened. What always happens when she starts messing about in the kitchen. There'll be burned milk in the cups and a drying milk scum all over the cooker. I'll clean it up when I get home.

Harry's sitting at the table sipping his milk. Typically, he's not made a move to turn off the cooker or move the pan. Too busy in his own little world, I expect. I punch him on the shoulder to wake him up. 'Are you here already?' he asks. 'Thought I'd have to go to school on me own.'

Quite apart from me, our walk is joined by Gerry Pettit and Wiggie. 'What are you doing here?' Gerry asks. 'You said you weren't going to bother with all the code-breaking rubbish.'

'Mam insisted, said if Alex Kirkwood was going I had to go as well. All very well for him, doing practice tests every Friday morning. Useless for the rest of us. We'd be better off twagging it to the park and annoying the ducks.'

'Not in this weather,' says Gerry. 'School is warm and dry. There's no proper lessons. All we have to do is sit still at our desks and stare out the window.'

'How boring,' says Wiggie. 'Do we have to sit there all day? Can't we simply walk out after writing our name at the top of the page?'

'Imagine what old man Reeve would do if we did that! Six of the best on each hand if we were lucky.'

'He can't do that,' I say. 'It's against the law. Six in total is all he's allowed.'

'Who's counting?' Wiggie replies. 'And who dares turn him in? Imagine what he would do: give us a beating every day and twice on Thursdays, have the police and the Social at your door claiming you're out of control. Grin and bear it. Sit still with a pen in your hand and a dumb expression on your face.'

'Should be easy enough for you,' says Gerry. 'You have a dumb expression anyway.'

Wiggie is not impressed. He and Gerry push and shove at one

another all the way down the street, nearly forcing an old woman into the road on the way.

'Council house brats,' she mutters once far enough away to avoid any repercussions. We all laugh. Having a reputation means you're someone in the world. As Mam says, all advertising is good advertising.

No assembly today. The school hall's taken up by over a hundred plain desks, specially brought from a Council depot in town. We carry in our own classroom chairs, sit down at the desk with our name on it. No choice this morning, strictly alphabetical order. Wiggie's in the next row by the window, Gerry in the same one almost next to me. Alex Kirkwood's next to him, one row further over. A pity. I could have copied his answers without bothering to look at the question.

Both Mr and Mrs Reeve are on duty, along with Miss Burton, who teaches the C stream. Attempts to keep them in order would be the true description. Looks after the flids in the class when they wet themselves. Not many of them are here today. Only the ones who can write their own names, I suspect.

Miss Burton walks along the rows placing the question paper upside down on each desk, together with an extra sheet for rough jottings. 'There will be no talking,' instructs Mr Reeve. 'If you feel ill or need to go to the toilet, raise your hand and Miss Burton or Mrs Reeve will assist you.' He says this in such a tone that no-one's in any doubt that raising a hand will put the person in his bad books for the rest of the year. 'On your desk is a sheet of paper with your name and examination number. When I tell you – not before!" A vile scowl. "You will turn your examination paper over and write this information on it in capital letters. I trust we have taught you well enough for you to know what capital letters are.' Miss Burton looks doubtful. 'Very well. Turn your papers over now and begin.'

The first paper is all about correcting any mistakes there may be. Question one's easy: 'The children look at there comic.' No

Monday

mistake on this one, so I leave it uncorrected. They're trying to catch us out already.

Question two has an obvious mistake: 'Nelson was a grate commander.' I cross out 'commander' and write in 'admiral' instead. Everyone knows an admiral is a higher rank than a mere commander. Some of the other questions confuse me but I plough on, doing much better than I'd expected.

On the next page is all the code-breaking stuff. What are they all about? Take this one: 'BEJC is to Christopher as BAGG is to…'

What? Who is this Christopher person? Am I supposed to know him? I give up completely on this section and turn over. Maths, easily the simplest section until the final few questions which are about long multiplication and division, the hardest involving decimal points. Nevertheless, I have a bash, finishing just as Mr Reeve instructs us to put down our pencils and sit back.

Wiggie is asleep in his chair, Gerry has chewed his pencil to a stump. Alex Kirkwood is still writing madly, scratching his head at the same time. 'Not so clever after all,' I think to myself. 'If I can finish all three sections, why can't he?'

No tests after lunch and no proper lessons either. Wiggie and Gerry have both done a runner, along with almost all of Miss Burton's class. The remnants have been amalgamated with us under Mrs Reeve's eagle eye. She keeps us quiet playing board games: Ludo, Monopoly, Cluedo. I avoid Cluedo, which stinks of police stuff. Miss Burton has been sent off to help with the little ones, who are disturbed by the disruption in the upper school.

Her influence rears its head on the walk home. Harry insists he has a story to tell me. Little Red Riding Hood. 'Not Red Riding Hood again,' I object. 'That's a baby story. Gran told it me when I was even smaller than you. Can't you think of a better one?'

'Well,' says Harry, 'if you know it so well, listen and tell me if I get it right. Miss Burton read it to us this afternoon, but I'm sure she got it completely wrong, especially the bit about the Grandmother and the wolf.'

I give in. Harry's going to tell me the story whether I listen or not. If he gets too boring I can always try and do long multiplication in me head.

'*Once upon a time,*' Harry begins. I nod in encouragement at the approved beginning of any fairy story. '*There was a little girl called Little Red Riding Hood, because she always wore a red coat with a big hood attached. Every day she visited her gran in the forest to take her milk and bread and to eat her apple pie. One day she was walking through the wood and met a big brown wolf with huge red eyes. "Hello, wolf," she said, stroking his head. "Hello, Red," said the wolf. "How are you today?"*'

'The wolf will eat her up,' I objected. 'That's what wolves do. Then the woodsman will come and rescue her.'

'How can he rescue her if she's been eaten up? Besides, the wolf is her friend. He says hello to her every morning and she gives him the crust off the bread because Grandma has no teeth and doesn't eat bread crust. Right?'

'Right.'

'*So the wolf went off in the forest, but later on Red Riding Hood met a woodman armed with a great big axe. This big.*' Harry throws his arms apart like a lying fisherman. He checks to see I'm watching. '*The woodman put his arms round Red Riding Hood's shoulders, which she did not like very much. Then he put his hand up her skirt. She didn't like that at all and ran away. The woodman was clever. He knew a shortcut through the forest to Grandma's house. Grandma had left her door unlocked because there are never any bad people in the forest and she knew Red Riding Hood was coming anyway. The woodman walked straight in and sat on Grandma's bed.*'

'Why's Grandma still in bed?'

'Because she likes to have breakfast in bed. Red Riding Hood comes early in the morning and has her breakfast in bed with Grandma, like we used to do. Right?'

'Right.'

Monday

'Grandma told the woodman to get his dirty clothes off her nice clean bed, but the woodman did not move, just propped his huge axe against her pillow. Then he did something naughty. He pushed his hand under the bedclothes and up Grandma's nightdress. Grandma was even more angry than Red Riding Hood had been. And she was a big, strong, grown-up woman. Instantly she jumped out of bed, grabbed the woodman's axe and cut off his head with it.

'Red Riding Hood was very shocked when she came in. "What do we do with a dead woodman?" she asked. Grandma had a clever idea. "We will call your friend the wolf," she said. The wolf was very pleased to be called. He sat down outside Grandma's house and ate the woodman all up. Every piece, even the bones. Then Red Riding Hood and Grandma had breakfast together and fed the wolf bread crusts with strawberry jam for his dessert.

'See, that's the proper story of Red Riding Hood and the wolf.' Harry looks exceptionally pleased with himself. Was I that bloodthirsty when I was seven? Surely Miss Burton can't have told him such a story?

Dad's out when we get home. 'Gone down the docks with one of his mates,' says Mam. 'Rumours on the radio about a special landing. "Seize the day," I said to him. "Get down there and find out what's happening." You boys see to your supper while I get washed. There's some chicken left in the cupboard.'

Which proves to be a half-picked carcass, not enough for two starving boys. Since Dad isn't here I have the run of the kitchen, boil up a handful of rice and chop the leftovers of yesterday's carrots while Harry picks every inch of chicken from the carcass. There's still some jelly left on the plate, which I mix in with the cooked rice, the carrots and chicken. Sprinkle with salt and a bit of white pepper and there's an instant supper. Grandma would have made it with oil, garlic and black pepper but I have to make do with what we have. It's still tasty and filling. 'Try this,' I say to Harry, handing him the parson's nose, 'it's a real delicacy.'

'Tasty enough,' he says, 'but too fat.' I grin. One day he'll find out.

'Wash up after yourselves,' orders Mam as she comes back down, her hair in curlers under a plastic head scarf. 'We may have guests tonight and I don't want to have to clear up your mess. Give us a taste of that rice. Not bad. You'll make a wonderful wife one day, our Danny.'

'Bloody nancy boy,' says Dad, pushing his way through the back door. 'You kids bugger off and do some homework while I talk to your mam.'

'No homework today, Dad. Only tests and games at school.' He aims a half-hearted fist at me as I rush past. Obviously he's in a good mood; he doesn't miss very often. Harry and I play dominoes for a while. It's boring playing dominoes with Harry. He picks up every domino in his hand, looks at it carefully, places it back on the floor, examines the next. Every time! Games take ages. Matters downstairs are more interesting. Harry and I creep out the bedroom, descend to the bottom stair, listen through the half-open door.

'Not that crew again,' Mam is saying. 'Every one of them is as ugly as sin. They get drunk so easy and spew up all over the place. Getting rid of them last time was like getting a limpet off a stone.'

'Come on,' says Dad. 'They only land here once or twice a year. And they spend a fortune. When did you ever object to a job because he was three parts to the wind? Money for old rope. Can't believe you'll pass up a chance like this.'

'They are so weird,' says Mam. 'You can't imagine the things they want to do. I suppose all they ever do up there in the frozen north is work out ways to fuck reindeer. Whatever, I'm not taking them on on me own. How many are there? Five, six?'

'I suppose so. No more than half a dozen. We could get Didi Moffatt over, she's always up for a good night. How about your Muriel?'

'No chance. She puts it around a bit but she's no idea of professional ethics. Quite likely to pack her bags and walk out when the going gets interesting. Anyway, Jersey would insist on

Monday

coming as well and he doesn't care for standing by watching. Nip round to Janice in the close, ask her if she's up for it. I'll pop by Lizzie Fraser. She was out of action last week but she should've finished by now. Get some booze in. Vodka's best for these guys, two or three bottles. On tick if you can. Meet the crew in the Victoria, stand them a couple of drinks. Bring them back here around eight when I've got the kids to bed and had time to put me face on. Make sure they pay for the taxi.'

We scoot back upstairs, pretend to be absorbed in our game. Mam pushes her head round the door. 'Right, you two. I want all the plates and dishes washed up and put away. I'm out to Mrs Fraser's for a while. I want everything spick and span when I get back. No sopping-wet dishcloths in the sink or water all over the floor. Wash hands and faces if you have time. And Danny, bring out the glasses from the under-stairs cupboard. The little ones Jersey likes to drink from. About a dozen or so. Hope your dad thinks to buy some crisps and peanuts from the offie.'

Harry and I both know to keep our heads down. We don't like big nights like this. They go on until all hours, making it impossible to sleep. With the worst ones we have the neighbours banging on the door to complain, especially those on the six-in-the-morning shift. Alex Kirkwood's mum is the worst. She has to be up at five, cycle to the bus station in time to be the clippie on the workers' bus at five thirty. Anyone so much as drops a pin within a mile of her after ten at night and she'll have the police on them. I've told Alex she ought to buy some ear plugs. He wasn't impressed.

I boil the kettle for some hot water to get the chicken grease off the plates, scrub them as hard as I can with the dish cloth. While Harry meticulously dries each one I rummage under the stairs for the box of glasses. These are tiny things, no more than a couple of inches tall. At Christmas Jersey brings round pink vodka, insisting everyone has a glassful, which is to be drunk in one gulp. Mam and Gran manage fine but Dad stubbornly refuses, sticking to his Christmas glass of Guinness.

Despite what people say, I know we're not poor because we have a second tea towel which we can use when the other one gets too dirty. I root it out from the airing cupboard upstairs, use it to clean a dozen glasses so they shine like new, lay them neatly on the kitchen table.

'You'll do for me, young Danny,' breezes Didi Moffatt, a fantasy in pink in a low-cut flounced dress, the neckline cut low to show off her large breasts covered in dark brown freckles. Didi's not a patch on Mam. Her bum is too big and her legs too skinny. She has ginger hair which she tries to disguise by dyeing it black. Except she only dyes it once a month, so the ginger's already showing through at the roots. Her face used to be sharp but now the bones have disappeared and she's getting round and puffy. She also wears too much make-up: heavy rouge on her cheekbones, brilliant orange lipstick. I'd never let Mam go out looking like her.

By contrast, Mam has stuck to black. The office look, she calls it. Severe skirt two inches above the knee with a foot-long slit at the back, white blouse and a loose black waistcoat. Black stockings, of course. Only a touch of rouge, enough to bring out her colour under the face powder, and the subtlest touch of pink lipstick. 'The working man's dream,' she says. 'Having it away with one of the girls from the office, a secretary or the boss's personal assistant. The kind he can only dream about. This lot we have tonight love it, gets them going every time, though they don't need much encouragement after three months at sea. Off you go, you two lads. Wash faces, pyjamas on. I don't want to hear a peep out of you tonight.'

A polite knock on the back door. That will be Mrs Fraser. She's always one for doing what she calls 'the proper thing'. We'd love to see what she's wearing but Mam pushes us away upstairs before answering the door. Harry curls up in bed, buries his head under the blankets, fully aware he won't get much sleep once the party starts. I lie listening to the faint sounds of the women's conversation downstairs, serious statements interrupted

Monday

from time to time by childish giggles. Girls are always giggling, whatever age they are.

Maybe I'm going deaf or getting used to the noise of Mam and Dad's parties but I doze off and only wake up to the sound of fighting in the street outside. It must be late because all the lights are out in the other houses. As the noise increases the lights come on one by one. Some houses remain dark but I can see the curtains twitching aside in upstairs windows. I creep out of bed and twitch my own curtains. Two men are attempting to wrestle one another to the ground. Quite a feat since both of them are so drunk they can hardly stand. Another, a huge man with a mop of dirty blond hair, is on his knees puking into the gutter while Mrs Fraser holds back his clothes to prevent him soiling them.

Downstairs is even more rowdy. Dad's shouting at the top of his voice. Mam's screaming abuse at someone. Didi Moffatt sings a popular song off-key in an incomprehensible Glaswegian accent. 'Come away, love. Come on upstairs,' she says to someone. 'And you, gorgeous. We'll make a threesome. I know what you like, love. No problem.'

Mam's shouting even louder, answered by a heavy, threatening voice. The dogs sound off on cue at the provocation. Dad's banging his fist on the table. Then all hell breaks loose. Chairs are overturned, glasses smash. Didi Moffatt screams. The two wrestlers stop their performance and totter back into the house, adding their bellows to the commotion. A crash. 'You fucking bastard!' Dad shouts. Mrs Fraser yells, 'You've killed her, you've killed her!' Growls and barks; the dogs are loose in the house. Another scream. A male one this time.

Blue lights in the street outside. Two police cars hurtle down the road, one from each direction. A black-painted Transit van follows, double parks, blocking the road completely. 'Call off the dogs,' someone shouts. 'Get those dogs outside. Shut up the lot of you.' His order increases the pandemonium. The blond man and the two wrestlers are ushered into the black van. A skinny man dressed in a Fair Isle pullover follows. Then two police stagger out under the dead weight of a huge brute who must be twenty stone and well over six feet in height. His trousers are torn and both his legs are bleeding from wounds. Not half as much as from the deep gashes across his face. I've seen wounds like this before, at a wedding Mam forced us to go to. Two fellers had a drunken argument and one smashed his glass into the other's face, outing one of his eyes. I look carefully to see if there's an eye hanging out of a socket, but it's too dark.

'What's going on? What's happening?' demands Harry, pulling at my pyjama sleeve.

'Been a fight,' I tell him. 'Mam and Dad are kicking up hell. Cop cars all over. Here's another one.' Not quite right. The flashing blue light's an ambulance, which nearly runs into the back of the Transit van. The driver and his mate hustle out, run round to the back for a folding trolley. A policeman stops them, seeming to demand bandages and cotton wool for the man bleeding all over his patrol car. The driver reluctantly hands them over. For only the second time this week our front door is open, allowing the trolley to squeeze through.

'Let me have a look. I want to see.' Harry pushes himself in front of me, presses his nose tight up against the window. 'Here they come. Look, there's a body on the trolley. A dead person. It's our mam. Danny, look, it's our mam. They've killed our mam.'

The world stops.

Harry's right, it is our mam, her clean white blouse stained a brilliant red, both arms lolling off the sides of the trolley. 'She's not dead. I saw her move,' I lie to Harry.

'She's dead. She's dead,' he keeps repeating. 'We must go and help her.' He lets go of my sleeve, races off to the top of the stairs, descends at top speed. Right into the arms of a policewoman.

'You boys can't come in here,' she says. 'You've nothing on your feet and there's broken glass all over the floor. Off you go, back up to bed.'

'Me mam,' shouts Harry. 'I want me mam.'

'Your mother has had a little accident and the nice men are taking her to hospital for a rest. Come upstairs with me and I'll tuck you in.' She grabs each of us by the arm, more lifting than guiding us back to our bedroom. 'Into bed you get,' she says, careful to stay between Harry and the door, mindful he'd be off in a flash if not watched. True to her word, she tucks Harry in before tiptoeing out and locking the bedroom door behind her.

A second later Harry is curled up beside me, like he used to do in the children's home, sobbing so hard the bed shakes.

'They've killed our mam,' he says. 'Our mam's dead. They've killed her.' He says that all night, even after he's finally drifted off to sleep.

Tuesday

'Don't you two come in here without your shoes on. There's glass all over the floor. I'm not spending the rest of the day mopping up your blood as well as everybody else's.' Grandma has her hair up on top of her head, an old pinnie of Mam's tied around her like the elastic band round a bundle of radishes, the coal shovel in one hand, a floor brush in the other. Sweat drips from stray strands of white hair, making rivulets through the thick foundation she plasters on her chest to hide the increasing number of liver spots.

'Get dressed and off to school with you. There's jam sandwiches for your breakfast in your satchels. I said don't come in here!' she screams as Harry tries to push past. I catch a glimpse of the wreck of the kitchen. Two chairs are in pieces all over the kitchen, looking like they have been flattened by giants. Blood and broken glass litter the floor, the odd sprinkling of white enamel glinting in the pale morning light. Jersey is busy righting the upturned table. I can hear Dad outside swearing at the dogs.

'I want me mam!' screams Harry. 'They've killed me mam.' He kicks at Grandma's ankles as she holds him back.

'Behave yourself, you little brat,' she screams at him, slapping him around the head furiously. I've never seen Grandma lose her temper with Harry before; he's her delicate little baby. 'Your mam's

Tuesday

not here. She's not well. Will you listen to me! Stop screaming. She's not dead, I tell you. She's in hospital. By the time you get home from school she'll be here. She's not dead; she just needs a rest and a little bit of care and attention.' Grandma looks daggers at Dad's back as he bends over the largest of the dogs. 'Go off to school, like a good boy. Let me fix things up here so it's ready for your mam when she comes home. Off you go, now.'

Together we prise Harry's fingers loose from Grandma's pinnie. I haul him away down the street, whimpering and crying for Mam. 'Tell me a story, Harry,' I say. 'This morning I need a good story.'

We're already halfway to school before he opens his mouth. '*Once upon a time*,' he begins, then bursts into floods of tears again.

'You can't go into school like this,' I tell him. 'What will the big boys say? They'll beat you up again and I won't be able to help, there are too many of them. Be brave!'

'I don't want to be brave, I want me mam.'

I wipe the snot off his nose, adjust his blazer. 'Look like you are telling me that story,' I say to him as we stroll through the school gates, just in time to hear the entry bell. 'You don't have to be brave all day, just until you get into class. Once you're in class the big boys can't hurt you. Mam will be home tonight and then you'll feel better.'

He nods, wipes his nose on the sleeve of his blazer, snuffles one more time before joining the end of his class queue. I amble into school, change into plimsolls, wander off to the empty classroom and plonk myself into a spare chair in the middle of the middle row. For ten minutes I sit there wondering where the others have got to.

Mrs Reeve bustles in, weighed down by a large bag of knitting which she throws onto her desk with a sigh before she registers my presence. 'What on earth are you doing here!' she cries. 'You should be in the hall with all the others, sitting your tests. Come along with you. Right now.'

She hustles me into the hall, a sea of bent backs and scratching pencils. Miss Burton fusses around like a mother hen until she can find my desk, verifying it by turning over the exam paper with my name typed on it. She points silently at the top, where I am instructed to write my name and school. Wiggie's seat is empty, Gerry's staring out of the window, his pencil already half chewed through. Alex is scribbling away like an old man desperately writing his last will and testament before he dies. I contemplate the word 'testament'. I must teach it to Harry; it's the sort of word he enjoys. Mr Reeve is glaring at me, as if to say, 'At least write your name, boy!' I do so, then look at the instructions:

'*Write an essay on any ONE of the topics below in not more than 1,500 words. You should be careful to use correct spelling and punctuation.*'

None of the topics looks very exciting. I was hoping for something on Lord Nelson again or the sinking of the *Bismarck*. '*My holiday*'. That's no use because we never have a holiday. '*A walk in the country*', just as unlikely. '*Swimming the Channel*' might be fun but I know nothing about it. Yesterday was '*An exciting day*' but I don't think Dad or Mam would want me writing about it at school. 'Home is home and business is business,' says Mam. 'Keep them as far apart as you can and don't open your mouth about either to anyone.' Pity she didn't follow her own rules last night. Dad's fault, I reckon. He never can understand the finer points of business, Mam says.

So I'm stuck with either '*My house*' or '*My future*'. Dad says I have no future, just be a slob and a layabout. He should know! Right, here goes.

'*My house is a very nice house. It has a front door and a back door. Only important people use the front door. There are five windows on the front of the house and four on the back of the house. Becos we are on the corner of our street and another one we are not attached to any other house and have a big garden. This is good for the dogs but they have to stay in there cage becos if they are in the garden they shit all over. Our front door is painted blue. Me and Harry share a bedroom somewear upstairs. Harry snores. I don't like blue.'*

I don't think this is 1,500 words but I count them all, just in case. One hundred and eleven. 'Brevity is the soul of wit,' says Mr Reeve when he delivers his sermon to the school in assembly every day. My essay must be very witty indeed. Alex has his hand up asking for more paper. I know he lives in a house no bigger than mine, so perhaps he's writing about his holiday or how many strokes you need to make when swimming the Channel. To pass the time I doodle on a spare sheet of paper, trying to remember all the ingredients Grandma has told me to put into a meal she calls a 'curry'. Most of the vegetables I know, except for some things call 'ladies' fingers' but she says I also need spices like 'core anger', 'come in', 'garam muscular', none of which I have ever seen. Next weekend I'll go with Grandma to the Paki shop and see what we can find.

'Stop writing and turn over your exam paper,' orders Mr Reeve. 'That includes you, Kirkwood.' Alex almost has to have the pencil wrenched from his grasp before he'll stop scribbling on his fourth or fifth sheet. We're released straight into the playground, though it's a good ten minutes early for lunch break. Gerry and I hunch up together against a classroom wall. 'What did you write about?' I ask him.

He pushes back his thin hair with one hand, trying to make it stay on the right side of his unruly parting, inspects his hand to check for louse eggs, lice having been all over the school for most of this term. 'Swimming the Channel,' he says. 'Don't know bugger all about it but it seems a stupid idea, so I said so. What's wrong with taking a good strong trawler? How about you?'

'My house. Did a pretty fine job on it, too. Short and witty, you can say. Old Alex kept scribbling away, crossing out, muttering to himself. Poor bugger had no more idea what to write than you had about swimming the Channel. Anyway, have you seen our Harry?'

A voice from behind: 'He's in the cloakrooms with the Blob.' A grim-faced Alex has shuffled up while we've been talking. 'Didn't seem at all well. Maybe Mrs Reeve has given him six of the best or the big lads in his class have had a go at him. The Blob had his arm round him, stroking his hair and all.'

Harry is a pretty lad and after the affair with Burnham down the Willows I can't help thinking he might be in some sort of continual danger from adults, even in school. The Blob smiles at me as I sidle into the cloakrooms, pretending to be there by accident. Harry's finishing one of his stories in the time-honoured fashion. '*And they all lived happily ever after.*'

'How wonderful,' says the Blob. 'You tell such tremendous stories, Harry. Why don't you write them down?'

'Cos I'm not much good at reading and writing, Mr Harrison. The letters are all blurred and keep moving around. What's P for Peter gets mixed up with B for Bear and A for Apple looks just the same as O for Orange. I don't even bother looking at the blackboard anymore; I just ask Jimmy what it says. Except Jimmy isn't much good at his letters neither.'

'Either,' says the teacher. 'Look at this, Morley, and tell me what it says.'

'I can't see it there, sir. Can I hold it?' Harry puts the folded square of green card right up against his nose. 'Dri-ving li-cence,' he says, 'for Thomas James Harrison. That's you, sir!'

'Quite right, Morley. Sit here for a moment, while I have a word with somebody. I'll be right back.'

'What's happened?' I ask Harry as soon as the Blob's out of sight. 'Did he do anything to you?'

'What do you mean, do anything? He was being nice to me. While everyone else was doing sums he let me sit at the back as long as I didn't cry too loud and disturb the others. When the bell rang he brought me out here and asked me why I was upset. All I could say was me mam had to go to hospital and they said she was dead. I didn't say anything about the party or the police or the

Tuesday

glass or nothing but he kept asking me questions, so I told him a story instead.'

'He really needs to go,' says the Blob as he enters the door side by side with Mr Reeve. 'An early assessment is imperative. I could take him over there now and be back for the start of afternoon class.'

'All very well, Harrison, but who is going to take your dinner duty?'

'Mrs Reeve could do it, sir.' A frown from the headmaster stops him in full flow. 'Or Miss Burton, sir. She had no classes this morning, just invigilation, and most of her regular class will be subsumed into Mrs Reeves', like it was yesterday.'

'Very well, Harrison, but be sure you are back on time or Daniel here will be believing you have kidnapped his younger brother.'

Harry holds my hand on the way round to the hard standing at the front of the school. Mr Reeve parks his car here. Alongside it is a bright red Vespa motor scooter. The Blob kicks it into life.

'On you get, Morley,' he shouts above the shrill noise of the engine. Harry clambers on to the pillion seat, wraps his arms around the Blob like a fisherman clinging to the mast of his sinking ship in a force nine gale. He doesn't even wave as they swing off along the road and out of sight round the nearest bend.

Instead of telling me a story on the way home, Harry's full of his ride on the Blob's Vespa. 'We went ever so fast, all the way into town. Then I nearly fell off when we stopped and Mr Harrison had to lift me down. A policeman stopped Mr Harrison and told him I'm too young to be riding on a motorbike and we should both be wearing helmets, but Mr Harrison said there's no law about how old the passenger has to be or about having to wear helmets and anyway it's more fun on a scooter with the wind blowing in your hair. The copper didn't like that but we was in a hurry so we went into this funny sort of shop place.'

'What did they do there?' I asked. 'What were they selling?'

Childhood, Boyhood, Youth

'Dunno. I had to go into a back room and sit in a big black chair. This man in a white coat, he put a horrible lumpy thing over my head and kept telling me to look at things on a lighted screen: letters, lines, dots and things. Some I could see like they were real sharp and others I couldn't see at all, like when I sit at the back of the classroom and Mr Harrison asks me to read what he's written. The man took ages. I didn't like it much but Mr Harrison looked real happy at the end and the man gave him a piece of paper and told him to bring me back in a fortnight. That's two weeks, isn't it, Danny?

'Coming back was great, we went even faster than the first time because we were late for afternoon school. Mr Harrison went so fast round one corner, when he leant the bike over he scraped all the rubber off his footrest and we nearly fell off. Can I have a ride on your scooter when you get one, Danny?'

All of this sounds strange to me but if Mr Reeve has organised it then it must be all right. What do I need to do for the Blob to take me for a ride on his Vespa?

Harry's still full of it when we get home, to find Grandma sitting in the kitchen peeling potatoes. 'Where's me mam!' shouts Harry. 'I want me mam. You said she would be here after school.' He starts kicking at the table leg, screaming for Mam. Grandma puts down the paring knife, carefully out of his reach, before flinging her arms around him and pulling him up against her.

'Your mam's on her way,' she says. 'Your dad's gone to fetch her from the hospital. I'm making her a nice soup. Help me with these potatoes so it's ready for her when she gets home.' Harry looks at me. I pick up the paring knife and start another potato, so he does the same, using one of our blunt old kitchen knives. Grandma starts singing 'My Old Man Said Follow the Van' and we join in.

By the time we've been through 'Daisy, Daisy' and 'I'm Henry the Eighth' there's a huge mound of naked potatoes on the table in front of us.

Tuesday

The post box on the front door rattles violently. 'You answer it, our Danny,' says Grandma. 'By the time I've squeezed out this chair whoever it is will have been and gone. Never know, it might be a man from the *Evening News* saying I've won the "spot the ball" competition.'

I struggle with the locks on the front door, have to stand on tiptoe to reach the bolt at the top, so I'm a bit flustered when I finally get it open, nearly poking my nose into a slightly grubby blue suit. 'Good afternoon, Daniel,' says the blue suit. 'Charmed to meet you again. Do you mind if we come in?'

As I say, I was flustered. Even then, if Mam had been in I'd have stood my ground, despite the policeman the blue suit had with her. 'Mam's not here,' I say. 'I'm not to let anyone in when she's not here.'

'Quite right, too,' says the policeman, pushing past me. 'Your father not here, neither?'

'Either,' I say. 'He's gone to collect Mam from hospital.'

'So you are here on your own,' says the woman from the Social in a tone of satisfaction. 'Just you and your brother.'

'And me,' sings out Grandma from the kitchen. 'A responsible adult and relative taking good care of the boys while their mother is having medical treatment. See, here we are together, a happy little family preparing supper in clean and comfortable surroundings. Not one of us in physical or moral danger. You two can just—'

'See how well we are getting on,' I add, fearful of how Grandma might have finished her sentence.

'That's not how it was last night,' says the policeman. 'Fighting and carrying on. Dogs tearing people to bits, blood all over. Neighbours called us, we called the Social. Just as we were told, children badly cared for, left all alone to fend for themselves.'

'Washed and tidy before they went to school, good breakfast inside them.' Gran eases herself up from her chair, still clutching a kitchen knife.

'Both parents absent, at the mercy of an elderly relative,' continues Miss Blue Suit. 'Officer, I shall be taking these boys into care immediately.'

'No, you won't,' cries Gran. 'Not unless you've got some paper from the court. I know my rights. And who are you calling elderly, you chit of a girl? I've not got an old-age pension yet and I've still got all me marbles. You just bugger off, the pair of you, and leave us alone.'

Blue Suit looks at the copper, who stares back and shrugs his shoulders. Without a warrant he's not going to try conclusions with an old lady defending her grandchildren in their own home. Apart from the damage she could inflict in her own right, the din would bring the whole street down upon his neck.

'You must be aware this matter will have repercussions,' snarls Miss Blue Suit in a voice which tries but fails to be neutral and official, adjusting her hat and wiping her hands on her skirt as if to get rid of the dirt she had picked up from Grandma's words.

'Thank you for a pleasant visit. Please come again,' I say to her and the copper as I let them out the front door. I smile a smile they take to be politeness as they pass, but which I know to be triumph.

Grandma is standing at the stove singing in French, something she does when particularly happy. 'Busybodies,' she says, 'do-gooders, hate the lot of them. Chop up the taters small, Danny. That way they'll cook quicker. Boil them down as hard as you can. We're going to mash them up anyway. No milk, no butter, no salt. Do you have a masher in this hell hole? Couple of chicken stock cubes, lots of white pepper. Does your dad still not eat garlic? Stupid man. Needs more salt.'

'Not very interesting, Grandma. Can't we put in some carrots or celery?'

'Not today, Danny. Nothing anywhere near hard or chewy. That's a taxi outside. Could be your mam now.'

Tuesday

People talk about walking over hot coals for a cause or for a person they love. Harry and me would have run through all the fires of hell. Dad is paying the cab driver. Mam is levering herself up from the back seat, one hand on the door, the other holding a huge bandage across her face. She staggers back against the car as Harry and I cannon into her.

'Watch it, you two little buggers,' shouts Dad. 'Your mam's still a bit wobbly.'

Mam's holding Harry's hair with her free hand. I grab her by the waist, help her round the back and in through the kitchen door, easing her down onto one of the three remaining chairs. 'Are you all right, Mam? Are you all right? They said you were dead.' Harry looks up from where he's kneeling on the floor, a knight begging a favour from his lady.

'I'm all right now I've seen you two.' Mam's voice is curiously muffled as if from the end of a deep mine. Dad has opened a bottle of beer and is drinking it in great gulps.

'Danny, come and help me. I'm an elderly feeble old woman who can't manage on her own, so the police say.' Grandma is stirring the soup. She hands me the spoon. 'Keep stirring while I add the potato. Don't stop or it will all stick to the bottom.' I stir as vigorously as I can, keeping my eyes firmly fixed on Mam as she strokes Harry's head, tears dribbling down her cheeks.

'Enough. Is there a ladle in this god-benighted place?' Grandma is rattling cereal dishes around, trying to find five matching spoons. 'You stop guzzling that ale and get some bread on the table. Harry, lay out the spoons. If there's no ladle, Danny, you'll have to pour straight from the pan. Can you manage, lad?' I ease the pan over, resting it on the edge of the stove. Gran holds a spoon over the bowl to stop the soup spattering her arms. Despite our efforts some dribbles down the side of the pan and onto the cooker. With five full bowls plenty still remain as seconds for everyone.

'Load of bastards,' says Dad, scratching at the stubble on his chin. 'Doing that to a woman. God knows what we'll have to live on now.'

'Have you ever thought of finding yourself a job?' Gran sneers. 'Plenty of work down the docks for them what wants it.'

'Hit her with a vodka bottle, he did,' Dad continues, completely ignoring her. 'Damn good job it didn't break like the one I hit his mate with. Dogs weren't much use, biting their legs. Teach them to go for the throat next time.'

Mam says nothing. She's sipping the soup under cover of her bandages, one painful spoonful at a time. Four, five mouthfuls. Pauses slightly, looks around as if she's never seen the place before, gently pushes Harry's head from her lap. Considers whether she has the strength for her next move. Levers herself up by the edge of the table. Staggers.

Gran and I rush to help her. Dad looks up from his beer. 'You all right, old girl?'

Mam moves unsteadily towards the staircase. Three of us is a squeeze, Gran and I either side of Mam. Instead of turning into her bedroom she opens the door of Salanne's room, always prepared in case of a sudden change of heart by Social Services. She sits heavily on the pink eiderdown on the bed while Gran pulls off her shoes. I hold her shoulders as she sinks back onto the pillow. Feebly, Mam waves the two of us away. At the door I pause to let Grandma pass through first, as Mam has taught us any gentleman would. Looking over my shoulder I see Mam has let fall her bandage, revealing her gums sucked back into the empty space where her four front teeth ought to be.

"Has it ever befallen you to become suddenly aware that your conception of things has altered – as though every object in life had unexpectedly turned a side towards you of which you had hitherto remained unaware? Such a moral change occurred, as regards myself... and therefore from it I date the beginning of my boyhood."

(Leo Tolstoy)

Boyhood

March

'Mam, where can I go to get boxing lessons?'

'What do you want boxing lessons for? Boxers get their heads smashed in and their teeth knocked out. Getting your teeth knocked out is no fun.' Mam grins, a beautiful all-white smile which flashes in the sunlight. This evening she has her teeth in, fresh from their stay in Steradent all day. Mr Rees, the dentist, had offered to make her a bridge for both top and bottom, which we all thought was a great idea until he mentioned the cost, almost twice the family annual income. Besides, the rest of Mam's teeth weren't up to much, so she had the whole lot out. Gran did the same just after she married Granddad. 'They were too much trouble,' she said. 'Always wobbling about and breaking. Far better to get rid of them.'

The grown-ups don't understand. If I don't get some boxing lessons soon I'll have my teeth bashed out anyway. 'It's the big lads at school, Mam,' I say. 'They pick on me because I'm smaller than them. Push me around, kick me when I'm not looking. I want to fight back, like Dad does.'

'If you fight back like your father does they'll kick you out of school and lock you up. A beer glass in the face and a quick runner is your dad's style. Not catch him bothering with a straight left and a sharp uppercut. Best is to run away as fast as you can.

You've got a mate who's a runner. Hang around with him and put some spring into your legs.'

'Wiggie's no use. He's in another class and spends all his free time in the gym. Anyway, if I run to the far end of the playing fields, I still have to come back when the bell goes and they'll be waiting for me like I never went away. I don't suppose I could take a knife to school with me?'

Mam is horrified. Not much upsets her. Today I've managed it good and proper. She rants and raves, sets about me with the tea towel, not doing much damage but forcing me to cower into a corner. At last she calms down, puts the kettle on, takes out her teeth, rests them on the draining board. I edge out from my corner towards the stairs.

'Not so fast, young man. Sit there at the table. Test the milk before you sit down, make sure it hasn't gone off.' She drops three tea bags into the pot, rinses two cups under the cold tap. Mam still moves smoothly. From behind you wouldn't think she's more than sixteen, or eighteen on a bad day, even if her hair is getting a bit thin and ratty. No expensive hairdos nowadays. On a normal day she's beginning to show her age, especially when she doesn't have her teeth in. There are small wrinkles around her mouth and a worn expression on her face except when she smiles, which she does now.

'Have a biscuit,' she says. I didn't know there were any. She must keep a secret stash. 'Pour the tea for me.'

I do as she says, adding a little cold water to hers to avoid scorching her gums.

'What have I always told you about the police?' she asks.

'Keep away from them and tell them nowt,' I reply.

'OK. Now I'm going to tell you exactly the opposite. Every Thursday night there's a youth night at the main police station on Lower Bedlam. You know the place?'

Of course I know the place. That's where they took Dad the night they locked him up, and me when they thought I'd broken into Kirkwood's newsagents. Can't imagine why anyone ever volunteers to set foot in it.

'They have this crazy idea of getting kids like you off the streets and out of trouble by teaching them useful things and telling them how to be good citizens. You've had quite enough of that from me; after all these years you can easily pass for a good well-behaved citizen. The point is, there's a man there, Bernie Finnegan. An Irishman, ex-army. He'd have been locked up for assault and battery long ago if he weren't a copper. You look in the local paper, see who's been arrested. See how often the arresting officer, Sergeant Finnegan, had to restrain the culprit. That means he gave him a good going-over before he brought the man in. Now, this Finnegan, he runs a judo class. Not too strict on the rules, more British commandoes than Japanese Zen masters. Go to his classes, see what you can pick up. He might knock you about in the process, but you must be used to that by now.'

If anyone else came up with a crazy idea like this I'd tell them where to go, but Mam knows what she's doing. Her advice has always been good enough to keep me out of trouble. Next Thursday I'm off down the Bedlam, see what's going on. For now, I'm on Harry duty, keeping him up to speed on his homework.

It's not very taxing and to be honest I'm enjoying it at the moment. He's reading aloud to me from a book: *Treasure Island*. I love all the stuff about Long John Silver and Jim Hawkins, the black spot and pieces of eight; only wish it didn't sound quite so old-fashioned. Harry is next up for those crazy code-breaking tests and the Blob says reading a good book is excellent preparation. Harry still hasn't cottoned on to the idea that you read silently, which can drive me mad sometimes when I am trying to sleep and he's reading the current edition of the *Hotspur*.

He looks like a fish from the deep nowadays, our Harry, with his great big goggle glasses and his surprised expression, as if he's only just discovered there is a world around him more than six inches from his nose. Since the Blob had his eyesight assessed

Harry has gone up a class every year, now proudly sits on the second row in the A stream and is the Blob's model pupil. Some say he's why the Blob has been promoted to deputy headmaster but I know better. Old man Reeve wanted his wife to get the job, but the education department thought it would look funny. 'Jobs for the boys', they called it. Harry says the proper word is 'nepotism', which comes down to the same thing.

When the Reeves retire, I suppose the Blob will get the headship and ask for his wife, Miss Burton as was, to become deputy. That's unless she fills his house with lots of squalling, grizzling brats before then. Perhaps she's already in the club. Harry says the Blob has sold his Vespa and bought himself one of the new Minis. Small inside, but enough for three little ones, I suppose.

I've homework of my own to do but I shan't bother. Boring history stuff. How one of the Georges went and lost the American colonies. Glad to be rid of them, I would've thought. Two months' sailing time there and another two months back. Some of the battles sound interesting but the bit I like best is in the later war when we burnt down the White House (except it wasn't called the White House then) and the Yanks had to re-paint it white once we'd gone away. 'No taxation without representation' sounds very intellectual. Frank says it's the wrong quotation. He says it's really 'no conception without copulation'. That one makes the girls all giggle and go red.

Funny having girls in the class for the first time. Not that they speak to us, always huddling away in little groups and talking about boring things like make-up and musicians. Strange that none of them seems to know anything about music. Their concern's how beautiful this one is, or how sexy the other might be and whether a third is married or not. They know the names of all the singers in the groups, but I bet they couldn't name one of Town's current first eleven.

Dad's home early on Thursday afternoon, just after I get in from school. Mam's been listening to the special channel on the radio and her hair's done up on top of her head, wrapped in damp towels. He doesn't spend so much time down the bookies nowadays, not since he's had a dose of having to work for a living. Not for very long. What did you expect?

After her teeth problem Mam couldn't work. Quite apart from feeling like shit, she didn't exactly look like God's gift to man. One day, Dad got off his arse (Mam's expression, not mine) and took himself down to the docks; got a job as a lumper. As luck would have it the days were getting longer, so he didn't have to get up in the dark for the morning tide, and he stuck it out for nearly three weeks. Packed it in a couple of days before the Social came sniffing around asking why he was still claiming dole if he was working. Dad denied it all, of course. It was obvious he wasn't at work that day and the gang master wasn't going to own up he was employing people off the books, was he?

All was fine then until the money started to run out again. Dad wanted Mam to go back to work. Instead, she went off and had the rest of her teeth out, which was when Dad fell in with Albert across the road. Albert is a funny-looking feller, all skin and bone, built like a stick insect. Any biology teacher would love to have him in her class: you can see every bit of his skull, the prominent cheekbones, how his jaw curves and is attached under his elephant ears. He's also what the newspapers call a 'cat burglar'. I always think this sounds funny, as if he's out stealing cats. (Jersey says during the war in his village the people ate all the cats and all the rats, too. I don't always believe everything Jersey tells me.)

Albert started taking Dad out on jobs which needed a bit of muscle. A crowbar here, moving a loaded dustbin under a window, keeping a watch out for nosey parkers. They never made a lot of money but what they did make was tax-free. Finally, they decided to turn over Kirkwood's newsagents. Now, you can't stand on the pavement outside a shop and climb in one of the upstairs windows. Besides, old man Kirkwood knows enough to keep all his doors and windows double-locked. But what's round the back?

Garages, is the answer. A lane with the back paved garden of Kirkwood's on one side and a row of garages, one for each of the shops, on the other. The sight of Dad or Albert hanging about there would have the cops swooping down on them in a second. 'Loitering with intent to commit a felony' would be the charge, Albert says. On the other hand, a kid kicking a football around, using the brick walls of Kirkwood's garden as a pretend goal, would only produce annoyed frowns whenever the ball bounced off one of the metal garage doors. Three days running I made a nuisance of meself round the back of the shops, until the guy from the chippie finally told me to 'bugger off and don't come round here again'. By that time the reconnaissance was complete and I could nip off back to Albert's to report my success.

Next day a police car arrived outside Albert's door and another at ours. Mam was annoyed at first, Dad having been stupid enough to get caught. She got madder when the cops found several hundred cigarettes stuffed under her bed. What did for her in the end was when the cops arrested me as well, as an accomplice. Hit Dad with my best frying pan so hard he had to be helped into the car. The frying pan was fine. 'Don't buy anything you don't have to, but if you do, buy quality.' Another one of the useful things Mam taught me.

So there I was in an interview room alongside Dad and Albert. No way they could claim innocence, what with the cigarettes at ours and carefully bagged up packets of cash at Albert's. The problem was me. 'We know how you got in,' said one of the cops, a chubby-faced man with virtually no chin, from which hung two rolls of flesh. 'Through the downstairs toilet window. Windows like that are designed to be small enough to be left open safely. There's no way either of you could have got through it, so you must have used the lad to climb in, then open the back door for you. We know he has been messing about round the back of the shop for the last week.'

'Nothing to do with me,' I said. 'I was tucked up in bed last night. Ask our mam. Ask Harry.'

'Who will both lie through their teeth for you. The only question here is whether the magistrate will have you put back in care or send you off to a junior borstal.'

Dad looked at Albert, who looked at the floor. 'My lad had nothing to do with it,' he said. 'You can't prove a thing.'

The two folds of skin wobbled. 'Your lad is already known to the police. When the magistrate is shown the size of the window she will reach her own conclusions. His family background is enough. Wherever it is, locked away until he's eighteen, I reckon.'

Dad looked at Albert. Albert raised his head, looked at Dad. 'All right,' said Albert. 'The lad had nothing to do with it. Take us back to the shop and I'll show you.'

There was a small crowd outside the shop when we got there, Didi Moffatt, Mrs W and Mam among them. To the cops' annoyance they followed us round the back to watch the performance. First, Dad moved the rubbish bin from its corner to a space under the window, making it look as heavy as possible. Then he made a stirrup for Albert out of his clasped hands. Albert perched gingerly on the bin lid. He pushed his head through the toilet window, eased his right arm after it. His left shoulder seemed to drop away as if it were dislocated. A scrabbling noise from inside as Albert's body squirmed forward like a caterpillar wriggling along a tasty cabbage leaf. One more wriggle and the left arm thrust itself through the gap, followed by the remains of Albert's body. The women behind let out a cheer as two scrawny legs fluttered in the air, disappearing out of sight into the toilet beyond.

'Lets me out,' I said to the chinless wonder holding my arm. 'You see he doesn't need me. I'm off.'

'Not until the inspector agrees. You'll come back to the station with me.'

'Not without me,' says our mam. 'He is entitled to a responsible adult. Since his father's in custody and about to be charged he cannot be regarded as "responsible". Either I go with him or he doesn't go at all.'

A nice little family excursion to Lower Bedlam, where Dad stays put until his bail hearing the next morning and Mam shouts and screams at everyone in sight until they threaten to lock her up with him. Threats don't stop our mam. She's leaning over the counter nose to nose with the desk sergeant when the inspector turns up. At first he tries the long-arm-of-the-law stuff, saying how proper enquiries have to be made and I should be taken into care until they're completed. Mam knows twice as much about care procedures as any jumped-up cop and gives it to him both barrels, finally suggesting his men have been guilty of kidnap and assault of a minor. I want to laugh and roll about on the floor but I've been well trained by Mam. Absolutely emotionless face. Sit upright, hands in lap, don't sniffle or jiffle. Mam and I wait to have the laugh at home.

That's why Dad is home early this Thursday afternoon. Six months in the nick have calmed him down, pulled him into himself. Made him more tricky. Those six months were the best I've had since I've been back home. Mam isn't easy, quite likely to lose her temper if things go wrong or if she's had a bad night at work, but the great thing is, she'll eat anything. Not only that, she opens up her purse on a Saturday morning, asks me how much I need for the shopping and hands it over. Because of her teeth all I was allowed to cook was soups: onion soup, bean soup, carrot and potato soup. I made all of it fresh with perhaps an extra stock cube to help it along. Before Dad got sent down I had to be careful what I put in them, but Harry and Mam were up for anything: garlic, coriander, even curry powder. Though I did get that wrong once, put in a tablespoonful instead of a teaspoon. We ended up having cornflakes and milk instead. Once Dad got back all that changed since he demanded 'real meals' with meat and two veg. Being inside must have killed his taste buds or softened his temper because he never complained again about a parsley sauce or a slice of apple and cloves with his pork chop.

'Where the hell are you off to?' he shouts as I reach for my mac.

'Just out.'

'Out where?'

'Down to Lower Bedlam. Seeing a copper.'

'He's not in trouble again, Mother, is he?'

'I'm sending him to get some lessons from Finnegan. The lad's being bossed around at school, needs to learn a few tricks to keep the bullies at bay.'

'I'll give them a few tricks,' says Dad. 'No little turd is going to push my son around.' He sits down at the kitchen table, looks greedily at the coal cupboard where his beer is kept. Mam and I both know this is as far as his parental protection role is likely to carry him.

'I'm off, then, Mam,' I shout, making for the door.

'Wait a minute, you'll need this.' She presses a shilling into my hand. 'Lesson number fifty-five: nothing in this world is free. It's a shilling entrance; you have to pay to be made a good citizen.'

Lower Bedlam was once the site of the local lunatic asylum. Some say it still is. From the front it looks like a modern office block: yellow brickwork and large windows. Round the back it's a proper cop shop: dull, dirty, grey, intimidating. To one side stands a prison with black-painted walls and windows right up by the roof. Actually it isn't a prison, it's the gym, where the cops are supposed to work out and keep fit enough to chase me and Wiggie or to half-dislocate Dad's arm.

There's a nice lady taking money at the door, the grandmother type with big heavy glasses, calling everyone 'darling' or 'my love'. 'Where's the judo?' I ask her. She points over to the far end of the gym where there's a set of mats tied together with a canvas cover linked to a wooden surround. I'm expecting a cop in uniform, not this bulldog in white pyjamas. He's bouncing on his toes, a volcano of energy desperate to erupt, muscles bulging on his forearms and calves.

'I know you, son,' he says to me. 'You're one of the Morley boys. Got away with that newsagent robbery.'

'That wasn't me, sir,' I say, all polite like. 'It was me dad and Albert. You should have seen the way he shimmied through the toilet window.'

'I heard about it. I also heard there was some lad out a couple of days before casing the place.'

'Just kicking a football around, sir.'

'Be careful I don't kick you around. Get changed. Find a suit which will fit you, then come back over here.'

If truth be told Finnegan's not as fierce as his looks or his reputation. We spend half the evening doing forward rolls and slapping our arms on the canvas before being allowed to try out throws on one another. 'Let me show you a standard shoulder throw.' Finnegan looks at me, considering using me as a dummy. Now, I'm only just over five foot and Finnegan is six-two if he's an inch. He picks on a lad six inches taller than me, who he proceeds to bury into the canvas. I understand. Getting his shoulder down under my armpit for the throw demands he be almost as much of a contortionist as Albert. My turn will come later when we progress onto ankle sweeps and pinning your opponent to the ground. I don't care; I can bounce.

Sitting with me on the sidelines is Alex Kirkwood. We take the opportunity for a quick chat. 'What are you doing here?' he asks.

'I've come to be made into a model citizen. Aren't you a model citizen already?'

'Of course I am. It's school. They play rugby there, not footie. All this throwing people around's perfect training.'

'Rugby? That's posh.'

'The sort we play at school is, but some of the lads have come down from the north. They follow teams like Wakefield Trinity and Halifax. Reckon it's the working man's game up there. Good thing is, it's right for all sizes, even for a titch like you. By the way, I never thought you were the one who did over the shop. How would you manage to climb high enough to get up to the window?'

'Enough of that chatter, the pair of you. Up on the mat, let's see what you're made of.' Both Finnegan and Alex think I'm going to be dumped good and hard, this being my first week. For over a minute we circle one another warily before Alex makes his first attack. I've already got this figured out, bend at the knees so as to shrink a good six inches. The lanky Alex can't get underneath. He tries again and again, getting increasingly frustrated. At last he gets careless, takes his eyes off me. I swoop in, have him over on his back in a second. That will 'titch' him!

'How did it go last night?' Mam asks next day. 'Any use?'

'Reckon I'll go back next week; give it another go.'

'Don't expect me to sub you every week. You'll have to find a shilling out of your paper money.'

Easier said than done. I spent all my savings on the frying pan Mam used on Dad and the rest on a few extras for the larder. 'Improve income, decrease expenditure in times of hardship,' is what Mam would say. Doing one is difficult; doing both is impossible.

April

After Dad came out of the nick he complained none of us had ever visited. 'I was there half a year,' he'd moan, 'and not one of you came anywhere near me. Yet you go see our Salanne every week, without fail.'

'Salanne was taken away through no fault of her own,' says Mam. 'You were locked up because of your own stupidity. Did you expect me to traipse all the way to Doncaster with two kids in tow so you could spend an hour moaning about the food while I spent the rest of the time telling you what an idiot you are? Next time you do something stupid, don't get caught, and if you do, make sure you're sent somewhere that's only a bus ride away, like Salanne's.'

Not every week, but most times, me and Harry go down the Home to visit Salanne. I like going there; it reminds me of what I've escaped, makes me careful to be more sensible than Dad and not get caught. Salanne is not as pretty as Mam. Her nose is too big and her arms and legs are thicker, more like Dad's. Her hair has funny light streaks in among the brown and would look fine if she bothered to wash it more often. What she does have is Mam's teeth. Mam's teeth as they used to be: bright, regular, with a slight gap between them. When she smiles her whole face lights up.

April

Today she's miserable. 'I'm going to be stuck in here for ever,' she moans. 'One of these days I'll run away when no-one's looking and throw myself under a bus. I don't even get to walk to school and back. They pile us into an old van and drive us there. Afraid we're going to abscond, I suppose.'

'No point in doing a runner now,' says Mam. 'You'll be sixteen in a couple of months. They can't keep you here after your sixteenth birthday, whatever the police or the Social say. Danny's moving back in with Harry next week so I can sort your bedroom out.'

'Aw, Mam! I hate sleeping with Harry. He snores and tells stories in his sleep. Bad enough having to listen to him reading "improving books" to me when he's awake. And his feet smell.'

'So do yours,' says Mam. 'Tell you what, when our ship comes in I'll buy us a new washing machine so you can both have clean clothes all the time.'

'You've been saying that for years,' I object. 'With Salanne at home there'll be even more washing. You know what girls are like. Clothes all over the place, wear them once then put them in the wash straight away.' I don't remember living at home with Salanne, but the lads at school tell me what it's like living with sisters.

'We'll see,' says Mam. 'I'm meeting with the people from the Social tomorrow to sort it all out. Relax, the pair of you. Maybe the Council will give us a bigger house.'

'I don't care,' says Salanne, 'as long as I get out of here. The sooner the better. Forget the birthday present, walking away from this place will be better than any present you can afford.'

Judging by the birthday presents Harry and I end up with, we can't afford very much, despite Mam having been back at work for the last couple of months. Harry gets a book, which is all he ever wants. I'd have liked a set of sharp knives. All I get is a new potato peeler. Dad is no more optimistic. I'm upstairs with Harry, who is droning on through one of the Squire's monologues in *Treasure Island* while Mam and Dad are having a bit of a barney downstairs.

'How are we going to feed another brat?' Dad demands. 'Five of us in this place is too many. Things are tight enough as they are.'

'And would be a damn sight better if you didn't piss half the money away and leave the rest at the bookies. If one person's to be thrown out of the lifeboat, it's the one I'm looking at now. I'm out three nights a week and extras on holidays when the crowds are over for Wakes Week. And what do you do? Sit on your fat arse and do bugger all.'

'I look after you, that's what I do. Listen, I was talking to this feller in the Yarborough the other night.'

'Since when has the Yarborough let in the likes of you? The Yarborough's all gin and tonics and double malt whiskies.'

'If you must know, I was seeing a man about a dog. Anyway, I was chatting to this feller. Works for Burnham. You know, the man what owns Burnham's Bargains.'

'A right poofter,' says Mam. 'If his cousin wasn't on the police committee he'd have been locked up over that affair outside our Harry's school last month.'

'Exactly,' says Dad. 'This feller, he says Burnham is going to ground. Purely operating on the q.t., he says. Hanging around outside schools or down the Willows is too dangerous. Words have been said in ears. No more hushing incidents up, he says. Next time, Burnham goes to court, followed by a long stretch inside. Now I sympathise, don't I? I've had my stretch, I tell him, and don't like to see someone in the same position purely for doing what nature's intended him to do.'

'Interfering with little boys! What sort of fucking nature is that?!' Mam's voice lifts an octave higher when she gets one of her fits of moral outrage, which is more often than you might suspect.

'Listen, will you? This feller, he's a sort of go-between, a recruitment officer.'

'A pimp, you mean? Is that why he picked on you, looking to get some career guidance?'

'Exactly. He wants to know where he can find a lad or two of the right age. Ones who know to keep their mouth shut. Ones whose parents are in need of the odd bob or two.'

'So you volunteered our Danny and Harry, I suppose.'

'No. I told him I might have some contacts who could help him out. We're meeting up Saturday lunch time. I said I'd have definite news for him by then.'

'Not news of my fucking kids, you won't. I'm no saint, but no dirty willie-fiddler is going to get his hands on my boys. And don't let me catch you trying it on with any of the other kids round here. If I don't tear you apart the rest of the estate will have you strung up by your bollocks from the nearest lamp post.'

I'm not sure if Harry's listening or not; it's hard to tell with him sometimes. The noise from downstairs subsides, to be replaced by Harry chanting, 'Yo, ho, ho and a barrel of rum!'

'That's enough for tonight,' I tell him. 'When are your code-breaker tests?'

'Next week,' he says. 'The Blob says I'll sail through them. We've been doing sample tests for the last three weeks. They're pretty simple once you get the idea. Like the one you told me about, a simple substitution code. Nought is A, one is B and so on, so BEJC becomes 1492, which was when Christopher Columbus discovered America and BAGG is 1066.'

'Is the Battle of Hastings! Even I know that. Is it really so simple?'

'Yeah, though the maths ones can be tricky. You know, one gap between the first two numbers. Two between the next two, three for the next, then the patterns repeat. Once you spot the pattern it's simple.'

'Why did no-one ever tell us that?'

'Because you're too thick to understand.' At which point Harry does a runner round the other side of his bed before I can catch him. First, Alex calls me a titch, now Harry says I'm stupid. So much for love and respect.

Old man Kirkwood doesn't exactly love me but he respects the fact I'm in the shop spot on six-thirty every Sunday morning, especially now Alex is finding it harder and harder to drag himself out of bed. My delivery bag gets heavier every week but my round gets shorter. Once a house puts up a television aerial on the roof there's a good chance they'll cut out Sunday papers. 'Supply and demand,' says Mam. 'Television's free and there when you want it. Papers have to be paid for.'

'What about the licence fee?' I object.

'Who pays that round here? Bet your gran doesn't pay her licence.'

Dead right. Gran rents a massive fourteen-inch television which goes wrong every six months or so. Mam is full of approval. 'Henry Ford said to buy what appreciates and rent what depreciates. Just like me.' Mam furrows up her lips when she says this, so I keep off the topic of televisions.

This morning Kirkwood's even more miserable than usual, letting the pint mug of tea go cold on the shelf behind him. 'We're going to have to cut down on the Sunday staff soon,' he says, looking at a space a foot above my head. 'The returns don't justify the outlay. In a couple of years, we won't be doing deliveries at all. Whoever wants their papers will have to come in and collect, or go without.'

As Harry says, I'm not the brightest button on the jacket but I know a hint when I hear one. I'm relying on my weekly half a crown to pay for the judo with a little left over for the odd bits of stuff from the Paki shop, a head of garlic or lump of ginger, or for bus fares into town. Then there's nine pence on a Saturday to get into the football. Now Town are back up into the second division the games are a treat not to be missed, especially with Blackpool coming up next week. Something has to go.

Walking back with an empty bag, I make a plan. Not a good plan, but the best I can do. If I walk everywhere, pay for the judo and keep the football I'll have nine pence left when Town play at home and eighteen pence when they play away, just enough to put by for a rainy day, like when Kirkwood finally gives me the sack. The flaw in the plan is it doesn't leave me any of those extras I've grown so fond of from the Paki shop. So far I've been good there, paid for everything. Matters will have to change. One big binge to see me over bare weeks ahead. Next Saturday will be my last visit of the year.

Saturday's bright and sunny, a little chill in the wind. A perfect April day, just right for watching football. I'm in town early, wearing a black parka Mam found for me on the second-hand stall on the market. The parka's too hot for this weather, but it has lots of pockets. In one of them is a recipe Gran found for me in one of her magazines. Mam quite liked the split pea soup I made her but Gran and Harry find it too bland. Gran's recipe is for something she calls 'dhal', which is a posh name for lentils. I've told Mam about it and she's ready to give it a bash: 'But for heaven's sake don't serve it to your dad. He'll shout and rave he's been poisoned and I don't fancy having to clean it off the walls when he throws his plate at you.'

The Paki shop's in a side street behind the market. 'Open twenty-four hours,' it says on the window. Some of the kids in the class above me come here to buy cider of an evening. They're well underage, only fourteen or fifteen, but big and hairy, not like me, who's neither. Funny thing is, on a Sunday you're allowed to buy booze there, but not baby milk. Weird.

The Paki's long and thin, with a nose which would cut paper. Some of the seamen round here have heavy brown complexions but his has a yellowish tinge to it as if he suffers from a mild form of jaundice. His eyes follow you everywhere, unblinking. By now he knows me, happy to take my odd shilling or ten pence. The shelves are loaded with peculiar packets of rice, grains and, thankfully, two different sorts of lentils. I put a packet of each into my bag, together with a head of garlic. At the back of the shop I pick out four large chillies: two for the meal and a couple more as supplies for the future. Calculating quickly, I reckon I've enough cash for a small piece of ginger. Next to the vegetable stand he keeps packets of spices: turmeric, cumin, cinnamon (Mam likes this instead of ground nutmeg on her rice pudding) and garam masala. With my back turned to him I stuff as many packets as I can into the various pockets of the parka. The recipe includes curry leaves. I'll have to make do with a dash of curry powder.

He looks at me steadily as I empty the shopping bag onto the table, turn it upside down to show there's nothing else in it. 'Five and thruppence,' he says, totting up his sums with a pencil on an old scrap of paper. I'd made it five and six in my head. Perhaps I'm getting a rebate as a regular customer. 'Anything else you'd like?' he asks.

I shake my head, refill the bag and make for the door. Before I can get that far he's slipped out from behind his counter and stands barring the exit.

'I beg your pardon?' This in an imitation of Mam's best telephone voice.

'Turn out your pockets. I want to see what's in them.' His voice is calm with no trace of an accent or any emotion.

'Just the normal. Chewing gum, marbles.' He stands unmoved, saying nothing. I say nothing, staring at the floor. No way I can do a runner. Perhaps I can talk my way out? He follows me as I retreat to the counter, watches as I turn out my pockets. I think about leaving one or two untouched, but there doesn't seem much point. 'In for a penny, in for a pound,' Gran would say.

He eyes the pile of spice packets before me. 'Why do you do this?' he asks. 'You are a good boy, a polite boy. Why do you steal from me?'

'Because I have no money and because you're rich and I'm poor.' Maybe I need more lessons from Mam on how to deal with angry shopkeepers.

'Where do you live?' he asks. 'On the Chatham Estate? I have been there. You have big houses. What? Four, five rooms, kitchen, bathroom. For your little family, one room for each of you. My family back home, we are seven. We have one room for all seven of us. My mother cooks on a stove outside, even when it rains. She washes our clothes in the river. The toilet is a hole in the road at the end of the street. Who is rich and who is poor, you or me?'

'It is no good having a car if you can't afford the petrol to put in it,' I say. 'We have a kitchen but I've no money for food.'

'Why do you have no money?' he asks, relaxing his shoulders and unballing his fists. I explain how everything I buy from him comes out of my paper-round money, which could finish at any time, how I have to spend an extra shilling a week so I can learn how to deal with the bullies at school.

'You work?' he asks.

'Every Sunday morning. Six until one or two. Don't tell anyone. I'm not allowed.'

'Do you want more work? Real work. Better money.'

The Paki can't possibly be the man Dad met in the Yarborough, but who knows how many people Burnham has out there working for him? Selling little packets of spice in a town like this can't be much of a living; less than social security. If I pretend to go along with him I can disappear later, say I have to go to the toilet or something.

'Yes,' I say, 'but I still have to go to school or the truancy people will be after me. My mam wouldn't like that.'

'It is hard work,' he says. 'Friday and Saturday evenings only. Come along with me.' He packs the spices into the shopping bag, tucking it safely under his arm. He knows I won't run off without my bag now most of it is paid for. As I stand looking around he locks the shop, then leads me to the main street.

I don't come here often. There's no need; there's nothing I can afford and little I can steal. For some time, I've had my eyes on a set of pans at Burnham's Bargains, but they're not the sort of thing you can easily tuck under your pullover. Three doors down is a heavy-duty door with large plate-glass windows either side, lace curtains hiding the interior. Mam's warned me about places like this. 'Only for transients,' she says. 'Girls who've run away. No idea how to protect themselves. Full of pox in a week, full of child in a month. Change the girls as soon as they start to show. You keep away from houses like them.' I've no intention of using any sort of 'house', especially ones that specialise in boys.

Inside is not what I'd expected. There are booths arranged around the outside, tables neatly arranged in the centre, each one covered with a spotlessly white tablecloth, laid out for a formal meal. The walls are covered with pictures of weird landscapes like the ones in some of Harry's books. Two brightly painted dragons' heads leer over the serving counter at the far end.

I've seen pictures of Chinamen, of course; my comics are full of them. Strange figures in long decorated gowns with black pigtails hanging down their backs. Usually they pull vicious-looking swords from under their gowns and chase the hero, threatening to cut off his head. This Chinaman has no gown and no pigtail, instead white trousers and a double-breasted white jacket buttoned to the neck.

'Chef,' says the Paki, 'I have brought you a new recruit. You said you wanted somebody Friday and Saturday nights.'

'He is too young and too puny,' says the Chinaman. 'And like all English people he is probably too lazy.'

I'm about to interrupt him and say something rude when the Paki grabs hold of my arm and squeezes so hard I almost cry out. 'He's a hard worker,' says the Paki. 'Seven hours every Sunday morning for the last three or four years. Needs some extra now he's getting older. If you keep him out of sight in the kitchen there will be no trouble.'

It's not true Chinese faces show no emotion; puzzlement in the present case. He leads us through into the back, a cramped but efficient cooking area lined with stainless-steel stoves and work surfaces. I stare jealously at the three-inch-thick chopping boards and the six-foot-high refrigerator, run my finger along the edge of a gleaming knife left on one of the boards, producing a thin trickle of blood for my pains. The Chinaman looks appreciatively at my pleasure, smiling as I suck the dripping blood.

'Keep going,' he says. There's no door to the next room, which is half the size of the kitchen. Two large sinks dominate the space, a wide area of stainless steel to the left, the world's largest draining board to the right. 'You work here. Start tonight at seven. Service finishes ten-thirty. You go home when the washing-up is done. Same tomorrow. Five shillings a night. In cash. You tell no-one. You stay as long as you are worth the money. After that you leave. Understand?'

'Yes, Chef,' I say. Ten shillings a week! Old Kirkwood can get stuffed.

'Give the boy his bag after tonight's shift.' The Paki hands Chef my shopping bag. 'Not before, or he may not come back.' He must be joking. For five shillings I'd stay here from now until closing time.

May

'Dad, what's up with the dogs? They don't look too good.'

'Useless bloody dogs, not worth their keep. If it's not shovelling stuff in one end it's pouring it out the other. About time you and your brother got round to clearing them out.'

'Not my dogs. I've got school and homework and all sorts of things. You're not doing nothing; why don't you clear them out?' He's slowed down over the last few years, put on a couple of stone or I'd never be able to get round him, out the door and up the stairs in time to avoid his fist. He's still handy, but not exactly nimble anymore. Whereas I, also having put on a couple of stone, am much lighter on the feet. Football at school keeps me fit, judo at Lower Bedlam teaches me to move, stuffy kitchens sweat off any surplus fat.

It's two months now since I started working for Chef at the Chinese, soapy water up to the elbow every Friday and Saturday night. Each week there are extra plates and pans as people in town become more adventurous in their eating habits. Sometimes I have time to snatch a quick meal, the leftover rice at the bottom of the pan or washed-out noodles with whatever hasn't been popular on that night's menu. I've tried using chopsticks but the cooks made so much fun of me I gave up. None of the regular customers bother; it's too much trouble. Even at home Dad's allowed the odd meal with bean sprouts and has developed a fascination for

May

chicken cooked with sweetcorn. The cooks are as friendly as they can be without understanding a word of English and I still don't know Chef's proper name. The Paki ('call me Abe') told me once but it didn't make any sense so I never asked again.

Most important is the ten bob a week I'm making. I'm determined not to fritter it away or let Dad get his grubby hands on it, so every Monday after school I call in at the post office and buy seven and sixpence worth of savings stamps. They have a picture of the young prince and princess on them. You stick them into a paper album and keep them for a rainy day. The insole of one of my football boots is peeling away so I hide the album under it. Neither Mam nor Dad is likely to investigate a muddy football boot. If they ever get cleaned I'll have to do it meself. Mam knows I have a job but hasn't told Dad. He hasn't bothered to ask where I get off to until midnight of a weekend evening.

The dogs start howling; someone must have walked round to the back garden. Raised voices, Dad's rising higher than any of them. 'They're my dogs. I treat them proper. What do you mean, take them for walks? They're working dogs, to keep my property safe from the likes of you, coming round interfering in other people's business. Spoil them and they're no good.'

I poke my head out the back window. Dad's confronting three men in uniform. One's police. I recognise him from the night of Mam's accident, his two folds of skin on the chin now grown to three with a fourth on the way. The other two are in a uniform I don't recognise, the letters RSPCA embroidered on the lapel. 'These animals are half starved,' says the older of the two, 'there's no proper bedding and there's excrement all over their sleeping area, almost covering the whole yard. They're covered in mange and obviously have fleas as well. Look at their food bowl, absolutely empty and looks like it has been for days, no water, no shelter.' The other two nod. Dad objects furiously.

'We'll take them away immediately,' says the younger man. 'Find them a good home if possible.'

'You're not taking my dogs,' shouts Dad. 'They're my property. This is theft. You've no right.'

'I'm afraid they do, Mr Morley,' says the policeman. 'We can do it now or after obtaining a magistrate's warrant. The warrant will involve legal expenses, which you will be required to pay. Now, you wouldn't want that, would you?'

Dad continues to object, but the appeal to his pocket carries a lot of weight. It's not as if he's emotionally connected to the dogs. As far as he's concerned all they are is a mobile man trap and burglar detection system. I hate the bloody things, all fangs and bad temper. Almost as bad as him.

For the next hour the RSPCA men battle to get the dogs out of their cage and into a waiting van without getting their arms bitten off. One by one the dogs are captured, fastened to a catch on the end of a long pole and led away. The copper stands well out of it, twitching gently whenever it looks like one of his companions is likely to have a lump taken out of him. Dad cheers on the dogs, making the noises he makes when one of the Saturday-night parties gets out of hand and guests require extra motivation to move on. He looks disappointed when the last dog is led away and there is no blood spattering the cage floor. About time I went to school, or he'll keep me off to clean up the mess in the yard.

Thursday's still judo night. Finnegan's taking us through the syllabus for a junior grading, so we have shoulder throws, hip throws and a variety of leg sweeps. I'm his demonstration model when it comes to the leg sweeps since he still can't contort himself enough to get in under my low centre of gravity. Though I've grown a couple of inches most of the weight is still concentrated in legs and thighs. Getting dumped with a leg sweep isn't unpleasant; it's only your own weight brings you down. With a shoulder throw Finnegan puts the whole of his muscle behind it as if he's trying to drive you through the canvas into the concrete floor beneath.

And then there are the extras, the bits which are not in the syllabus. Mam was right: this is British Commando judo. Take a shoulder throw: keep your opponent's arm straight and locked at the elbow joint. He either accepts the throw or you dislocate his elbow. Sometimes both. Then there are chokes and strangles. As juniors we're not supposed to know these but they're one of Finnegan's favourites. He demonstrates them with glee. Rules say that if you tap the canvas or your opponent's arm, that's a sign of surrender. Finnegan ignores any taps until he feels you beginning to slide away. He's been a trifle more careful recently, since Alex went out like a light during one demonstration.

Me and Alex are the best. No-one can get in against my guard, while Alex's lanky legs are a constant threat of a leg sweep. As long as I stay on my feet I can fight him to a draw. Once on the mat into groundwork my lack of arm muscle and upper body strength loses every time unless I can sneak in with an illegal strangle hold. Alex also cheats in his own quiet way, using the weights at his school to build up muscle for rugby. Unsupervised access is forbidden, as is use by anyone under sixteen, but Alex and his mates sneak in during lunch break when the teachers are having a quiet ciggie in the staff room. We all wriggle our way through the world in our individual manner.

'You're very twitchy this evening, Mam. And Dad's got his best jacket on, as well as a shirt and tie. What's up?'

Mam fiddles with the second button on her frilly white blouse, undecided whether to have it fastened or not. She wants to show off her fake pearls, but do they look better against her skin or on top of the blouse? 'What do you think of the skirt?' she asks. 'Is it too short?'

'An inch above the knee,' I reply. 'Perfect for a respectable married woman. Do you want to be a respectable married woman on a Saturday night? Four-inch slit in the back, figure-hugging round the hips, light chocolate-coloured tights. Hardly working gear, Mam.'

'I'm going upmarket,' she says. 'Saturday night down the Vic's no good these days. A change of venue, change of day and a change of image is required.' She says this as if addressing the board of directors at Barclays bank. 'Your dad gave me the idea. He's been hob-nobbing with some feller down at the Yarborough. You know, the posh hotel by the station. All the businessmen stay there, stuck out in the wilds with the likes of us when they'd rather be at home in Leeds or London. This feller, he's a barman, so gets to know all the customers, supplies them with whatever they require.'

'And Burnham,' I add.

Mam looks at me out the corner of her eye. I'm not supposed to know about the argument with Dad about Burnham. 'Little animals have big ears,' she says. 'We're off tonight for a quick reconnaissance, make sure the Yarborough's as good as this feller says it is; your dad has made an agreement with him for a Sunday-night special. That's when the customers are at their lowest: a week away from home, another week to come and bugger all to do in a strange town when all the locals are out on the razzle. Me and your dad turn up like any ordinary couple. I plonk myself down in a corner with a drink, while Dad sits at the bar like he and the barman are the greatest of buddies. When the barman spots a good mark he points him in my direction and Bob's your uncle!'

'I suppose the barman takes a cut?'

'Of course, but it's a cut from a much bigger cake than usual. And more comfortable in a cosy hotel room than a quick knee-trembler behind the Vic.'

I must admit, I'm quite shocked. Mam's never been so open about her business before, always speaking of it in veiled and general terms. Anything which goes on at home is behind closed doors after Harry and I've been sent off to bed. There may be a lesson to be learned here, but I'm not sure about what. 'So, what's with these clothes, then? No stocking tops, properly fastened blouse, pure white bra underneath.'

'A sales pitch, Danny. Don't sell the product, sell the image. You'd be surprised how easy it is to sell a dodgy car. When I worked on the car lot, the first thing we did with a new banger was to give it a thorough wash and shine; make it gleam like new. The punters had no idea about how the engine should sound or what the grinding in the gearbox meant. What they saw was great bodywork. I'm doing the same. Show off the bodywork. Not in a tarty way, more like how they wished their own wives looked, all smartly turned out, well dressed and ready for anything. Not like when they get home and their missus has been looking after the house and the kids for a fortnight, hasn't had time to wash her hair and gives him a mouthful about how he's been off enjoying himself while she's been working her fingers to the bone.'

'Whew!' I say. 'Did you swallow a marketing manual?'

'Common sense,' she says. 'Know your product, know your market, know your clientele. Your dad, greedy sod that he is, wants me to go in for overnight stays. Extra cash for little effort, he says. Not a chance, I tell him. What does it look like to the client when he wakes up in the morning and looks straight at me teeth on the bedside table? He'd tell all his mates and that would be my career at the Yarborough over for good.'

'You ready, our lass?' I must say, Dad does look smart in his best gear, though it won't be long before his jacket doesn't fasten round his growing waistline. He seems to have forgotten all about the dogs, no longer coming home to tell us about a feller he's met who has an Alsatian or a Doberman for sale. He, too, is taking the move upmarket seriously. Less effort for him, I suppose.

They go off to wait for the bus, while I cut round the back to walk into town the short way. No point spending money on buses. Coming home is a different matter. By then it's drunks only, the women on the two till ten shift already wrapped up home in bed. Mrs Kirkwood, Alex's mam, is the regular conductor on our route. The late shift is the most unpopular among the conductors, what with the drunks and all, so it's left to the likes of her to volunteer duty as extra overtime. That's why the Kirkwoods have both a fridge and a washing machine and Alex has a clean ironed shirt for school every day.

Mrs Kirkwood is five foot nothing, a whole inch shorter than me. See her on the top deck of the bus sorting out passengers who don't know if they are in Brigg or Belgium. 'Here, love. Seven pence. Dig out your pocket. I'll take this, here's your change. Hey, you don't go to sleep. Where's your money? What do you mean you ain't got none? Show me or you are off this bus now.' She clips and passes out her tickets, hoovers up the cash from both the meanest and the drunkest passengers. Except me. She pretends I'm not there. That's not being rude, it's her way of avoiding asking me for my fare. Odd times when she asks me, I know an inspector has got on and is demanding to see tickets. A rare event: not many inspectors volunteering for duty at eleven thirty of a Saturday night.

Chef's always happy to see me. He knows what chaos the kitchen would be thrown into if the pans and plates were left to pile up. Tonight the restaurant's packed, waiters gliding between the tables like agitated ghosts. Funny how they manage to move fast while appearing to be wafted on a light breeze. There are a few plates and glasses left over from lunch time. I'm annoyed about this. As far as I'm concerned my shift tonight ends when everything has been washed and dried. Why can't the lunch-time washer-upper do the same?

'He was in a hurry to get to the football,' says Chef, though I have not spoken. 'Strange, this English fascination with kicking a ball around.'

How can you explain? I've tried talking to the girls at school about footie, but they're just as deaf. Since Town got relegated last season I've hardly been to a home match. I got disillusioned that time three years ago when almost the whole town turned out for the game against Stoke City to see Stanley Matthews in his last season. Over twenty thousand of us there, the biggest crowd since before I was born. You should've heard the groan when the teams were announced and the announcer said Matthews wasn't playing because he was injured. And we lost.

I finish the lunch-time leftovers and fill the sink ready for the first run of plates from the early starters. Little to do for a while. I watch the cooks throwing ingredients together, mixing them from huge aluminium pans large enough to take a whole pig. The shortest of the three squeezes himself into the far corner, where he attacks mounds of raw vegetables with a variety of razor-sharp implements, reserving especial fury for attacks using a hatchet with an eight-inch blade. For a moment I'm convinced he's thinking of his wife back home who has exiled him to foreign parts. More likely he's thinking what he would like to do to Chef if he doesn't give him a pay rise.

Being short, and recognisably underage, still in short pants, I'm supposed to keep out of sight of the customers, but it is hard to resist. With luck all they'll see if they catch a glimpse of me is a squat Chinaman in a dirty white apron. I peek out round the service door while one of the waiters holds it open with his backside, trying to manoeuvre out a large order without dropping it all over the floor. Unusually there's someone I recognise sitting at one of the tables: Marusia Strumov, surrounded by her family. Her birthday, probably. I kissed her once, at her last birthday party. No, that's not true. She kissed me. One of those silly games where the loser pays a forfeit and the winner gets to choose who to kiss. She chose me and made a real meal of it, tongue halfway down the throat and all. Shan't let her do that again; like sucking on a wriggling slug.

She winks at me and I pull back guiltily. Not before spotting another customer. Burnham in brand-new cavalry twill trousers, lilac shirt and paisley cravat tucked neatly around his neck. Smiling as he adds a tasty titbit to the plate of his dining companion. Someone else I know: Jake, Jersey and Muriel's younger son. I wonder what Mam would have to say about that? Or if Dad has taken a backhander?

July

I'm sprouting hair everywhere. Hairs on my legs, hairs on my arms, hair around my willie. Worst of all is the hair on my upper lip. Wearing short trousers while sporting a fluffy moustache is embarrassing. I clip it off with the kitchen scissors but it keeps coming back, thicker and more luxuriant than ever. After school I creep into Mam's room, rummage in her dressing-table drawers. She has oceans of creams, reefs of lipsticks, shoals of hair clips. Neatly stacked in the second drawer down are the combs, an expensive Mason and Pearson hairbrush, hairspray, three pairs of tweezers, a compact bag containing nail clippers and files and finally what I've been looking for: a safety razor.

Mam doesn't believe in using creams to get rid of her unwanted hair, says they make her skin come out in spots. The razor's as sharp as I'd expected, Mam being extra careful about such things. At first it pulls a little, so I rub soap on the lip before trying again. Not completely satisfactory but much easier than before. I admire myself in the mirror. Nice and smooth, except for a little touch of blood at one corner, which I dab off with a handkerchief, there being no toilet roll as usual. Nor is there any hot water, so I run the razor under the cold water tap to clean off any hairs and most of the soap.

All's fine until Thursday evening. The fleet's in again and Mam is prettifying herself for a night's work. 'Stephenson's boat's on its last trip,' she says. 'The company have sold it on to the Spaniards. That's the third one to go this year. Won't be any left soon at this rate.' She wanders off upstairs for a bath, dressed only in her bath gown and a pair of fluffy slippers.

'Daniel! Come up here, right this minute. I want a word with you, young man.'

I ponder which of my considerable misdemeanours she may have discovered. Perhaps the three packets of cigarettes I swiped from the newsagent in Barnswood which I've not yet managed to flog at school, or the copy of *Lady Chatterley* which Dad gave me to look after for him.

'Have you been rooting about in my things?' I stare at the floor. 'Have you been using my razor?'

'Yes, Mam.' There's no point in denying it; the evidence is all too plain. Mam would never use soap for shaving, and if she did she'd clean it much better than I've done.

'I won't have you poking about in my private stores. Not even your dad dares to do such a thing. Now, what've you got to say for yourself before I kick you downstairs and hand you over to your father for a good walloping?'

'It's not fair, Mam. I look ridiculous. Great hairy moustache, as tall as you nearly and in short pants. All the girls laugh at me. It's not fair.' Before I know it I've dissolved into huge sobbing tears. What would the kids at school say if they could see me now?

Mam flings her arms round me and pulls me tight, pats me on the back like when I was little and couldn't go to sleep. 'You're choking me, Mam,' I say, wiping my cheeks on her bath gown.

'Right,' she says. 'Keep your thieving hands out of my drawers. Buy your own bloody razor. You must have enough money stashed away from that job of yours. Get me up at ten on Saturday. We're going shopping down the market.'

In the end it isn't the market we end up at. There's nothing on our usual stall which fits an odd shape like mine: slim waist, big bum, short legs. Instead, here we are in Burnham's Bargains being as nice as we can to a middle-aged shop assistant who obviously wishes we'd stayed at the market. Mam wants trousers with twenty-inch bottoms. I know better and insist on fourteen inch or even smaller. We compromise on seventeen. 'Fashions change,' she says. 'In a twelvemonth you'll be wanting them skin-tight or thirty inches wide like Granddad used to wear when he was young. The rate you're growing we can afford to wait and see. Don't worry if they're six inches too long, you can turn them up. No, I'm not going to do it, you can do it yourself.'

The trousers look cavernous. Is my bum really that big? I stare down into them, regretting my old shorts, especially now the summer weather is beginning to peek through. I wriggle into them. One item Mam and I have both agreed on, they have a zip fly. She refuses to keep sewing buttons on (not that she ever did) while I like the idea of being able to hold my pee until the last minute without having to fumble with buttons. Mam knows an awful lot about trouser buttons, she tells me.

Next Monday, cheered by the purchase of my new trousers, I set out to find Henderson. Henderson's two years older than me, a good foot taller and perhaps two stone heavier. Though not really one himself, he hangs around with the thugs. They push everyone about, especially short arses like me. I'm picking on Henderson because he's the biggest and physically the most prominent of the gang. A fight with him would draw a crowd, happy to see one of the thugs get a punch on the nose or me mashed to a pulp. No-one is going to help if I get into trouble, least of all the teachers, who have despaired of keeping any of us under control anywhere except in the classroom, and sometimes not even then.

Henderson's surrounded by six of the gang, discussing what our defence should have done to Scunthorpe's centre-forward and what they fancy doing with Debbie Marchant once they get her round the back of the gym again. Henderson has a grating, braying voice which he's inherited from his dad, who sells the cheapest vegetables on the market. The way he's talking about Debbie, she might as well be a vegetable.

'Don't talk like that about a friend of mine.' I give him a firm push in the middle of his chest, sending him a step backward, more from surprise than the power of the push.

'What the fuck's it got to do with you, titch?' He squares his shoulders, sticks out his mottled red chin like he thinks it could knock me over on its own. His mates laugh, start forming a circle, convinced a rumble's about to begin.

'Who are you calling titch, you mouldy tub of lard? You're as rotten as your father's vegetables and as yellow as his bananas.' I growl up phlegm as hard as I can, then gob straight in his face, hitting just below the left eye.

Henderson goes crazy, which is just what I want. He rushes at me, swinging his fists like mad. Another reason I've picked on him: he's a lousy fighter. The smart boys stand their ground, measure their distance, then kick you in the crutch. I'm under his flailing arms, hoick him over like a sack of coal, dump him on the ground. A small crowd's gathered, egging me on. Henderson's warier now, coming forward in a crouch before swinging a roundhouse which might've done for me had it landed. Ducking under it, I use his momentum to pitch him on his back in a manner of which Finnegan would be proud. Not quite as I'd intended, far too purist, landing him on his back. I'd aimed to dump him on his shoulder, smash his collar bone, put him out of action for good. Instead, here he comes again, lumbering towards me. There's nowhere to go, hemmed in by the crowd as I am.

His arms around my back, he tries to squeeze the breath out of me in a bear hug. I lurch left, then right, sweep away his trailing leg, sending the pair of us tumbling to the floor. Now I'm for it; those two extra stones will do for me, for sure. Henderson sits on my chest, banging my head into the playground tarmac. There's no way I can throw him off. Keep calm. Think. Breathe. I reach for his neck, remembering one of the British Commando tricks Finnegan taught us must never be used on a judo mat. Playgrounds don't count.

There are arteries running down each side of your neck, carrying blood to the brain. Stop the flow of blood and you pass out. I dig my thumbs as hard as I can into Henderson's neck, squeeze with all my might. He's still banging my head into the tarmac, now with an increasing lack of fervour. Suddenly, he stops altogether, rolls off, lies in a crumpled heap on the floor. Slowly getting up I brush myself down, check the back of my head for blood, stroll away apparently unconcerned across the playground.

'What's all that about?' Neddy Grainger, the maths teacher, asks.

'I don't know, sir. Some of the big boys letting off steam, I suppose. You know they always have lots of energy they need to get rid of.'

Neddy sighs, decides there's nothing he can do and wanders off back to the safety of the staff room and correcting 4C's homework.

'Fred Henderson at the door. What can he want?' Mam's in curlers and her old black dress she wears when she thinks about doing some housework. She leaves her copy of *Woman's Own* on the kitchen table, then ambles over to answer the door to Fred Henderson. He has his son in tow. A great mistake, I think. Mam will eat the pair of them for breakfast.

'Your lad's been trying to kill my son,' opens Henderson senior, with no preamble. 'Are you going to do something about it or am I going to take the lot of you to court?'

Have you seen the Michelin advert, with that man made out of car tyres? Imagine him dressed in a worn blue overall, his face a bilious crimson. This Michelin man works in the cold store at Salveson's when he's not on his Saturday stall on the market. The rolls of fat must be useful, keeping him warm at work. Like his son, he has a chin the size of the prow of a ship, which he sticks out in front of him when he's angry or excited.

'Daniel, come here,' orders Mam. 'Did you try to kill Mr Henderson's son?'

'No, Mam.'

'Lying little bastard. You should see the bruises on his back! Left him lying there unconscious. Walked away without even a "by your leave". My lad could have been dead for all he cared.'

'Did you do that, Daniel?'

'Yes, Mam.'

'Why did you do that, Daniel?'

'He came at me, tried to punch me. Then started banging me head onto the playground. Had to defend mesen, Mam.'

'There you are, Mr Henderson. A typical schoolboy fracas. Sounds like your lad started it. Fifty-fifty. Got what he deserved. Look at him, great lump that he is. Our Danny's giving him a couple of stone, six inches shorter, two years younger. If anyone ends up in court, it's your lad. I've a mind to complain to the headmaster about all the bullying what goes on at that school, led by your son, picking fights with kids younger and weaker. Made a mistake with my Danny. Knows how to look after himself, does Danny. Takes lessons in self-defence from the police, especially to keep himself safe from bullies like your Jack. Now, get out of here and don't bother us again. And you, young Jack, let this be a lesson to you. Keep your fists to yourself and lay off me and mine or you'll have me to deal with.'

This may not be much of an argument coming from her eight and a half stone but young Jack Henderson seems to find it pretty convincing. He slinks away with his father, the pair of them arguing with one another as they proceed up the street. Mam is all smiles. She loves putting one over on anyone who comes between her and her boys. Now is a good time to ask for a favour.

'Mam,' I whine, trying to ignore the throbbing at the back of my head, 'tomorrow night is parents' evening.'

'Yes? Never had any of them when I were at school. I've not been to yours and don't intend to start now. Why should I bother? Two years' time and you'll be off out of it. No question of you failing any exams, because you don't have any. Or are you expecting me to explain to the teachers why you're always getting into fights?'

'It was only the one, Mam. And I was well away before any of the teachers showed up. Don't suppose Jack Henderson will go crying off to them after the mouthful you gave his dad. No, there's a problem with the options for next year.'

'What options is that? You mean you get to choose whether you go to school or not? You do that already.' Mam is enjoying herself. Time now to press ahead.

'We have to do all the standard stuff, English, maths and so on, but we have a choice of the extras. Like, the boys have a choice between doing physics and chemistry or French, and the girls can choose biology or French. So, I'm going to choose French.'

'What? Because there are more girls in the French class?'

'No, Mam. Because Gran says all the menus in the big restaurants are written in French. She says she'll help me with some of the words.'

'Most of the words your gran knows in French you won't find in the grammar books. Still, sounds like you're being sensible for a change. Far more sensible than picking fights with the likes of Jack Henderson. What did you do to make him take a swing at you, by the way?'

'I gobbed in his eye.'

Mam giggles, calls me a disgusting little tramp.

'But the options,' I say to get us back on track. 'There are another set. The boys can do woodwork, metalwork, technical drawing or art. The girls can choose home economics or art.'

'So, I suppose you want to choose art, for all the girls. You can't fool me, our Danny. Options for you come down to chatting up as many girls as possible.'

There is a portion of truth in this. It's obvious which girls are going to choose art as an option. They're the ones who wear the shortest skirts, the loosest tops and the shortest hair. 'Not so, Mam. Girls in our year don't fancy the likes of me. They're either in love with some pop singer or mooning about Jack Henderson and his kind. I'm lousy at woodwork and metalwork and I can't draw for toffee. What I want to do is home economics.'

I go and put the kettle on while Mam finishes laughing. 'Two sugars,' she says as I pour milk into our cups. 'What do you want with home economics, baby care and stuff? You'll have a wife to look after the babies and clean house for you.'

'Just like you, Mam,' I say as I pour the tea and rescue her toast from under the grill. Shutting our mam up is no easy task, but those four words work better than any long-winded speech. 'There is some baby stuff and sewing but most of it's cooking. Now, you know I love cooking, Mam. But the teachers say I have to do metalwork instead. I have to do something when I leave school, not be a layabout like Dad or go on the boats. One day I'll be the world's greatest chef, so you don't have to go out to work and I can cook you fabulous meals in my restaurant every day.'

'So, what do you want me to do?' Wouldn't it be great if she was like this all the time.

'Go to the parents' evening. Insist I be allowed to do home economics. Say it's unfair to ruin my prospects of a good career. If both boys and girls can do art, then why can't we all do home economics? Or metalwork, when it comes to that! All the subjects are in the same timetable slot, so as far as the school's concerned it doesn't matter who's where.'

'What time is it?'

'Seven, tomorrow night.'

'Walk down with me.'

Wednesday evening, we walk the four hundred yards to school. An uncomfortable walk, me holding up the left leg of my trousers to avoid treading on it. Shortening the trousers hadn't been as easy as I'd thought. At first I tried standing in them and tucking the surplus cloth under. Then when I came to take them off it all unravelled, so I pinned them up with safety pins, almost pinning myself into them in the process. Once they were off it became obvious more was pinned up on one side than on the other. The solution was to turn the trousers inside out, pin up the extra until both sides looked equal in the mirror.

Rather than sew all the way round, in case they needed doing again next term when I'd put on a couple more inches, I tack-stitched them fore and aft, port and starboard. You can see the stitches through the fabric if you look carefully enough. Anyway, tonight when I came to put them on I got my toes caught in one of the resulting loops and pulled out two of the tacks in the left leg, which is now trailing behind me like the shit out of a fish's bum.

Mam is amused by my plight. 'Another good argument in our favour,' she says.

All the class teachers sit behind individual desks. Ours is the maths teacher, Gerard Grainger, or GG, which we now render as Neddy. He's not a bad sort, not like Hattersley, that sod of a history master. Neddy's polite to Mam as he carefully goes through my end of year school report: English (good), history (poor, disastrous), geography (average), maths (excellent), PE (average), art (below average), metalwork and woodwork (idle).

'Yes,' says Mam, 'it's those I need to talk to you about. My lad...' She goes on for a good half an hour. 'And look at his trousers,' she concludes. 'As well as cooking, he needs to learn to sew and look after himself. I won't be around for ever. No girl's ever going to bother with a weed like him. It's the job of this school to prepare him for real life.'

Neddy's not going to give in or take the responsibility of acceding to such an outlandish request as allowing a boy into the home economics class. 'I will refer it to the headmaster,' he concludes.

'And if I don't get a positive response I'll refer it to my cousin on the education committee,' says Mam in her best telephone voice as we leave.

'I didn't know you had a cousin on the education committee,' I whisper.

'I don't,' she says, 'but he doesn't know that. Pull your trouser leg up, Danny. When my boat comes in I'll buy you a proper suit and have it fixed up by a real tailor.'

'It's a bloody slow ship, Mam,' I say.

August

'Hey, Danny, there's some Chink at the door.' Harry's leaning out the bedroom window, desperately holding on to the windowsill with one hand and his glasses with the other. 'Has he come to chop us up into little pieces and bake them into a steak and kidney pie?'

'Letting your imagination run away with you as usual. Come on in before you break your neck.' I beat Mam to the door by a short head. Despite the warm weather Chef is clad in a long mac with a woolly sweater and crumpled trousers beneath. His only concession to the English summer is a pair of off-white plimsolls. Without his whites he seems somehow smaller and more foreign.

'Daniel, I wish a word with you.'

I'm about to send him round to the back door when Mam edges me aside. 'Come on in,' she says. 'You'll find us all in a bit of a mess. It's always like this when the kids are on holiday.' She leads the pair of us through the living room. The carpet is as clean as we can get it. Dad's chair has a blanket draped over the back to hide the stains and Gran has lent her favourite coverlet for the sofa. Four cushions have appeared from somewhere and are plumped up, two at each end. The kitchen's equally spotless; perfect, if I say so myself. The cooker doesn't gleam (there are limits to what wire wool and elbow grease can achieve) but there isn't a trace of grease or food stains anywhere. My best frying pan stands proudly on top, the inside shining like the summer full moon. Perhaps the kettle lets down the effect a trifle, being blackened by age, but it has the appearance of an old family heirloom from another, pre-war era. Of course, the floor's swept and mopped, a clean piece of vinyl on the table and the chairs newly wiped and carefully arranged. Chef looks appreciative. Poor sod probably thinks the place always looks like this.

'Daniel,' he begins. 'I have a staffing requirement you may be able to help me with. You know Ho, who prepares the vegetables?'

Of course I know Ho, who hides himself away in the darkest corner of the kitchen and never talks to anyone, even the other cooks. What I didn't know was that he's called Ho.

'He has had a small problem.'

'Is he sick? Cut off one of his fingers? Had a traffic accident?'

'Worse,' says Chef. 'He is arrested. No passport, no visa, no work permit. He will be deported as soon as the authorities can decide where he must go. They say he should go to Taiwan, but he insists he is from Hong Kong. Rubbish, of course. On the run from the mainland. At least they won't send him there. So, I need a vegetable chef for the busy times. During the week, no problem, only enough work to keep the other two going most of the time. They can do the prep work between them as well as the washing-up. Weekends are different: we need all the help we can get. What I want is someone I trust, someone who already knows the business, to prepare the vegetables Friday to Sunday. If that person can also do the washing-up, so much the better.'

'What hours are you talking about?' asks Mam. 'Danny still has his schoolwork to do.' Both Mam and I know I haven't done any homework for most of the past year.

'Start at six on Friday,' says Chef. 'Finish when the washing-up is done. Eleven to two-thirty Saturday and Sunday lunch times; six to finish on Saturday.'

'Seventeen hours in total,' says Mam. 'That's a long time for a lad of thirteen. He's not supposed to be working at all until he's fourteen, and then not after ten at night. What were you thinking of paying him?'

Chef pretends to think. We are not fooled. We know full well he's had everything worked out before he even left the restaurant. 'I was thinking of doubling Daniel's pay, which is very generous since he won't be doubling his hours. A whole pound a week, which is a fortune for a lad of his age.'

Mam may not have any certificates from school but she's been in business long enough to be able to able to calculate pay rates in her head. 'That means you're paying him a shilling and thruppence an hour. Slave labour. The current rate round here's four shillings.'

'For skilled labour,' says Chef. 'Preparing vegetables and washing-up is definitely unskilled labour. Besides, he is not paying any tax or national insurance, which makes his pay thirty per cent better.'

'Only an extra thruppence,' says Mam. 'And you're saving on employer's national insurance as well. A street sweeper makes more than three shillings an hour.'

'And doesn't pay tax.'

'Nor do you, besides breaking the law by employing him at all, exactly the way you broke the law employing someone with no work permit or visa. A good three bob an hour seems a reasonable rate to me.'

'Dearest lady,' begins Chef, launching into another set of intricate mental arithmetic. They sit together in the kitchen for the next hour fencing with one another while I mooch around, making them cups of tea and offering plates of last month's biscuits.

In the end Chef stands up, bows to Mam, shakes her hand and bows once more. She shows him out and he bows to her again at the door. 'That's settled,' she says. 'Start this Friday at six. Two pounds fifteen a week. A bit over two bob an hour. I tried to get him up to half a crown but he's a tight one, the old Chink. If I were you I'd see if you can open a junior bank account. You can't go on hiding your money in your football boots for ever; your dad will find it in the end, just like I did.'

She disappears upstairs. Two pounds fifteen! What am I going to do with so much money? Buy a bike, perhaps? Another pair of football boots? A fish kettle? Best hang on to it for a while. Jobs round here have a way of disappearing as quickly as they arrive.

We have other visitors in a couple of hours. While Mam's turning herself into a domestic superwoman I have to make sure Harry's properly turned out and knows his lines. Mam and I may be on a high but this is one of his depressing days. Visits from the Social have a depressing effect on the pair of us.

While he's getting dressed he tells me a story he swears the Blob told them at school. *'From the Russian,'* he says. *'A real Russian story about the witch Baba Yaga who lives in a house in the woods which stands on a huge chicken leg. It turns round and round, then hops off into some other part of the wood so no-one knows where she might turn up. One day it appears right in front of two boys who are out gathering blackberries for their grandmother's apple and blackberry pie.'*

Grandma always adds blackberries to her apple pies in the autumn. Harry must be very depressed if he has us gathering autumn blackberries already.

'The two boys are lured into Baba Yaga's house by the promise of sweets and are immediately turned into mice. She locks them in the kitchen, feeding them on cheese rinds and mouldy bread. Matters become worse when a woodman falls under the witch's spell and is turned into a cat. For days the boys eat nothing for fear the cat will catch them if they venture out. In the end a beautiful princess arrives along with her fairy godmother, who turns the witch into a cockroach. The princess picks up the cat, kisses it. Of course, it turns back into a handsome woodman, who marries the princess

and takes the boys to live with them in the palace. The mice cannot be turned back into boys, however much the princess kisses and cuddles them. But at least they now live in a huge, safe golden cage, fed on the best gorgonzola cheese and well away from cockroaches.'

Another ring at the front door. I grab Harry's trouser belt to prevent him hanging out the window again. 'We know who it is. Remember your lines and behave yourself.'

Mam is at the front door, the sound of her telephone voice echoing through the house. 'Please come in. Excuse the mess. You know what it's like with two growing boys rattling round causing confusion all day. Daniel, Harold, come down. We have visitors.'

Instead of our usual rumbustious entrance we creep into the living room like a pair of domestic mice seeking their cheese rinds. The invaders have seated themselves comfortably, three on the sofa like monkeys, the fourth on Dad's armchair. Mam sits facing them like a captured spy in a movie being interrogated by the KGB. Two of our guests I already know. Miss Harris has learnt something from three years on the job, now sitting stiffly in a charcoal skirt and jacket designed not to show dirt or stains. Next to her sits a woman who looks nearly as old as Gran, her face covered in wrinkles and fluffy hair which she's tried to hide with too much face powder. The hair on her head is dead straight. At one time it must've been mousy brown but has begun to turn white. She's made the mistake of trying to dye it black, with the result it now shines a dull purple in the light. She has the thinnest mouth I have ever seen, no more than an inch wide, lips pressed together so tight it would need a crowbar to open them. I imagine they'll belch fumes like Dad's on a Sunday morning after he's spent a night on the beer.

Our Salanne makes up the trio. For a change she's washed her hair and there's even a trace of pink lipstick on her pale lips. She's wearing her school skirt, which she tucks around beneath her thighs and pulls down to cover her knees. Her blouse is clean but hasn't been ironed. From time to time she looks up towards the policewoman in Dad's chair, tugging at her skirt every time she does so. The policewoman has a nose too big for her face, evened up by her eyes, which are far too small. In her woolly uniform she looks like a blue teddy bear which has been left out in the rain too long.

Mrs Thin Lips is the boss. No-one speaks until she gives them permission. She's the Senior Protection Officer, she tells us, Mrs Hattersley. There can't be two Hattersleys around, I think. She must be the wife of that bastard of a history teacher. No wonder he's so bad-tempered. Mam's leaning forward, as if to catch every drop of wisdom from her lips.

Mrs Hattersley speaks extremely quietly, just like her husband. For him it's a way of forcing us to be quiet and pay attention, giving him an excuse to clip us round the ear hole if we miss a word of the doings of assorted kings and queens. She looks like she's ready to throw a board duster at me or Danny if our attention wanders for a tenth of a second.

'Salanne is sixteen at the end of this month. As you know, her protection order expires on her sixteenth birthday and in normal circumstances the girl must be returned to the family home.' Mam smiles, sits back a little. 'However,' Mrs Hattersley continues, 'where a girl is deemed to be in moral or physical danger the order may be extended to eighteen or even twenty-one. Our task today is to determine whether or not that order is to be extended.' Salanne lifts herself from the sofa. Mam gestures to her to stay put. Harry and I look at one another. We've been prepared for difficulties but haven't been expecting them to be so sharply phrased.

Mam smiles. 'Well,' she says, 'you've only to look around to assure yourselves my daughter will not be in any physical danger. The house is clean and tidy, there is food in the larder, and Salanne's room upstairs is ready for her to move in. You may inspect it and anywhere else, if you wish. Miss Harris has been here several times over the years. I'm sure she will have told you everything is in order.' Not quite, I think, looking at the living-room windows. Although they're no longer thick with dirt, there are wiped smudges across them on the outside and ground-in grime in the corners where Harry hasn't been able to reach. An improvement, I suppose. At least it shows effort and commitment.

'Her physical well-being is not in question, Mrs Morley,' drones on Mrs Hattersley, adjusting the heavy frames of her glasses, giving her the look of a starving vulture. 'It is her moral welfare we are concerned about. Constable, I believe you have some comments you wish to make.'

'What is your profession, Mrs Morley?' asks the policewoman in a voice like a seagull with a throat infection.

'I am an ordinary housewife,' replies Mam, 'devoting myself to the welfare of my children and the care of the household.'

'Is it not true,' continues the policewoman in an inquisitorial manner she must've picked up from court-room dramas on the cinema, 'that you are fact a common prostitute?'

'That's slanderous,' says Mam, rising to her feet in a movement I know she has rehearsed. 'You have absolutely no reason for making such an accusation. I have no criminal convictions of any kind and have never even been arrested.'

'There was a violent affray here three years ago when this property was being used as a brothel.'

Mam remains standing. 'Again, a slanderous accusation. Some friends came round for a bit of a celebration, which was invaded by foreign interlopers. Things got out of hand when my husband tried to eject them, that is all. Something like that can happen to anybody.'

'Not to me,' says the expression on three faces, though nobody dares say anything. Mam resumes her seat. Produces a spotlessly clean handkerchief, which she uses to dab away non-existent tears from under her eyes.

'Then there is your husband,' continues the policewoman. 'Who I notice is not here today.'

'It's his day at the employment office,' says Mam. 'He never misses his day. Does everything he can to find himself a job. Times are hard, now the fishing is going off.'

'Your husband served six months for burglary. A second offence. A burglary in which your older son, Daniel, was involved.'

'Partly true,' says Mam calmly. 'My husband fell into bad company and was led astray. He got exactly what he deserved, as I have often told him. Since then his behaviour has been exemplary. Daniel had nothing to do with the burglary, as you well know. He is a good boy, works hard, plays hard. Ask Sergeant Finnegan if you don't believe me. Daniel attends his sports club every Thursday evening, pays his dues, regular as clockwork. I believe he is one of Sergeant Finnegan's star pupils.' Mam sits back in her chair, straight as a guardsman outside Buckingham Palace.

'We are not altogether satisfied,' says Mrs Hattersley. 'There are questions to be answered.'

'And I have answered them,' Mam continues. 'There is no reason to keep Salanne locked up any longer.'

'She is not "locked up",' objects Miss Harris.

'As good as,' says Mam. 'If you want to extend her detention any longer you will have to go before a magistrate setting out your reasons in writing. And none of your slanders and defamations. We're a respectable family which can offer my daughter a good home.'

'A family which frequents low public houses,' puts in the policewoman.

'If you call the Yarborough a low public house,' Mam sneers, 'frequented by the top businessmen and councillors in town, out like us of a Sunday night for a quiet drink with their wives. Why don't you arrest them? Start with that poof Burnham, if your boss will let you.' Mam is going off script now.

'Mam,' I say. 'Why won't they let Salanne come home? I want Salanne to come home now!' I burst into tears. Sort of. Harry gets up, moves over to Salanne and starts stroking her hair. Salanne picks up his hand and presses it to her lips. She has been fully rehearsed as well.

'Time for a nice cup of tea,' says Mam. 'Daniel, if you can give me a hand.' While we're in the kitchen I catch the sound of the two women from the Social whispering to one another. Big ears Harry will fill us in later on what's being said. For now, I'm more concerned with checking each cup for old tea stains and finding matching saucers. We've borrowed some from Gran and she's not as meticulous as I am about washing up.

Whispering ceases as I bring in the cups on one of Gran's trays, hand around sugar in a cereal bowl and milk in Gran's milk jug, 'a present from Ilfracombe'. Mrs Hattersley looks at her cup as if it's a time bomb or an offering of rat poison. Sipping, she almost smiles in her surprise. Lapsang Souchong I got from Chef. He says it should be drunk with lemon rather than milk. I can't believe even Mrs Hattersley drinks her tea with lemon.

'Very well,' she says, 'we have had a quick discussion and there does not seem to be any firm evidence of moral harm which would necessitate Salanne staying in care beyond her sixteenth birthday. Until then, since the school holidays are upon us, we suggest she should spend her days here in order to find her way back into the family. Salanne can be off the care home premises from eight in the morning until eight in the evening. As long as there are no complaints from the police or any other agencies in the intervening time, she will move back here on her sixteenth birthday. Until then, she will be required to sign out of the home when she leaves it and back in again at night. Are we all happy with the arrangement?'

'Delighted,' says Mam.

'Thank you very much,' say Salanne and Harry in unison.

'An excellent solution,' I say. 'May I show you out? I trust you have enjoyed your tea. I'm sorry we only had plain biscuits. I like chocolate biscuits myself but people like us can't afford such luxuries. The weather is nice today; I hope it keeps fine for you.' They scatter off into the street: Salanne into Miss Harris's car, Mrs Hattersley to an upmarket Rover and the policewoman to a squad car where one of her male colleagues sits at the wheel guarding the small fleet, which presents an inviting temptation to the likes of Gerry and Wiggie.

Me and Wiggie are cramped up in our den under the hawthorn bushes. We don't use it so often nowadays. The den's changed and so have we. Instead of sweet wrappers and comics on the floor there are used condoms and the sort of magazines which feature women in various stages of undress. Neither of us care much for these. The women seem unreal, uninviting, lacking the softness of the likes of Debbie or Marusia. Certainly we aren't the ones who've abandoned the johnnies. Whoever needs to hide away here to have sex must be desperate.

'I've got a job you might be interested in,' says Wiggie. 'You know how you did the lookout piece on Kirkwood's newsagents that time?'

'Not me,' I say, lying through my teeth. 'I were just kicking a football about in the back yard.'

'Yeah, yeah. Tell me another one. Albert says you did a good job of it, spotting the window was open and so on, even if you weren't the one what climbed through. There's a new posh estate up Hunstone, full of expensive German cars and stuff. Albert reckons he can knock over three of them in one go. What he needs is a couple of lookouts, one at each end of the road. Perhaps help him lump the stuff out, a radio or a television maybe.'

'What's it worth?' I ask.

'Depends on how much we pick up. Last time he give me a quid. Could be more this time.'

'That's not a lot. You've already got a couple of juvenile convictions for nicking stuff from shops. Get caught on a proper burglary and they'll put you away. Youth custody, they call it.

Somewhere to keep you until you are old enough to go to prison proper.'

'Aw, come on. How much will you make sweating away in that Chinky place you work in? Me and Albert will make more in one night than you will in a month.'

'OK,' I say. 'What day are you talking about?'

'Saturday. Everyone's out partying on a Saturday night. What about it?'

'I'll think about it,' I say, knowing full well I won't. Doing one job like this means I have to give up the restaurant, which means I'll be stuck for ever as Albert's lookout until the police have us both put away. And what would Mam say if I got arrested before our Salanne was allowed home? Dad might not care, but she'd never speak to me ever again. What if Mam never did speak to me again?

September

Mam and Salanne have been shopping. 'Your sister has to have some nice clothes,' Mam had argued. 'She can't go on wearing her school uniform or other people's cast-offs now she's a grown woman. Next week she has a job interview at the Co-op, needs to look presentable.'

'What about the new fridge, Mam?' I asked. 'I thought you were saving for a fridge. We need one now there are five of us.'

'Danny, I have a plan, only you have to help me out. There's enough money in reserve for a fridge, exactly as I promised you. But there's nothing extra for Salanne or for a new suit for you either. How much have you got saved up in your bank account? Lend it to me and I'll pay you back as soon as I can.'

'When your boat comes in, Mam?'

Mam giggles. 'You daft sod. I'll slip you a couple of quid every week until I've paid what I owe you. When Salanne gets her job she can buy her own clothes.'

'As long as Dad doesn't take it all off her.'

'He'll get nowhere near. Now, get your bank book out and come with me. We'll call into the electricity showrooms first; choose which fridge we're going to have.'

So, here they are, back from Bon Marché and Burnham's Bargains, Salanne dolled up in an A-line skirt six inches above her knees, tight ribbed sweater and kitten-heel shoes. Tights, of course. All the girls are wearing tights nowadays, hardly a stocking top to be seen, even in the strongest wind. 'Are you going to your interview like that?' I ask.

'Like what? This is what everyone is wearing now.'

'Not the girls on the till at the Co-op.'

'You can't see what they have on underneath their overalls. It's my skills I'm selling, not my appearance.'

I begin to object, but Mam gets in there first. 'Salanne has a longer skirt and a delightful pink blouse for her interview. She's well aware it's the bodywork which sells, not the engine. Sell the sizzle, not the sausage. Why do you always buy the toothpaste with the red stripe down the outside? It's exactly the same as all the others.'

Mam in businesswoman mode again. Salanne listens silently, sucking up Mam's words of wisdom, which she must have heard twenty times already. To be fair it hasn't been an easy time for her. She's not used to having a man bossing everyone around or to two excitable boys running up and down stairs, causing a row first thing in the morning. Getting dressed has been another problem. In the Home it's all girls and women, so she can slop around in her underwear or even less. Here there's Dad and us, as well as Mam moaning at her to cover herself up.

Salanne's mood oscillates between sullen sulk and screaming virago. Mam and Dad hate both. Harry and I have fun winding her up, making comments about her clothes, suggesting the ugliest men on the estate fancy her, hinting her armpits smell, farting loudly when she's eating. This last is guaranteed to produce comments about disgusting little boys, leading to us farting even harder and louder, a joyous release on evenings when I've made one of my hotter curries. Finally, Salanne loses it, shouting and screaming while we roll about on the floor hugging ourselves in fits of laughter.

There are good times, of course. Like when the two of us are alone in the kitchen. Sal can boil an egg but not much more. Unlike Mam she's keen to learn. After the Home my special meals once or twice a week are a real treat, especially Sunday lunch, which has turned into Sunday dinner, giving me a couple of hours after the restaurant. We chop vegetables together, me five times faster from months of practice, talk about different flavours, how much time things take in the oven, the difference between boiling and stir-frying. She admires my new wok, bought second-hand from Chef with money quietly saved from Sal's clothing fund.

She's happy, too, to listen to Harry's stories, which have become longer and more complicated. Sal is proud to have passed some exams, CSEs, she calls them, in English and maths. Her school's been a pilot school for them, which is why she stayed on an extra year. 'There was nowt else to do,' she says. The maths exam is why she's being interviewed for the job at the Co-op. 'None of the others know how to count!' she says, throwing back her hair, newly cut and shaped by Mrs Thompson's niece, who runs a backstreet hairdresser round the corner. Harry holds her hand, gives her a kiss on the cheek, then farts loudly as he rushes out the room.

'You're disgusting,' she shouts after him.

'You never say nice things like that to me,' I whine. 'I know he's the angel of your dreams, while I'm the devil in your heart.' I've no idea where that came from, it just spilled out. Don't know what it means or if it's true. I put my coat on and thunder out the front door, slamming it behind me.

It's raining. But then it's summer, what do you expect? I call in at Abe's on the way to work, see what he can let me have cheap. 'Curry leaves,' he says, 'and this ginger is past its best, so half price to you. Have you seen what has just arrived? Brinjal pickle!'

'What the hell is a brinjal?'

'It's an aubergine.' I look puzzled. 'You know, a big purple fruit like a huge pear or a long quince.'

'Yeah,' I say. Trouble with Abe is he thinks he's still in Islamabad or wherever he comes from.

'How's it going with Chef?' he asks.

'You know, so-so. Not a lot of career progression. I'm chief veggie slicer already.'

'Do you fancy a job as assistant cook? I'm aiming to open my own place in the autumn. The first curry house in the whole county. I'll make a fortune. You could be in on the ground floor.'

'I'm on the ground floor already and it's still hot and sweaty. Besides, I know nothing about proper curries like you have in Islamabad.'

'Islamabad is west Pakistan. They don't understand real cooking there. I'm from the east, Bangladesh, which has all the best recipes. I could teach you. By the time you leave school you could be running one of my new restaurants in Hull or Lincoln.'

Quite how Abe has tapped into my fantasies I can't imagine, but this is real life, not airy-fairy dreams; I have the responsibility of keeping a growing family. 'Listen, Abe, I'm touched you think so much of a scrawny young thief off the estate, but I have to turn you down. I've got a steady job with Chef. He treats me right and pays me regular. I can't afford to take a chance, not with Salanne being at home now and all. Isn't it easier for you to bring in a friend or a brother from home?'

Abe groans. 'You've no idea how difficult it is to get a visa nowadays unless you are married to an English girl or something. I don't suppose your sister would marry my younger brother?'

'Not a chance,' I say. 'Even if he's as beautiful as Omar Sharif.'

'He's more handsome than me.'

'That's not saying very much.'

Abe laughs. 'Don't give up on Chef, then. When I open, come over some nights, lend a hand in the kitchen, peel a few onions or something. I'll slip you a couple of quid. By the time I open you will be fourteen and legal, so neither of us will have to worry.'

'Not until November,' I say. A month which causes problems for me.

Early September and school is starting. Wiggie isn't there; he's at the magistrate's court. Not at the juvenile court, because his birthday is in June and at fourteen he can be given a custodial sentence. Sent away, is what that means. He's packed a little bag in case he's bussed off to the borstal in Boston, a wind-swept barracks in the back end of nowhere. Alex has been there and tells us all about it.

'Ten-foot-high fence all around,' he says, 'with another three feet of barbed wire on top. All the buildings are Nissen huts, left over from the war, except for the screws' barracks which was the officers' building, and the canteen.'

'So, what were you doing there, goody-goody Alex?' asks Gerry Pettit. 'Banged up after a bank job or stealing your mother's takings?'

'Playing rugby,' says Alex. 'The governor thinks it's character-forming, insists all the boys play. Only home games, you understand. Some of the screws play as well. Dirty bastards, they are. A fly half with only one arm. Makes up for it with the way he puts his boot around at anything that moves. I've still got the scars.'

We're interrupted by Frankie Harrison, still the smallest lad in our year. 'Got a message for Danny,' he says. 'Some Chink downtown give it me. Gave me a bob and all. One of your admirers, Danny?'

He keeps well out of reach as he hands over an envelope which has been used two or three times before, the opening closed over with sellotape so I have to rip it open from the bottom. 'Do NOT com to work tonite. Danger,' is written in thick pencil on the back of a waiter's order ticket. Am I being given the sack? Not likely. Chef would simply tell me to piss off and never come back. Anyway, what's this about 'danger'?

'Bad news, Danny,' sneers Frankie. 'Got his daughter up the duff? Found out who's been nicking the takings?'

You can go off people. Going off Frankie is easy. Tomorrow's Saturday. I'll nip round to Abe's early, see if he knows what's going on.

Abe is full of it. 'Cops, customs, Social Services, the whole lot,' he says. 'Looking for illegal workers, like Chinks without visas.'

'And veggie cutters under fourteen,' I add. 'Did they find anything?'

'No-one.' Abe smiles. 'Chef must have been rushed off his feet last night. Short of a waiter, a cook and a washer-upper. You will be in for overtime pay this lunch time.'

Dead right. Lunch-time washing-up runs into evening prep. No overtime pay, though, Chef considering extra hours worked are payment for his advance warning. Could be, he had to make payments of his own elsewhere.

Tuesday morning there's still no Wiggie. 'Off on his holidays,' says Frankie. I have my new timetable. Two lessons of French each week, a class of childcare and a whole afternoon of home economics. 'Another poofter, like cousin Jake,' sneers Frankie when he sees it. By the time I've decided whether to punch him on the nose or kick him in the bollocks he has disappeared in the direction of the metalwork shops. Learning how to file and temper a stiletto probably. He'll need it when I get hold of him.

Childcare isn't so bad, especially as the teacher's highly embarrassed having a boy in the class. She's had the lessons carefully planned out: periods, personal hygiene, contraception (our school regards itself as being 'progressive'), conception and birth, before even getting to looking after the actual child. I take note, especially of the contraception bit. Most of the rest I know by rumour and listening to Mam talking to Salanne. The girls aren't embarrassed, asking detailed questions, turning to see if I'm blushing. With my ruddy complexion they can't tell even if I do.

By contrast, home economics is a disappointment. How to boil an egg. Making tea. Cooking fairy cakes. As it is, I end up as a sort of second teacher, helping the girls who've never been anywhere near a kitchen. Several of these are from one of the care homes, where all food comes from the canteen. I'm used to their incompetence, having lived so long with Mam and now trying to bring Salanne up to speed. By the end of the second week I'm the only one the teacher trusts within a mile of her collection of half-blunt knives. I object to them. 'They aren't safe,' I say. 'A sharp knife does not slip; these wobble all over the place. You must let me sharpen them.' By the end of week three I at last have a whetstone in my hand, going at the knives with a will.

School, then, is satisfactory, as my overall school report card says of me. But you can't have everything. Salanne's quit her job at the Co-op. 'It's so boring,' she says. 'All these old biddies wandering in. No idea what they want, not shopping, keeping out of the rain. Some days there's nobody. The manager won't let me read a magazine, insists I sit at the till, sit up straight like I'm expecting the queen to walk in any minute. Piss-awful pay and all.'

Dad wasn't amused when Mam told him. 'She'll have to pay her way,' he said. 'All very well you buying all them new clothes for her and young Danny rustling up his expensive meals. At this rate she'll be here until she's fat and forty. Buggered if I'm going to keep her. She gets herself a job or she's out of here.' He put on his coat and stomps off to the bookies to lose some more money.

'Don't worry, love,' says Mam. 'He's all mouth and trousers. You'll have to get a job, though. No money from the Social until you've got enough stamps on your card. Didi Moffatt knows someone at the frozen food factory, why don't you try there?'

I carry on peeling vegetables in the corner. No-one notices the cook, either in the restaurant or at home. 'She won't last,' I think. 'Isobel Moffatt only managed a month. I'll give her three weeks at most.' In the end it was two, finishing in a huge scene one Monday morning.

Mam had had a busy Sunday night with one of her regulars who had brought a couple of friends down from Doncaster. Dad had spent all night drinking in the bar of the Yarborough, so neither of them was up. Harry wandered around the kitchen getting in the way, slopping jam down his new school tie and tipping the contents of his satchel all over the floor. Leaving the kettle to boil, I barged into Salanne's room, shaking her and shouting it was time for her to get to work.

'I'm not going,' she said. 'Fucking lousy job. You won't catch me anywhere near there again.'

'You've only been there two weeks,' I say. 'Give it a proper chance.'

'It's shit,' she says. 'Do you know what we do? They give us a plastic overall and a pair of wooden clogs with a copper band round the bottom. Supposed to keep your feet dry but the water gets everywhere. What we get is the freezing trays from the fish fingers. All the fish gets frozen as a lump, then sawn off into fingers. Me and the other girls have a huge tub of water full of soap. The water's supposed to be piping hot, but give it half an hour and it's almost cold. So we wash them trays all day in cold water in an unheated shed with the water slopping all over us and the wind blowing up our skirts. Which is where the foreman would be if he had half a chance. Fuck it all, I'm going back to sleep.'

'No, you're not, young lady.' Dad was full of fury and hangover, shaking Salanne and pulling her out of bed. Sal tried to pull down her nightdress which had risen up to her navel. Dad shook her. She screamed loud enough to wake the whole street. Mam was there, battering at Dad with her fists, shouting at him to let go and get out. Dad slapped her with the back of his hand. Sal bit his arm hard enough to draw blood. I was trying to get in between them, pushing them apart. 'Get off me tits!' shouted Sal, whether at me or Dad I'm not sure. Mam got back up, hit Dad on the back of the head with a perfume bottle. He staggered off holding his head, pursued by a string of swear words from Sal.

'Fucking mardy little mare,' he shouted as he crossed the landing, banging the bedroom door behind him. Sal sat herself down on the bed. Mam cuddled up, put her arms round her shoulders, gave me one of those looks mothers develop for such family situations. I scooted off downstairs, turned off the kettle before it boiled dry, lugged Harry out of his chair and pushed him in the general direction of his new school before helping myself to his leftover toast and jam.

End of September and Salanne still hasn't found herself a job. Dad's a bear with a sore head. I can't see what he has to complain about. Mam's happier with Sal at home and says that her Sunday-night business venture's a huge success. Harry loves his new school and has started teaching me French. We both started at the same time but he gets five lessons a week while I only get two. He's also in the top class while I'm surrounded by kids who can hardly speak English, never mind French. I like to fox him with questions like, 'What is "brinjal" in French?' Trouble is, he keeps coming back with the answer.

Six weeks and I will be legal at Chef's and not have to sneak around anymore. The school has regulations about how many hours you can work but none of us pay any attention to the school rules. The boys wear their ties five inches long, the girls use theirs to tie up their skirts, hoiking them up to eight inches above the knees, not always with success. Beth Coe has such short, fat legs you can see her knickers whenever she takes a deep breath.

There are constant conversations in the kitchen at night when me and Harry are in bed, and Sal has gone out to hang around outside Kirkwood's newsagents with her mates. 'I'm not having it,' says Dad, 'her slopping around, hardly a word to anyone, lazing about like Lady Muck. She'll have to earn her keep somehow. Take her out with you on Thursday, young lass like her will bring the youngsters in like flies round a jam pot.'

'Fucking typical,' says Mam. 'All you think about is money. She's not done it yet. How do you think she should start? Half a dozen anxious punters all over her, back behind the Vic?'

'Yeah, you're right. What the girl needs is a gentle introduction from a caring older man. I'll take care of her myself, bring her along nicely.'

'You're disgusting. Ready to bang your own daughter. Don't know why I stay with a pig like you. Leave the lass alone. I hear you've been making a nuisance of yourself with her I'll have your prick off with one of Danny's new kitchen knives.'

'Talking of Danny, if you're so keen on looking after your brats, where's he getting all this money from? Have you been holding stuff back and slipping it to him? Or is he Albert's new sidekick, knocking over the Hunstone housing estate? Won't be any more coming from Albert's direction, not for a couple of years yet.'

'He's got a part-time job,' says Mam. 'About time you noticed he's not around of a weekend.'

'I'm too busy trying to earn us a crust,' says Dad, as if he isn't any more than a casual minder and dedicated beer drinker. I don't like the idea of him knowing I have some money. Perhaps I'll take my savings books round to Gran's for her to look after.

'Mam,' Harry says, 'are you ill?'

'Why do you say that?'

'You keep taking them pills in the morning. Regular as clockwork.'

'It's a business thing,' says Mam. 'Ask your brother about it.'

So Harry asks me and I have to explain all the stuff I learned in childcare: all about periods and pregnancy and contraception. Salanne sits at the kitchen table pretending to read a magazine. You can almost see her ears twitching.

'We get none of that at school,' says Harry. 'Biology's all about earthworms and plant life. Your school's much more fun than mine, even if it does have girls.'

'Nothing wrong with girls,' pipes up Salanne.

'What's with these pill things, then?' continues Harry regardless. 'The safe way's not to do it. I don't understand why people bother anyway.' I'm completely of Harry's opinion, though I do find the girls in my class more interesting than I did before, now their shapes have begun to change.

'They stop women getting pregnant,' I tell him. 'Mam doesn't want any more children. Having you was such a disaster it put her off children for life.'

'Can't Dad use a johnnie?'

'Not reliable,' I tell him. 'This new pill is one hundred per cent effective.' I don't tell him about the times Mam has had to go off to old Mrs Thomas to have 'something taken care of'. The longer he's sheltered from the seamier side of Mam's business, the better. The sooner she gives it up completely, the more I'll be pleased.

'The pill makes you fat and makes your tits grow,' says Salanne, looking at me for the first time. I'm obviously taken as a fount of knowledge in the area of modern contraceptive methods.

'Might do you good,' I say. 'You could upgrade to a B cup, but you'll have to buy a tighter roll-on than the one you've got.'

'I'll have you know I'm already a B cup, and a full one at that. And I don't have or need a roll-on, only a suspender belt.' Harry sits with his mouth open, taking it all in. So much for protecting him from the intricacies of what Gran refers to as 'women's business'.

November

'He's a good boy. Never done no harm to no-one. Good as gold at home. Been led astray, that's what it is. Some dirty old man's got hold of him, turned his head. That's where all them nice clothes have come from, chisel-toe shoes and things. He never got them out of his apprentice money. They'll lock him up for ever. Jersey's no help, shouting and swearing, saying he'll never speak to him again. "Unnatural," he says. Not my lad. No lad of mine is unnatural. What am I going to do? What am I going to tell Mother?'

'You don't need to tell Mother anything. It's not as if Jake's been arrested. Taken in for questioning is all. If a lad can't have a pee in a public toilet, what's he expected to do? Piss in the street? A storm in a teacup, that's all it is.' Mam has her arms round Muriel's shoulders, stroking her hair and making soothing noises from time to time. Muriel's in full flow, alternating between condemning Jake for being such an idiot and declaiming he's done nothing and the police ought to keep their noses out of other people's business.

'About time you got yourself down to Lower Bedlam, see what's going on,' says Mam. 'Find Jersey and take him with you. Keep an eye on him, don't let him start a fight. You want him as noisy as a jet fighter, make the cops glad to see the back of the three of you. Threaten to call your solicitor.'

'We don't have a solicitor.'

'Of course you don't, but the one thing the cops hate is some snooty lawyer turning up and spoiling the day for them. I'll come along with you as well, if you want.'

Muriel mulls over Mam's offer. 'No,' she says. 'He's my boy and I'm the one to look out for him, whatever he's done.' The two sisters hug one another, Muriel tugging her worn coat round her as she marches off into the evening gloom.

'What's up, then, Mam?' I ask, clearing away empty teacups and soggy tissues from the table.

'Her Jake. Police picked him up in town. Simply hanging about by the "Wyne Pipe". Can't imagine what he was doing there.'

'Cottaging,' I say. 'Hanging around the public toilets looking for a pick-up.'

Mam's shocked. 'How come you know about cottaging and them toilets? Is that what they teach you at school?'

'Everyone knows, Mam. If you really do want a pee, you go somewhere else. But I didn't think our Jake went in for the low life. I thought he was properly fixed up with Burnham. Saw them together a couple of months ago in the restaurant, billing and cooing like a pair of love birds. Perhaps they've broken up now Jake's grown big and hairy.'

'Jake and Burnham! Didn't think they mixed in the same circles. Wonder how they came to get together.'

'Maybe Dad set it up,' I say, quickly dodging the teacup Mam hurls at me.

'Don't you ever say anything like that again. Your father would never do such a thing. He's a good man, a family man.'

'Such a good man he was ready to pimp out me and Harry,' I spit from the safety of the other side of the kitchen. 'If it wasn't for you it would be me being fed tasty chicken pieces by Burnham down the Chinky.'

'Little boys have big ears,' sighs Mam, sinking into the sturdiest of the kitchen chairs. 'He's not a bad man, your dad. A little lazy, too ready to spend whatever money's in his pocket.'

'And yours,' I add.

'And mine,' she agrees. 'Knows what he has to do to keep the business running. Always ready to put himself out, even if it means getting a bit of a thumping on the way. I couldn't live without him. He's not perfect, but what man is?'

Ask anyone round here and the answer would be 'Fred Parker', the man who gives up his wage packet the minute his boat docks, never swears, never drinks more than the odd half, smokes one pack of Woodbines a week, has never raised his fist to Mrs Parker in twenty years. Rumour has it even Fred's going to the dogs. He's been seen mooching around the streets at odd hours and on odd days. Perhaps not so perfect after all.

The kids at school know all about it. 'Stephensons have gone bust,' says John Davison. 'Only two boats left and both of them sold off to Iceland. My dad says there won't be a trawler left in town in twenty years' time. Says I should get out of here or get a job as a bankruptcy expert. Not with my maths, I won't.'

John knows a lot more. 'Cops let your cousin Jake out late last night. His mum and dad caused such a fuss down at the station it was either arrest the whole family or let Jake go. No charges, they say. No poofter's going to admit Jake was trying to pick him up, are they? Best bit. Jake's been Burnham's bum boy for nearly a year, since when he was fifteen. Now, the cops and the courts don't like that and Burnham was on a heavy warning anyway. Your Jake, he was after Burnham for money to keep his mouth shut. Asked once too often and Burnham told him to piss off. So now Jake's giving the cops chapter and verse, all the lads Burnham's been messing around with, including him. Which is another reason there are no charges; not against Jake, anyway.'

What a family mine is! Which is what John Davison was dying to say but was too afraid of me sticking one on him, leave him lying unconscious in the middle of the playground. Matters are no better at home. Dad and Salanne are having a right barny. Sal has been sacked from her job at the warehouse, having only lasted a record three days. 'It's shit,' she says. 'Lumping about them packages, nearly getting killed by the forklifts, fellers making rude comments about me tits.'

'You're just a lazy cow,' shouts Dad. 'Think the world owes you a living. Me and your mam, we work our fingers to the bone to help you live in luxury and all you do is slop around all day painting your face and getting in everyone's way. Even Danny's more use than you.'

'Thank you,' I say, but neither of them's paying any attention to me. As usual.

'If you can't do nothing else you'd as well get out with your mother. This house is no charity. You either work or you get out.'

Salanne brings the argument to an end in her normal manner, storming out the door and slamming it behind her.

'Typical woman,' says Dad. 'Can't hold a sensible conversation for more than five minutes. And your brother, off with the fairies in one of his books again. Get upstairs before I boot you up.'

I'm surprised at this; didn't even realise he recognised I existed. Harry's upstairs trying to get on with his French homework. 'Is it true eating cheese before bedtime gives you nightmares?' he asks.

'Not as far as I know. Where did you get an idea like that from?'

'In the textbook. He says he has a "*cauchemar*". I've looked it up and the index says it's "a nightmare".'

'Stupid,' I say. 'I've got something much more useful. How about "*pommes de terre au citron*" for Sunday dinner?'

'*Avec champignons*,' adds Harry. 'Have you heard about Mr Parker?'

'John Davison says he's lost his job now Stephensons have gone bust.'

'Alan Parker told me his dad's got a new job in the chemical works. Three cycle shifts, five and a half days a week, and regular overtime. Not as much as working on the boats but steady, not likely to drown in a storm or have the boat sink under you. Alan's over the moon about having his dad home all the time, take him to the football and things. Do you think Dad can do that?'

'No chance. Nor Sal either.'

'Neither,' says Harry. Pedantic little so-and-so.

'Daniel, may I have a quick word before you leave?'

The comics always describe the Chinese as 'inscrutable'. Chef isn't inscrutable; he has two new expressions: angry and worried. This afternoon he's worried. Perhaps I've done something, blocked up the sink, chopped up one of his obscure vegetables in the wrong way? He stands by the serving hatch, rubbing his thin, knobbly hands together. Ideal for wringing the necks of chickens, I always think, squeeze them like a garrotte. They've got thinner over the last three years while the wrinkles on his forehead have got deeper and longer.

'Can I help, Chef?'

'Of course, Daniel. I know you are always ready to help, always willing. I have a slight problem.'

Here it comes, I think. Wondered how long it would be before I got the sack, to be replaced by one of Chef's relatives. With luck Abe will open his curry house soon and I can wash his dirty pots and pans instead. 'Anything I can do?' I ask aloud.

'We have a problem with the freezer and the refrigerator.' He gestures at the pair of stainless-steel towers which dominate one corner of the kitchen. 'The repair man cannot come in until Tuesday morning, just in time for the first serving of the week. But we have food in there which will not be fit for consumption if it is left until then. The last thing I want is customers getting ill and the hygiene inspector closing me down. It was bad enough last month when some busybody accused me of serving dog in the meat balls. Admittedly the lamb was a little on the tough side, but dog! That's ridiculous! Now, I can't leave this stuff lying around to go rotten here, either, so if you'd do me the favour of taking as much of it away as you can it would be an immense help.'

Chef's talking out of his hat. Sunday to Tuesday's no problem with fresh vegetables or the meat, which takes over a day to thaw out anyway, even in the heat of the kitchen at full blast. He's making a charitable donation, though how he knows we need it I'm not sure. Mam didn't go out to work this week, not even for her Sunday-night regulars. She hasn't been out for three weeks past and has stopped paying me back the money she borrowed towards Salanne's new clothes as well as her 'kitchen money' for food and supplies. 'Not well,' she says. 'The doc has me off for a month at least, insists I finish the whole course of antibiotics. We're on short rations for a while. No more smarty-pants foreign concoctions from you, my lad.'

That must be it. Abe's hardly seen me recently. Even when I've been in his shop it's only been for the odd clove of garlic or lump of ginger. Funny how things which were a luxury a couple of years ago have become necessities in our home kitchen now. Even Dad hardly notices the odd whiff of garlic in his soup. Abe and Chef are great mates ever since they opened up within a couple of months of one another. They must've been talking, Abe saying I seem to be short of cash.

'As you say, "always ready to be of assistance",' I say to Chef, keeping up the pretence I'm doing him a favour rather than the other way round. Two bulging plastic bags with the logo of Burnham's Bargains are propped against the freezer. I'm careful not to open the doors, avoiding embarrassing both Chef and myself, aware the freezer must still be stuffed full of produce which he'll be careful to have used and replenished by the time it comes for my shift on Friday evening.

Getting them home is difficult. Too far to walk, but buses are few and far between on a Sunday, even Alex's mam having a well-earned day off. I wait for nearly an hour before my 3X turns up, the driver annoyed I take so long lugging the bags onto the seat beside me.

Childhood, Boyhood, Youth

'Dinner's going to be late again,' grumbles Dad. 'A man might starve to death of a Sunday in this house. I were ready to cook it myself. It were only your mother what stopped me eating before you got home. Off chatting with your mates or some lass, I suppose. Here, I've got something for you.'

'What's this rubbish?' I ask. 'It's not cod or haddock or even rock. If you want good food, I have to have proper ingredients.'

'Listen to him! God's gift to British cooking! It's hake, that's what it is. Perfectly good fish. The Spaniards buy all we can land. My mate Bri gave me these. Came in Friday morning, too late for the main sale. Still good enough to eat. Fillet both of them and we'll have them with chips.'

I throw another glance at the sad-looking specimens in front of me. Even with Chef's generosity there's nothing else ready I can use. Anyone round here can fillet a fish in minutes. The flesh is soft and friable, not up to any kind of frying; the four fillets would collapse into a mush. A good job Abe's been talking to me about how his family deals with dubious fish in Pakistan. Not that Dad will countenance a curried version, but I can invent, mock up a solution from Chef's carrier bags, something Dad won't throw all over the floor.

A sauce, then. Carrots, onions, celery, a whole mess of mushy tomatoes I'd normally throw in the restaurant's bin, the last of my allspice, a big spoonful of the black peppercorns I buy in bulk from Abe, some grated lemon peel. Some ginger? No, not a good idea. Cook it up, cover the fish with it, pop in the oven for twenty minutes to cook the hake. Ready to serve by five o'clock dinner time.

Harry spoils it by moaning me and him have to share one of the fillets. 'You got the better piece,' I tell him, 'and I had to do the cooking.'

'But I bet that means I have to do the washing-up.'

'Of course. I've had enough washing-up for one week.'

'Stop bickering, you two,' says Mam. 'You get on my nerves,

constantly going on at one another. If it's not you two fighting it's your sister throwing her mardy fits and flouncing off like Lady Muck.'

'Oh, Mam,' whines Sal.

Never mind. Home sweet home. A normal Sunday afternoon, except Mam's not in a rush to doll herself up for another trip down the Yarborough.

Tuesday after school I take myself off to Abe's. He's leafing through a catalogue offering low-cost catering equipment. 'Getting it started, then?' I ask.

'Signed a lease on an old café near the market. Doesn't need planning permission or change of use. Not as big as I'd like but it will do as a start. Now my brother has a visa he can come over and help me. Open next month, with luck. You can always muck in if you want.'

'Sorry, Abe. I told you before, I've got one job. I can't handle another. On the other hand, you might think about taking on my sister. She's had experience in the food industry, knows her way round the kitchen.'

'Daniel,' says Abe, stretching back his shoulders and opening his chest, a movement I've seen him make often when confronted by a customer asking for tick. 'I hate to disappoint you, but what I've heard about your sister's work record does not inspire me with confidence. Washing fish trays for two weeks is not exactly "experience in the food industry", is it? Anyway, my brother doesn't approve of women working outside the home. You English can do what you like, but he's never going to take on a woman to work for him, unless it's at home, as his wife. I don't suppose your sister is looking for a husband? That would make the visa situation far easier.'

'I can't see Sal wanting a husband for a while yet after escaping the Home. Getting out of one prison and into another's her view on marriage. She wants to have fun first.'

Childhood, Boyhood, Youth

'Not like you, Danny.'

'No. I want to have fun, but I know I have to work for it. No money, no fun. But I'm not going to be washing up for ever, I'm going to do better than that.'

'Already chopping the vegetables! I admire you, Danny. You are, like me, not prepared to take "no" for an answer. Work hard and get on, that's my motto.'

'And keep your mouth shut,' I say. 'What have you been saying to Chef?'

'Only that you hadn't been around much the last few weeks, seemed a bit down in the mouth.'

'That's my business,' I say. 'But thank you, anyway.' We shake hands, turning our different ways.

'Here, our Danny, lend us a quid.' Sal, dressed in a pair of my old jeans, too long for Harry, too short for me. Jeans are now trendy for girls, but only the expensive brands make ones which fit them. Sal's bottom fills out the lower part while she has hauled the thirty-two-inch male waistline into her narrower profile with one of Dad's cast-off belts.

'Not a chance,' I say. 'Haven't got a penny.'

'Come on. I know you're the money bags in the family, working all hours for the Chink. Mam says you even have a bank account of your own, bulging with cash.'

'Post office,' I say. 'It's empty.'

'Oh, come on. Say, ten bob. Enough for the cinema and an ice cream.'

'Look, I'll show you. Here it is, balance of one pound ten.'

'What have you been spending it all on? Some classy girl somewhere who wants champagne cocktails all the time? You don't buy records or even any decent clothes. All you've bought since I've been here is that cooking pan.'

'Cooking pans are expensive.'

'Not that expensive. You're just being mean, hiding your

money away in an old sock in your mattress like some mad old woman. I'll have to ask Mam, she'll let me have some.'

'She's got no more than me,' I tell her. 'All we have is the money from the Social and Dad spends all that down the bookies and round the pubs. You'll have to go to the cinema another week.'

'But it's *Blue Hawaii* this week. You know I love Elvis films.'

'Ask me on Sunday when I've been paid. But only five bob, no more.'

'Mean sod.' Sal smiles as she says it. I've promised to make her favourite chicken chow mein for supper tomorrow so she needs to keep in with me. No idea where I'm going to get the chicken from.

She's not smiling later. Words have been said with Mam, who has no more in her purse than I have in my post office account. Mam's also told her where the money for the family food comes from at the moment and how my two pounds ten shillings doesn't go far between five people with good appetites. Sal's ability to hold down a stable job has been called into question, in rather cruder terms than those used earlier in the week by Abe. Time for me to slope off round to Grandma's, see if there's an episode of *Z Cars* on her new rented television.

On Sunday, as promised, I slip Sal five bob. With difficulty she manages a quiet 'thank you'. No-one bothers to ask where she's going in her best dress and a collection of Mam's old make-up. Mam's not worried and Dad doesn't care. They are out together tonight for the first time in a month, Mam even sharper dressed than usual, like a businesswoman about to close a multi-million-pound deal.

I lift my eyebrows at her. 'Preparing the ground, Daniel,' she says. 'I have foolishly let matters slide these last few weeks. Much remains to be done, contacts to be made.'

Dad stands around looking foolish. He's been 'confined to barracks' this week, kept from both pub and bookies. 'Ready money is required for our investment,' Mam has told him. 'We have a valuable property on our hands, one which requires nurturing with time and money, one with an important selling proposition which will not last forever. Keep your cash for Alan on the bar, some more for a round or two of drinks, this week and next. See if you can't borrow a few quid from your mates. Nothing stupid, mind. Don't want you locked away with Albert. Keep it legal. Leave it me to prepare the ground here. Hurry up, or we'll miss the bus.'

They're up to something. Confirmed when they are back in the house by half past nine; unheard of to be so early on a Sunday night. Whatever business was transacted must have been out of the ordinary. Nothing is said all week. But I mean, nothing! 'Hello.' 'Where's tea?' 'Pass the milk.' That's all. No complaints about dirty shoes or not washing behind the ears. No complaints to Salanne when she fails even to bother applying for a job. Harry and me, we talk, of course, in the privacy of our bedroom. Mainly school stuff, him checking my French, me trying to explain the intricacies of the female anatomy. Apart from us, the house has come to a standstill.

'What's up?' asks Harry.

'No idea.'

'Is it always going to be like this?'

'What do you mean? Everyone not speaking?'

'You know. Mam getting her teeth bashed in, Dad on the piss all the time, Salanne grumping around like she's got thistles in her knickers. This estate. This house. No-one at school lives like this. What's the point? Why us?'

'Listen, misery-guts. Sal's got her exams, I'm on my way to being the greatest chef in Britain, you're at a smart school on your way to being a top lawyer or a doctor or a manager. Together, we'll pick ourselves up, crawl out of here. Take Mam with us. She knows business, knows how things should be done. So, she's not great at doing it herself, but you and me, we can pull it off if we work hard and listen to what she says, not what she does. Then I can have all the cooking pans I want and you can have a whole library of books.'

'Fat chance,' says Harry, shutting his French dictionary.

'No garlic in the meal this afternoon,' warns Mam next Sunday morning. 'Tasty, not bland, nothing what will linger on the breath. Traditional, maybe. Chicken, the nice roast potatoes you do with lemon on top, peas, carrots. No, not peas, you always do them with mint.'

'Black pepper?' I ask.

'Yeah, black pepper don't linger. Not too much lemon; too much gives me wind.'

Having a firm order for Sunday dinner's unusual. Normally I'm permitted to go my own way, produce a surprise as long as it's not too far out of the ordinary. A standard Sunday roast is a problem for me, trying to fit it in after lunch-time serving. Roasting can't be hurried; no point in burning the outside and leaving the inside raw. And where do I buy a chicken on a Sunday? All the shops are shut on Sunday morning, except for the beer-offs, and they don't sell chickens.

I hammer on Abe's shop door, shouting at him to come and open up. Today he's dressed in a red and black floor-length dressing-gown he calls a '*djellaba*'. 'Most fetching,' I say.

'What the fuck do you want?' he asks.

'I'm glad you've developed your colloquial use of the English language,' I say. Colloquial? Amazing the words you can pick up from a younger brother at a grammar school. Abe has a huge metal freezer plugged in in his back room. The restaurant's due to open sometime next week and he's been stocking up in advance.

'A slight emergency at home,' I say. 'Someone, meaning me, has forgotten to buy the chicken for dinner tonight. I was thinking maybe I could buy one off you? Give you the money when Chef pays me this afternoon.'

Abe looks concerned, eyes narrow, teeth clenched. 'Has it come to that?' he asks.

Such questions are too subtle for a fourteen-year-old. I consider. Light dawns. 'No, we're not completely broke,' I say. 'I'm not trying to con it out of you. A genuine oversight,' I say, not quite accurately. 'There's always fish, but not on a Sunday.'

'Pay me on Friday,' says Abe. 'If you are cooking a whole chicken this afternoon, you'll need all the time you can manage.' He hauls open the door of the freezer, six inches taller than him, pulls out drawers, rummaging around inside. The chicken's immense, ten pounds if it's an ounce. 'This one should do you,' he says. 'Fill a sink at the restaurant with warm water, not too hot, and soak the bird in it. Add extra hot water when the first lot cools down. With luck it will be properly de-frosted by the time you get home. Don't forget to save some money for Friday.'

I thank Abe, not quite as enthusiastically as I ought. Another set of 'thank you's can wait until Friday. Chef isn't happy to have one of his sinks taken up with my dinner, only giving in after I explain my difficulty and enumerate the menu. 'Complete with apple pie and custard?' he asks dismissively. Chef has little appreciation for traditional British cuisine or the British palate in general.

If the week has been quiet, Sunday dinner is arctic. Dad demands both legs, Sal will only eat the whitest meat from the breast, Mam picks at the wings, leaving most of the bones in pieces on her plate. Harry declares there is too much pepper on the carrots. Ordinary politeness is forgotten, Sal and Dad reaching across the table to grab the potatoes, Harry picking at the chicken carcass with his dirty fingernails.

Then, all of a sudden they're gone. Sal's in the bath, Mam's trying on clothes, Dad's rootling in the wardrobe to find an ironed shirt. With difficulty I intercept Harry before he can disappear out the door in the direction of Grandma's television set. 'Washing-up and drying's to be done,' I say. 'You know the drill. Get some hot water in the sink, then find a clean tea towel.' The last is said merely for effect. We still only boast two tea towels and the one I've been using all afternoon's now covered with fat stains, soggy from wiping our meagre surfaces.

By the time the pair of us have finished the house has come to life once more. Mam has her hair down, using a hair dryer to force it to flip on the edges, using an old towel to prevent it wetting her best dress, a bright red creation reaching just above the knee, fitting tightly in all the important places. Dad appears in a suit I never knew he had, slightly too small for him, the jacket lapels a good six inches wide. It can't possibly be the one he was married in, can it?

The pair of them are getting increasingly flustered, waiting for something. Maybe the taxi's late or a friend is meant to call. Dad's beginning to sweat, pacing round the kitchen, getting in Harry's way as he arranges crockery on the shelves. Salanne finally makes an appearance. The perfect schoolgirl. A flared plaid skirt, above the knee but not art student length, white see-through blouse, a lacy white bra hinting at its existence beneath, bobby socks and sling-back dark blue patent shoes. There's been some disagreement about the latter, I'd dimly heard over the noise of the dishes, Sal wanting Cuban heels and white knee-high boots, Mam insisting on restraint.

A hooting outside. A taxi for this special occasion. The three of them make a fine sight as they cross the road together: mother, father and daughter on their way out to the Yarborough and another jolly evening.

Breathe.

Harry cries himself to sleep.

"In youth the powers of the mind are directed wholly to the future, and that future assumes such various, vivid and alluring forms under the influence of hope – hope based, not upon the experience of the past, but of an assumed possibility of happiness to come – that such dreams of felicity constitute in themselves the true happiness of that period of our life."
(Leo Tolstoy)

Youth

September

'Once upon a time,' begins Harry in the traditional manner, 'in a country a long way away there lived a very ambitious king. The king had to be ambitious for he was a most minor king indeed. His land was much smaller than that of most princes, not as large as a duke's or an earl's. Even mere counts had lands more extensive than his.

'Besides being ambitious the king was both cunning and unscrupulous. A nearby count had a single daughter but no sons, so the king seduced the daughter and agreed to marry her on the promise she would be the count's heir. The marriage was not an overwhelming success but the couple managed to grind along without killing one another. They agreed on one thing: how beautiful their daughter was.

'Another king wished to leave on a crusade. The minor king agreed to guard his kingdom for him until his return. Somehow the crusader failed to return, though he had been fit and healthy when he left the crusade, so the king gathered the lands into his own. An argument over rights and boundaries led to a full-scale battle with a duke who had no military experience and was completely unable to direct his army efficiently. Gradually the kingdom grew and grew until it was one or the largest between the Arctic and the Antarctic.

'One day the king's neighbours called a conference. They agreed he had become too dangerous and powerful to be faced by one of them alone. A defensive alliance was necessary. Should one of them be attacked, the others would rush to his aid. "But let us not make our agreement public," said their leader. "To do so would give him an excuse to attack us and would warn him to build up his forces in advance to such a level that even together we could not resist them." All agreed and a secret contract was signed.

'In the meantime the king's daughter had grown tall and even more beautiful, a striking blonde girl of sixteen years. All the kingdom's subjects were in love with her. Even the women admitted she was beautiful, charming and good-natured. None loved her as truly and as passionately as William, a young captain in the king's guards. He, too, was tall and handsome, though not charming and good-natured but fierce and passionate, as is right for a soldier. His passion was returned by the princess, who sighed with desire every time she glimpsed him in the courtyard of the palace.

'"We must be married," she said to him one day. "My passion for you is huge, but I have no wish to make the mistake my mother made. If I were found to be with child my father would cut off your head, but not before having you tortured and dismembered first. You must approach the king and ask for my hand."

'The captain was, as I have said, fierce and passionate, as well as being the bravest of all the king's men. However, he could not decide which he feared most: the punishment which would be visited upon him should he impregnate the king's daughter or the king's anger at being asked for his daughter's hand in marriage by a mere captain. Between his fear of punishment and the wheedlings of his beloved he had little choice. Finally, he crept up to the king on bended knee and respectfully asked if he might be allowed to pay his respects to the princess. Proposing marriage seeming a precipitate step at this point.

'The king's anger was awesome to behold. He threw cups, plates, jewels and crowns around the palace chamber, cut down wall hangings with his sword, smashed his sceptre in half on the oak dining table. Only the intercession of his wife and daughter prevented him from cutting William into tiny slices in front of his courtiers. As an act of clemency he had the captain placed in solitary confinement in the darkest, dampest, dingiest cellar in the whole palace. No-one was permitted to visit him. Even his food was lowered through a trap door in the ceiling, using a rope to which he attached his waste bucket once it was full.

'Soon after, it fell out that the king engineered a disagreement with one of his neighbours, a rich and powerful prince who had many followers willing to fight for him. The king was not stupid; he realised he could not afford for his army to be outnumbered and needed every soldier who could be found, especially ones who were fierce and brave. An emissary was despatched to the dungeons to make an offer to William. On condition he never met the princess ever again he would be released and returned to his military post.

'The captain crossed his fingers and agreed to all the king's terms. Anything would be better than fighting off the rats in his cellar and drinking the water which ran down the walls. Within days he was dressed in his best armour and leading his company out to battle against the prince.

'The campaign was hard and fierce. At one moment the prince's men were in the ascendant, the next the king's troops had stood firm and were advancing. But the prince had the larger, better drilled army, reinforced by men supplied by his neighbours who had remembered the terms of their alliance.

'The main body of the king's army was finally surrounded on a small knoll, hard pressed and about to surrender. Looking on, protected by his personal guard, the king was gloomy. He ordered his equerry to bring his fastest horse so he could flee the battlefield, leaving the bulk of his army to their fate. "A dereliction of duty," thought the captain. "Such is not the manner in which a great king should behave." He gathered up his sergeants, gave them careful directions and led the whole of the king's personal *guard in a huge cheering mass against the enemy, splitting their formations apart and capturing several of their generals as well as the prince himself.*

'Naturally, the king was delighted. He had considered confining William to the cellar once the campaign was over, but William was now so popular with the soldiers the king feared a military revolt should he do so. Besides, he needed the cellar in which to confine the rival prince while he took over his principality. The captain was reminded of his promise never to meet the princess again and made the commander of a border fortress as far from the palace as possible.

'But love conquers all and the captain and the princess found many opportunities to meet and swear their undying love and passion to one another. "My father is yet young and we will never be allowed to marry as long as he is alive," wailed the princess.

'"There is yet hope," answered the captain.

'As strong a blow as the defeat of the prince had been to the alliance, its members were now more convinced than ever that the king had to be cut down to size. Accordingly, they gathered together every man they could find from dukedom, kingdom, principality, county and earldom to form the largest army the continent had ever seen. With much noise and fanfare, they marched against the kingdom, declaring they would strip it of its power for ever.

'Our captain was brave but also pragmatic. His border fortress could not stand against such might. In correct form he made an agreement to give up the fortress in return for being able to retreat with its garrison in good order and fully armed. Other fortresses followed suit. "A sensible tactical decision," said the captain to the king and his generals in the war cabinet. "As individual forces we can be picked off one by one, with little loss to the enemy. Now we have consolidated and present a much more potent fighting unit, able to stand on ground of our own choosing, at a time of our choosing."

The generals nodded sagely and confirmed William's appointment as head of the army.

'On the day of his choosing, on a hill of his choice, General William drew up the king's army in defensive formation. At the peak of the hill stood the king himself, beneath his personal banner, his trusty steed close by again in case he had cause to flee the scene. The site was well chosen. All day long the alliance's troops battered the king's defensive line without making any progress. Fighting continued into the next day. The king's troops stood fast but there were so many fewer of them now, while the alliance's army had only appeared to grow.

'Another attack was launched, spears and arrows filling the air. For a while there was mayhem before the attackers withdrew for a rest. The king's soldiers sank to their knees in exhaustion. A sergeant stared around him, considering the bodies with which he was surrounded. "Look there!" he cried to his companions. "Look there! The standard has been lowered. His majesty has saved us, he is surrendering. Hurrah!"

'"Hurrah!" echoed the soldiers, relieved to have escaped with their lives.

'But it was not the king who descended the hill to talk terms with the generals of the alliance, but General William.

'"Hurrah for the general!" they cried.

'"The king is dead," shouted William. "A spear has gone straight through his back and out of his chest. For the sake of the kingdom, I must make peace with our enemies." He shifted the leather jerkin on his shoulders to hide the blood which stained both arms, hiding the right hand full of splinters from a spear shaft and concealing it behind his back.

'Out of respect for a brave man the alliance concluded a generous peace treaty, where the kingdom lost only half its territory. The week the treaty was signed William married his princess and declared himself king. It is possible they lived happily ever after.'

'You're a cheery soul,' I say to Harry. 'Where do you get all this stuff from?'

'Shakespeare,' says Harry. 'We do it at school. Great stuff once you get round the funny language. Sex, adultery, battles, betrayal, jealousy. Just like home.'

One betrayal's still raw. Difficult to say who's angriest about it: Gran or Muriel. Now the boys have left home, Jersey's done a runner. Although he calls himself Polish his ancestral home has become part of Russia, so he's pleaded political asylum with the Americans, who have awarded him a permanent resident's visa. Apparently, the negotiations have taken five years; five years during which he's said nothing to anyone in the family, including his wife and his mother-in-law. One day he was here, the next he was in Chicago.

'Left without a word,' complains Muriel. 'Cleared out and left me with nothing. What am I going to do now?'

Do what you always did, is my feeling. Live off the Social with a little bit of Mam's business on the side. I'm getting to be really judgemental nowadays since I left school. To be fair to Muriel, she's not afraid of hard work: serving in the shop, picking peas or beans in the summer, just that she never lasts at anything very long. I'm not going to be like her, I'm going to stick with it, get ahead, not let other things get in the way.

I'm not sure whether Mam's with me on this or not. She was dubious when I stayed on an extra year at school to do those new exams. 'What good's a CSE in history going to do you?' she asks, amazed I have a qualification in the subject I hated most.

'Not only history, Mam,' I tell her. 'Look, maths, English, French and top grade in home economics. Five subjects in all. Aren't I a clever sausage?'

'Too much bloody sizzle for your own good,' she says. I think she's proud of me in her funny way. Really, it's Harry she should be proud of. He's the one who steered me through the bits of trigonometry on the maths syllabus and reminded me French conversation needs verbs and prepositions as well as nouns. Then there's all the reading aloud of 'good books'. Suppose it rubbed off on me somehow.

Today, I take myself off to the local technical college, having told Mam I'm going into town with Gerry. He may be a snide little shit but Gerry can be helpful when he feels like it. For the past year he's been an apprentice painter and decorator, earning even less in his fifty-hour week than I do in Chef's kitchen. 'But I'll have a trade when I'm finished,' he says. 'Branch out on me own, charge what I like, work when I want.'

'How come it's decorating?' I ask him. 'Brickies earn more money. You were never any good at art at school.'

'Too small for a brickie,' he says. 'And when it rains you stop. Painters work indoors, they never get rained off. You ask a brickie. He'll tell you laying bricks is a proper trade, but if you can piss, you can paint. Four more years for my City and Guilds and I'll be earning more than any brickie or chippie, nearly as much as a deckhand. That's what you need, a City and Guilds. Get the Chink to take you on as an apprentice, put you through day release at the college.'

Which is why I'm on my way to an impressive three-storey building about a mile from home. Gerry's right: I need a qualification. He's wrong about taking five years to achieve it. No way is Chef going to take me as an apprentice. Having an apprentice involves intimate contact with the authorities. Chef keeps as far away from anyone in authority as possible. Thanks to Mam he also pays me more per hour than the minimum enforced by the wages council for the catering industry. Why should I give up a nice little earner?

Instead I'm here to sign up for the one-year intensive course: City and Guilds 147, General Catering. Nine till five, five days a week. No pay. Applicants divide into two groups. One is the sons of people already in the trade, owners of small cafés or bed and breakfasts on the sea front. The other's a group of girls who can't think of anything else to do, not wanting to wash dirty fish trays in cold water or sit upright at the Co-op checkout while old biddies wander around buying nothing.

Harry says I'm 'an anomaly', whatever that means. I'm interviewed by a skinny man with a huge paunch, as if everything he's ever eaten has gone straight to his belly, forgetting it's also meant to reinforce the rest of his frame. Mr Berry, as he announces himself, tries at first to persuade me to take the day release course. He has the first page of my application form in front of him. He's taken in my address on the Chatham Estate and the name of my secondary school. 'Not a promising candidate,' I'm sure he's thinking. 'A year older than all the others, been slopping around doing nothing for the past year until his parents have got fed up and thrown him out to us to keep him out of trouble. Don't see him lasting more than a week.'

'Daniel,' he begins, 'the catering trade is a very difficult one. It involves long hours at times when other lads your age are out enjoying themselves. What motivates you to spend a year of your life training for such an industry? Do you have any experience of catering at all?'

I explain to him I've been working for Chef for some time. Deliberately, I keep the exact amount of time vague, since only two years of it has been legal and none of it was on the books. Mr Berry's unimpressed. He probably thinks I'm either lying or exaggerating, that I've been there once or twice then packed it in.

'What have you been doing for the last year?' he asks.

'I've been at school,' I answer, suppressing a smirk. He looks at me strangely, mystified why a lad like me should voluntarily spend an extra year at school when all the others have been dying to get away as quickly as they could, leaving at Easter instead of in the summer if their birthdays fell in the right half of the year. Perhaps I've been in borstal or some such special institution?

He turns my application over and stares at the second page in surprise.

'You have five CSEs,' he exclaims. 'Three of them at grade one, including home economics! Why didn't you tell me before? You start next Monday. Go directly to the catering block at ten. You will need a set of whites and a collection of professional knives. Bring your birth certificate with you and your CSE certificates. Welcome to the college, Daniel.'

He goes so far as to shake hands with me as I leave. Looks like I'm turning into a good citizen after all. First job is to visit Grandma to retrieve my post office book. She's sitting in her kitchen sipping mint tea dosed with several spoonfuls of sugar. The flat's taken on a musty smell, as if the windows are never opened. Her television's on, as it always is nowadays, showing an England cricket match. They're losing to the West Indies, as they always are nowadays. She shifts around, puts the kettle back on the hob. I realise it's not the flat which smells, but Gran. She's developed a stale, sour old woman's odour which no amount of deodorant or perfume can disguise. I wonder if that was another reason for Jersey to decamp to the States.

'I need my bank book, Gran,' I say.

'Getting married, then?' she asks. Her standard answer, more in hope than expectation. She doesn't bother with Harry who, besides being too young, hardly seems to notice girls as much as exist. As far as I go, she knows I spend as much time as possible eyeing up girls' breasts and bottoms. She's taken all the credit for getting Muriel's son Ben married off and now expects to do the same with me.

'No, Gran,' I say. 'I need some things for college.'

Like Mam, Gran doesn't know how to handle this. On the one hand she's looking forward to being able to tell all her friends she has a grandson at college. On the other, it takes me out of the marriage stakes completely, or at least lessens my chances. The favourite has been nobbled with an extra ten-pound penalty, is the way Dad would see it. Still, 'what cannot be cured must be endured', he would say. One must look to the future, find an acceptable girl to line up for next July when my course finishes. What she doesn't know is that I'm already fixed up.

November

'You'll never believe this,' says Mam. 'Your father's got hissen a job.'

'A proper job?'

'More or less,' Mam says. 'His mate Barry, the barman at the Yarborough, he's fixed him up. The boss has started doing wedding receptions on Saturdays, so he needs Barry to work on them while your dad looks after the bar. Then Barry says he needs extra help on a Sunday as well. As a hotel they're open all day for residents, except no-one ever checks who's a resident and who isn't. Absolutely heaving come four o'clock, what with the lunchtime boozers running over and the evening ones just beginning. So, that's your dad fixed up, eleven to eleven on Saturday, twelve to eleven on Sunday. A good steady job for a change. Means we can't go out of a Saturday, but he says it's better for us; he can tap up some customers for later. Might even have a phone put in, so he can dial through with an order. I can be a real call girl, like Christine Keeler. We have to move with the times, steadily glide upmarket. You can imagine him working in a bar. He's as happy as a pig in shit.'

I don't bother to ask about Dad's dole money. There's no way he's going to declare his new occupation to the people at the job centre. He'll turn up on his day every week and collect his money as normal. May even manage to attend the odd job interview, mumble his way through it, pretend he's mentally defective or talk about his time in the nick. No sensible employer fancies taking on a wally jailbird.

Having him out the way on Sundays is ideal, means I can cook whatever I want for dinner without him moaning or throwing it on the floor. To be fair, he hasn't done that so much recently. Whether it's because he's got used to meals which aren't straight meat and two veg or because we have regular company for Sunday dinner I'm not sure. Gran comes every week now, bringing a pie or a home-made cake with her. She's pretty good when she puts her mind to it and I've not got enough time after leaving Chef's to bake, as well as making two other courses.

Janet is the other guest, my girlfriend of two months. She comes over here on Sundays. Wednesday evenings I pick her up from work and we share a newspaper full of fish and chips on the way home to her house. Janet works at a stationery shop which sells posh pens and things out the front, and printed flyers, business cards and restaurant menus out the back. Mondays and Wednesdays they open late, finishing off one week's orders before setting up the next run. Another pound in overtime goes very nicely on top of her basic fiver a week. A fortune when you are sixteen and have no rent to pay.

She's not happy with our arrangement. I'm working Friday and Saturday nights when all her mates are out snogging on the back row at the Gaumont cinema or dancing at the Mecca. Monday and Wednesday she works late and Thursday I'm at Lower Bedlam for the judo, which doesn't leave us a lot of time together. I'm reconsidering the judo. Alex Kirkwood has been to an adult grading and returned with a newly dyed orange belt. I still have my white one with its three red bands, the most I can attain as a junior. Alex's mam has paid for his senior licence; no way Mam's going to pay for mine. Without one I can't enter a grading whether I want to or not. With my lack of upper-body

November

strength, how far would I get against grown men of fourteen or fifteen stone? Giving up judo would allow me one more evening with Janet.

The miracle of Dad getting a job opens up better opportunities. After dinner Harry and Gran go back to hers to play Newmarket or Fives and Threes. Harry wins most of the time nowadays, even when Gran cheats, which she does with regularity. Mam primps herself up, then goes off to service her regulars at the Yarborough. Which leaves the house empty for me and Janet to do whatever we fancy. And I know what I fancy. With luck Janet will feel the same.

Sundays almost live up to expectations. Janet and I declare we're deeply in love. It's not true, but it's what you say to each other. We're on a journey of exploration, mapping out unfamiliar bodies and crevices. I know all about the female anatomy from childcare classes. Nothing prepares you for the reality, the soft yielding parts, the enticing curve of the hips, a slowly hardening nipple. We map one another, tracing out bones and muscles, naked parts and those with lesser or greater concentrations of hair. Our tongues and fingers are busy for hours at a time climbing mountains and trailing along crevices.

'Almost', I say, for there's one thing we do not do: the one thing for which I'm most desperate. 'You'll have to wait until after we're married,' she says, though neither of us expect we'll ever marry. 'I'm not going to the altar looking like a barrel or find meself sitting at home with a kid while you waltz off with Marusia or Debbie. I know you fancy both of them. You have to be happy with what you get; your mates would love to be where you are.'

Where I am, is tucked up in my bed, legs wrapped round Janet, left hand stroking her right breast. Not a huge breast, but neatly formed. Large enough to curve underneath, firm enough for the nipple to point upwards without the help of a bra or corset. I keep an eye on the clock. Her last bus is due at ten. If it's a slow night

Mam will come home around ten-thirty; Harry's supposed to be back by nine-thirty (though I've threatened him with castration if he's as much as a second early). We'll need to be up and dressed soon to avoid discovery. A fake discovery since I'm sure they all know what's going on. 'What the eye doesn't see, the heart doesn't grieve over,' says Gran.

Janet gets up and starts dressing. I insist she dresses first, so I can watch her, and undresses last, after I am tucked up in bed. Having her revealing and covering is almost as erotic as actually having her flesh sliding against mine. I wonder if Mam's customers get the same charge? Janet's given up wearing her roll-on, which makes the dressing and undressing even more seductive. In return I've been forced into a clean change of underwear every Sunday. Mam must know what's going on, since she now changes the sheets on Sunday morning, without fail. I wish she would iron them first.

College has been a disappointment. Most of the cooking's stuff I've done already at school: roast beef and Yorkshire pudding, lamb chops, a variety of boiled vegetables. Again I find myself in the role of assistant tutor, helping the girls baste their roasts or in de-boning a joint. They think I do this because I fancy them. I wouldn't mind, but what with Janet and Chef there isn't much time or opportunity. I do it because I'm bored. Mr Berry tells me the complicated stuff comes later, but I'm not convinced. The lads whose parents are in the trade seem quite happy. Their ambitions only stretch as far as serving up the same old mush week after week.

What is new to me is the waiting. We serve in the college restaurant twice a week, me in my one and only pair of black trousers, white shirt and blue tie, feeling a right twat, face red with embarrassment. At home everyone grabs what they can as soon as the dishes hit the table. Here is far more refined with all the cutlery carefully set out, plates individually wiped, water glasses and water jug. Gravy comes in a gravy boat, not spooned straight out the pan like at home. I have to use a napkin to wipe stray breadcrumbs from the tablecloth, address the customers as 'sir' and 'madam'. Chef's waiters do no such thing. They stand by with their notebooks until the customer orders, plonk the plates down in front of them when it's ready before gliding back to the shelter of the kitchen. I must have a word with Chef about this.

Then there is wine. Chef now serves wine, of course, which has turned his restaurant from a foreign oddity into one of the most fashionable places to go. He has one red, a Bulgarian cabernet, and either a Lutomer Riesling or a Blue Nun as a white. His waiters bring the bottle out uncorked and leave it on the table. In the college restaurant we present the wine to the customer, uncork it in front of them, then gently pour. I haven't quite got the hang of this yet. However hard I try I always end up with a drop of red wine on the tablecloth. And which wine? We have whole lists of wine areas to memorise: Bordeaux, Burgundy, Moselle, Barolo, Roussillon, Songulare. The college doesn't stock many of them but we have to learn the varieties anyway in preparation for our test at the end of the year.

Abe's dismissive. 'Pure snobbery,' he says. 'One wine is much the same as any other. If you must have alcohol with your food, drink beer.' But then, Abe doesn't drink, so how would he know? His brother is the same. When they opened their curry house they decided there'd be no alcohol. 'That's crazy,' I told them. 'This town is built on fish and booze. You're not selling fish. If you don't have any booze, you'll go bust inside a week. All very well trying to educate the customers' palates but you also have to give the customers what they want.' Now there are three different varieties of beer on the menu. No wine, no spirits but Worthington's, Watney's and Hewitt's, our local brewery.

On the way to work on Saturday I pass Abe's shop. I don't have to, but I enjoy a chat about recipes and what strange products he may have had the courage to present to the world. Abe's busy nailing a large sheet of plywood across a space on the door where the glass used to be. Someone's also tried to smash the shop window, which has proved more resistant, now showing a series of star bursts. Fed up with their inability to break in, the attackers have scrawled graffiti in red paint, which has run in scarlet strips down the shop front and onto the pavement. 'Pakis out,' it reads. 'Paki go home.' 'No imgrants here.'

'A right mess,' I say. 'Any idea who did it?'

'Could be anyone,' sighs Abe. 'Stupid buggers can't even spell. At least they didn't touch the curry house. I blame all this fuss in the newspapers, "rivers of blood" and stuff. Papers and politicians. Shoot the lot of them!'

Not much chance of a friendly chat this morning. Better off checking Chef hasn't received the same treatment. Chef is philosophical. 'People do these crazy things,' he says. 'Everywhere countries are busy throwing out the English, so the English have to retaliate and throw out the foreigners in return. Come, I have something for you.'

He takes me through to the kitchen where two of the cooks are busy unpacking a large cardboard box with the name of a catering supplier printed in faded letters on the outside. I know what's coming. Chef has negotiated a good deal with the suppliers, from whom he buys direct rather than paying higher prices at Burnham's Bargains. Besides, he gets a discount for bulk orders. 'Look what has come,' he says, and points to the surface on which I cut my weekend's supply of raw vegetables.

It's magnificent, a gleaming steel fish kettle, big enough for the largest sea bass or salmon. I've been wanting one for ages, promised it to myself as a Christmas present. Now it's arrived a month early! Chef's agreed to take a pound a week out of my wages to pay for it, which will keep me in his debt until after I've finished college. What with a super set of knives, my post office account is as naked as Janet on a Sunday night. Never mind, I love it and life is all about priorities, Mam says, and if my priority is a fish kettle, instead of downing vast amounts of beer with my mates in the Ram, what the hell.

Dad's not impressed. 'What the fuck's this?' he asks a couple of days later, echoing everyone's thoughts.

'A fish kettle, Dad. It's for steaming fish.'

'Why do you want to steam fish? Fry the bloody stuff. Get a decent bit of cod and fry it. Not that disgusting hake or dabs you keep serving up. Where the hell are we going to keep it?'

'Don't worry about storing it. I look after the kitchen. All you have to do is eat the food.'

'Cheeky bastard,' Dad mutters. He puts on his coat and hurries off. Down the bookies, I expect. He no longer tries to take a swipe at me since I've grown almost as tall as him at last. I'm far more agile, too, and I think Mam's warned him about some of the tricks Finnegan's taught us down the judo club.

He comes in later with a dripping bass, dumps it in the sink. 'Put this in the kettle,' he says. 'See what you make of it. George was going to save it for his cat but he give it me for nowt.'

I tip the contents into the sink. A horrible-looking dark fish, mouth as wide as the estuary stares, back at me. 'Rock,' says Dad. 'Let's see you turn that rubbish into a decent meal.'

Dad's bloody useless. This is monkfish, not rock salmon. A monkfish isn't like your normal fish. For a start it has a long tail with a bony spine all along its length. No-one around here has any idea how to fillet or prepare it. My chance to show off. I set to, cutting off the head, making a note to send it back to George for his cat. The outer skin has to be eased off gently, leaving it wrapped in a slimy inner layer. Into the fish kettle with some water and dried rosemary. Careful how long to steam it; too long and it ends up like chewing gum. I peel it off the central bone, portion it up, serve with a choice of Chef's special dips, soy sauce and lime wedges.

'Where's the chips, then?' asks Dad. He's wary of the dips, especially the one with the chilli. Harry plunges his pieces into one after the other, mixing hot, sweet, sour promiscuously, a beaming smile on his face. '*Goujons de lotte avec sauces Chinois*,' he tells me later. 'I had a devil of a job looking it up. Monkfish isn't in the dictionary at the back of the textbook.'

'I already know that,' I say, pleased to be one step ahead of swotty Harry for a change. 'We have it all in the French class at college. Next week I have to write out the teaching restaurant menus, in French and English.'

'Better bring them back to me for spell-checking. In French and English.'

I take a swipe at him with my pillow, taking care not to dislodge his goggles. He giggles, curls up on his unmade bed, wrapped around my pillow. 'What's new on the Rialto?' he asks, quoting from the Shakespeare play he's reading at school.

'You've heard about Mrs Moffatt?' I ask. He shakes his head and sneers, Didi not being one of his favourite people. 'She's gone and got herself arrested. "Running a disorderly house". Police turned up at three on Sunday morning after the neighbours complained. Found her and a couple of others, not a stitch on between them, with half a dozen fellers from the oil exploration company. Said they were celebrating having traced oil deposits off Skegness. Cops didn't care, ran in the lot of them. Seems the biggest of them all tried to resist arrest, ended up with a broken collar bone and dislocated shoulder.'

'Your friend Sergeant Finnegan, I suppose?'

'Could be. Alex told me all about it, so I guess that's where it all came from. I'm glad dad doesn't run his Saturday nights here anymore.'

'So am I. I was always afraid Mam would get beaten up again or the cops would arrive with some hard-faced bitch from Social Services and take us back into care. Good for us he's stopped, but not for him.'

'How do you mean?' I ask.

'You wouldn't know,' says Harry, 'you get in so late after

work, but you should see the state Dad's in when he gets back on a Saturday night. Barely standing this week. Customers keep buying him drinks, so he's on the piss from midday to closing time. Mam keeps him more or less under control on Sundays, but he's still three parts to the wind even then.'

'As long as he's sober the rest of the week there's nothing to worry about, especially if someone else is paying,' I tell him. Harry doesn't look convinced. He's seen too many people round here boozing away every penny they have. I remember going to Russell Coe's house once. All they had in their living room was a rocking horse. No furniture, no carpets, just a rocking horse. Russell's dad was run over and killed by a bus in the end. Never knew if he was too drunk to notice or if he did himself in deliberately. Can't see Dad doing the same, worse luck.

'Never mind,' I say. 'Mam will look after him.'

'And who'll look after Mam?' asks Harry, staring like a frightened owl.

'We will,' I say firmly.

January

A new day. A new year. Mam and Dad are flat out. Dad was behind the bar until well after midnight last night and Mam had a particularly busy time of it with a couple of friends, all in constant demand from businessmen marooned in the Yarborough over the holiday. Harry's reading in bed. I'm not at my best, either. Chef was generous last night, letting me go at ten, even though the washing-up wasn't finished. The restaurant was fully booked last night, as it has been every night over Christmas. Extra pay for me for filling in over the busy time, glad to be able to squirrel away a few pounds in the almost denuded bank account. Janet hasn't been pleased. Having expected to see more of me over the college holiday she's actually seen me less, last night being a rare exception.

Most parties don't get going until after ten anyway, so I wasn't the last to arrive at Alex's place. His mates were still drifting in from various pubs which are not too religious about asking the ages of their clients as long as they have plenty of fluff on their faces and money in their pockets. The usual motley crowd, an uncomfortable mixture of kids from the estate and grammar-school lads from round and about. The glue which holds us together is the girls, none of us being too choosy about education or accent as long as the girl has a pretty face and an attractive figure. Some of the romances will last, but not many once work and other things intervene.

Alex's mam's off to a party of her own with her new boyfriend, a cook off one of the trawlers. Mam doesn't approve of him. He's a South African who's not completely white and doesn't speak with an Afrikaans accent. 'Some sort of wog in disguise,' says Dad. I wanted to ask him if it was the wog or the disguise he objected to, but this is the season of goodwill so I just let it go. One day I'll bring Abe home for supper.

So, we are on our own to enjoy ourselves. The grammar-school kids all seem to have plenty of money and have brought along LPs to play on Alex's new Dansette record player: John Mayall, Beatles, Alexis Korner, Rolling Stones, all the trendy stuff their sort rave about. At home Mam and Gran settle for Tom Jones and the Carpenters. Everyone got into the swing of things, bopping about then falling into heavy clinches when the slow pieces came on. Alex looked strange, with his girlfriend a good foot shorter than him, while his mate Robin was trying his best with a horsey-looking girl two inches taller than him with the biggest pair of breasts I've ever seen trying to burst out of her dress. Debbie Marchant was around somewhere, though not with anyone in particular. Or rather with everyone, and not particular, just like it was round the back of the bike sheds at school. She used to charge ten bob a time, but that went up to a quid when builders came on site to repair the gym roof. Not sure if she was charging last night or if it was freebies all round, given it was a holiday. I'd join in but Janet wouldn't approve and I'm not sure I wouldn't catch something.

Midnight, we were all outside on the street counting the new year in, dancing and singing as a drizzle of snow settled on the road. That's when it all went downhill. Everyone was kissing everyone else and I got shirty when Alex seemed to be hanging on to Janet's lips longer than I thought appropriate. Me and Janet had words about it in the middle of the street, then Alex came back over and got in the way. Lots of pushing and shoving. Nothing serious. Then Albert wandered down the road on his way back from the pub, a half-full whisky bottle in hand. 'Here, you kids,' he said. 'Don't you know it's Christmas? Have a drink and be friends. There's plenty of time in the future for any argy-bargy.'

I pulled Janet away back into the house, where we sat snogging in the corner of the sitting room, me still angry at her earlier desertion. Alex floated in later, his arm round Albert's shoulders, swearing eternal comradeship and decidedly well pissed. Bad timing. Enter Mrs Kirkwood and the new boyfriend, fresh from a dinner dance at the Winter Gardens. She took one look at Albert and blew her top. 'Who let him in here? I'll have no gaol birds in my house. Get him out.'

'He's my friend,' objected Alex. 'I invited him in. You can't just throw him out like that.'

'You watch me.' Mrs K had her best late-Saturday-night dealing-with-drunks face on, looking like she could pick poor Albert up and throw him bodily out the door. Drunk as he was, Albert knew how to make a rapid exit. When I looked round, he was gone, taking the remains of the whisky with him. Alex was furious and just as drunk as Albert.

'I'm not staying here to listen to my friends being insulted,' he shouted. We stared as he grabbed his coat and stormed out into the new year, slipping and sliding on the newly fallen snow. I suppose he must have gone home eventually, but none of us stayed around to find out. We all made our excuses to Mrs K, thanked her for a lovely party and took our embarrassment elsewhere.

Which is why I'm not at my best this morning, having had to walk Janet home to her house 'over the marsh' before getting to bed somewhere around three. At least I'm not working at lunch time, but I'll have to get in earlier than usual tonight to clear off the leftover washing-up before getting down to chopping the vegetables ahead of evening service. I toy with the idea of making a pot of tea and taking it up to Mam and Dad with a side dish of

January

aspirin, but decide I'll only get sworn at. Instead, I make toast for me and Harry, hoping he's not going to spill jam all over his sheets.

I spend the afternoon leafing through my Christmas presents. Mam has bought me a cookery book by the television chef Fanny Cradock. This is my third browse and I still haven't found anything in it worth cooking. The inevitable meat and two veg in various combinations, shepherd's pie, Victoria sponge cake, a Christmas pudding which is fifty per cent Guinness. I leave the book in an obvious place in the kitchen to become well-thumbed and greasy, as if it is a book I refer to frequently. Gran's present, a new re-issue of Elizabeth David's *French Provincial Cooking*, I pour over with glee. Probably provincial French men find the recipes banal and boring, meals they have had every day and grown to hate but here on the Chatham Estate they're a breath of fresh air. I turn down page after page until there are more pages turned than unturned. My new year's resolution: to make my family every recipe in the book by the end of the year.

Mam finally pitches up around six, as I am getting ready to go to work. She's walking gingerly, clutching her head in both hands. 'I must be getting old,' she says. 'Can't take it anymore. This is the worst hangover I've ever had in me life. Starts somewhere around the shoulder blades and just keeps on going. Does a double circuit around me skull then drives a nail straight through both eye sockets and out the back of the neck. Didn't have that much to drink, either. Too bloody busy. Bang, bang; one after the other.'

'Careless talk costs lives, Mam,' I say. 'Don't want Harry to hear you rabbiting on like that.'

'You're right. Pass the aspirin. A quick cup of tea and I'm back to bed again. Maybe I'll give up drink altogether.'

'Until tomorrow,' I say.

'Fucking snide bastard. Piss off to the Chinky before I throw this teapot at you. Now look what you've done, woken up that bloody headache again.' She shuffles off in her Christmas present, a pair of fluffy pink slippers with a rabbit face on the front. She's always complaining her corns are giving her gyp, what with standing about half the night in tight shoes with four-inch stiletto heels, so I decided on something practical. Not sure what Dad gave her, if he gave her anything.

It's dark by now and Harry's still in bed, stuck into one of his books. They're huge, like those old Bibles you see in church sometimes. He has three of them, from me, Mam and Gran, and he's finished one of them already. I should've bought him the collected works of Jeffery Farnol instead, but at five bob each I'd end up in debt to the book shop as well as to Chef. I give him a shout to let him know I'm leaving. The snow from last night has settled and frozen, today's fresh fall floating on top, hiding the ice underneath. There is no way I'm taking a chance on walking fast on this stuff. 'De-risk the process,' Mam would have said. 'Worth spending sixpence on the bus to earn a quid at work.' Funny how she can be so right about most things and still make a total mess of her life.

By Tuesday the holiday rush is over but there's still a week of the college holiday to go. Our house is full of colds and sniffles. Dad blows his nose every two minutes. Harry lets his run until I shout at him how disgusting he looks. Mam looks miserable. 'I'm bloody fed up with this,' she says. 'Having a fucking hangover when I've not touched a drop for days.' I feed all three of them a powder I got from the chemist. Gran says rubbing Vicks on their chests is better, but nothing's going to get me rubbing Dad's chest. I'd rather listen to his snot running.

'I'm supposed to be babysitting tonight,' moans Harry. 'Can't go with a cold like this. She'd never let me in.'

'Don't look at me,' says Mam. 'I'm going to bed with a hot-water bottle.'

Dad says nothing, but none of us expected him to. He'll be off down the pub and dosing his cold with double brandies as soon as they open. They all think they've put one over on me, but I know better. They've played right into my hands.

'I suppose that leaves me,' I moan. 'All of you shake off your responsibility and leave me to take over as usual. Don't know why I bother coming back to this house. It's "Danny do this" and "Danny do that". If it's not the cooking, it's the washing. Now it's the babysitting. Next you'll want me to do a fan dance.'

'That will be fun.' Harry smirks. I flip him round the ear with the tea towel.

'Better be off then,' I say.

'Hold on,' says Harry. 'You're not due for two hours yet.'

'Have to get meself in the right mood,' I say. 'Chase a cat up a tree, kick a dog. No point babysitting if you can't have a bit of fun as well.'

Harry's mystified, but I can see from the glint in Mam's eye that she may have caught on. Still pullover and heaviest coat weather. Pity my shoes leak. If the snow's dry enough it may not matter. I make the way over the marsh, call in at Janet's house. She's still at work but her mam is home, wants to feed me tea and cake, keep me talking until Janet gets in. 'Can't stop, missus,' I say. 'Have to pick Janet up from work. Just dropped in to tell you she won't be in for tea. Don't worry, I'll see her safe home.'

She fusses around until I make my escape. Janet's mother's the main reason we'll never marry. If you want to know what your wife will look like in twenty years' time, take a look at her mother. I'm ready to admit Janet isn't the most beautiful girl in town, but she has her good points. She's fashionably slim. Not Twiggy shape but narrow and rounded in the right places. Her smile is pleasant, her teeth regular and her lips engagingly full. Her hair, almost white it's so blonde, is thick and curly, when long and straight is fashionable at the moment. At sixteen her attraction is undeniable.

Her mother's also slim, to the point of beginning to disappear altogether. Like Gran she's begun to bend over at the shoulders and lose weight from her face as well as her body, accentuating its main features. She now looks like the moon on the Ovaltine adverts, her nose pointed and downturned, her chin sharp, almost aggressive, so upturned is it. Harry's suggested I buy her a broomstick for Christmas; she looks unnervingly like a witch out of one of his story books. Do I want to be married to someone who looks like she should be in *The Wizard of Oz*?

Nevertheless, Janet's attractive now and will probably remain so for the next five or six years, or until children start to wear her down. I put my arm around her and give her a kiss when she comes out of work, looking every inch the calm and efficient shop assistant glorying in her basic five pounds a week. She's not too happy with this display of affection outside her place of work, whatever we may get up to in the back alley behind her house or in the quiet of my bedroom on a Sunday afternoon.

'Where are we going?' she asks.

'Round our Salanne's,' I say. 'Harry's supposed to be babysitting, but he has a cold. Salanne would be furious if he passed it on to Robbie.'

'I don't like Salanne's place. It smells.'

'What do you expect with a baby? Boiling all them nappies. All babies smell. They puke and shit.'

'Then they grow up to be horrible boys like you, who fart and belch. Don't know why I put up with you.'

'Because I'm so loveable,' I say. 'Come on. Don't want to keep Sal waiting.'

Salanne's flat's at the other end of our estate, in a great block fifteen storeys high. There's a lift, which never works, and flights of cement stairs which no-one ever cleans. Don't know how Sal manages, trying to get the pushchair and her shopping up and down stairs every day. The front door's painted a military grey, as required by the Council. All the doors here are the same, either because the Council deem all the residents to be equal or because it's cheaper to buy the paint in bulk. The doors are already scratched and peeling, making them look older than their eighteen months.

Inside, Salanne's place is neat and tidy, everything in its place. Not much furniture, of course. A table, couple of chairs, a sofa she got from the Sally Army and an old carpet Gran was throwing out. One wall's been painted a brilliant orange, the brush strokes showing off the amateurish application. It's blazing hot inside, fired by electric heating common to all the flats. Sal insists the windows have to be kept shut to keep out draughts, which she claims are even worse up here on the sixth floor.

Sal herself is sat on the sofa with her tits hanging out, giving Robbie his late-night feed. I keep out the way. Last time she gave him to me he puked all down the back of my best shirt, the one I keep for my Sunday-night dates with Janet. Janet is not as wary, happily picking up the baby and declaring him 'a real love'. She won't say that once the pee starts seeping through his nappy. Salanne fastens herself up, lays a towel on the table and assists Janet in changing the nappy, which contains more than the odd half pint of liquid. This was the part of childcare classes I always did my best to avoid, but the girls seem to enjoy it.

While the mess is being cleared away Owen makes an appearance from the bathroom, all done up in his interview suit and brown shiny shoes. I like Owen. He doesn't show off, doesn't drink too much and never refers to what Salanne was doing when he first met her. It was a slow night down at the Victoria, when neither she nor Mam was doing much business. They got chatting, nearly got themselves thrown out of the pub for getting too familiar with one another. Within a week Sal was so enamoured she had declared to Mam she was leaving the business entirely and had gone back to her old job at the checkout at the Co-op. Dad was furious, of course, losing a good source of income. 'No money and still expects to be fed and kept for nowt,' he grumbled.

Too much for Salanne. 'Fuck it. I'm off,' she said, and we didn't see her for another month, shacked up with Owen at his mum's place. Took nothing with her, including her pills. So here she is in her cosy tiny Council flat with baby Robbie puking and shitting all over. I don't mind the little bugger, really. It's the look in Janet's eye when she picks him up I don't like. I may not be able to persuade her to open her legs, but thoughts of another little Robbie just might. As for me, the mere thought is enough to put me off sex for life.

Tonight's a chance to find out. The moment Owen and Salanne are out the door we are stripped off and tumbling in their bed between smelly sheets which haven't been changed for weeks. We don't care; our voyage of exploration's far too much fun. Both of us like to keep the lights on; Janet so she can see what I'm up to and me so I can find Janet's tiny nipples without having to search too hard. About the time when I'm getting totally frustrated and Janet is having to fight me off we are interrupted by the deep roar of a motorbike outside. Instantly we dive out of bed and into our clothes before Salanne and Owen can make it up the stairs.

Janet hasn't managed to fasten all the buttons on the front of her dress, but what can anyone expect? We didn't spend an evening on unpaid babysitting for nothing. The noise and bustle has woken Robbie and he's whimpering in his carrycot. Salanne and Janet pick him up, cooing and making silly noises. Owen takes me downstairs to look at his bike, a sturdy BSA 500 he got cheap from a customer at work because it needed a lot of attention. As a bike mechanic himself all Owen needed to pay for was parts. 'Nobody wants British bikes anymore,' he says, stroking the saddle. 'It's all Hondas and Suzukis nowadays. Better performance, higher maintenance, which is great as far as the boss is concerned. He gets commission on the sales then makes money on the repairs as well.'

I look on enviously. Even a little Honda 50 would be beyond my budget, if I worked for Chef eight days a week. But then, Owen only has two pots and a battered frying pan in his kitchen, while mine looks as good as Fanny Cradock's.

Janet comes bounding down the stairs carrying both our coats. Her cheeks are red. She and Salanne have been swapping confidences. Knowing Salanne she's told her to be wary of randy young men who are only after one thing. Rather than take the bus we walk back to her place, stopping off in the side alley for a goodnight kiss and a protracted fumble, as if we hadn't done enough of that already. She has her own key and I give her a last peck as she pushes through, before turning off down the street. The wind has got up, bringing with it flurries of sleet. I wrap my coat round me as tight as I can, thrust hands deep into the pockets, encountering a hard hand-sized packet inside. Puzzled, I pull it out. A three-pack of condoms still in their wrapper, the Durex logo prominently displayed.

Good old Mam. Always ready to look after her boys.

March

'The lad's a fool. Who in their right mind's ever going to give him a job, college or no college? All he does is fanny about all day in a pinnie. I pity that poor lass of his. Even if she ever gets him into bed she'll find she's landed herself with a right poofter. Send him down the docks, sign on as a deckie learner. Get him out the way for a while.'

'No lad of mine's going on the boats. He's perfectly happy where he is, working for the Chink. There's a full-time job waiting for him at the Paki's place when he leaves college. Properly qualified and prepared to do a good day's work. Not like some round here I could mention.'

'Working for a dirty Paki; what sort of job's that? He's better off on the boats.'

'There are no more boats, Dad,' Harry interrupts. 'Get down the docks yourself, see how few there are nowadays.'

'The lad's right,' says Mam. 'Even on a Thursday night it's hardly worth going out. Worse than December in a blizzard. If it weren't for the Yarborough, we'd starve.'

'I slog me guts out behind that bar, morning, noon and night, to keep you and your brats in the lap of luxury.'

'And drink it all away before you get home. There's no luxuries here. Look around. There's holes in the living-room carpet, all the kitchen chairs are ready to fall to pieces. Even the mangle's on its last legs. God, you give me a headache, the lot of you.' Mam puts her head in her hands, stumbles over to the sink, pours herself a glass of water to wash down a couple of aspirins.

I watch from one of the rickety kitchen chairs where I'm trying to translate this week's teaching restaurant menu into French as part of an assignment. Almost as much fun as trying to work out the calorific value of each of the meals on offer. Mam's been worrying away at me to apply for jobs for when I leave college. A bit previous as usual; there's nearly four months to go before I finish. Dad wants extra money coming into the house so he can spend seven nights a week down the pub. Judging by the number of packets of Durex Mam has stuffed into my overcoat pocket over the winter, she thinks I'm looking to move out with Janet, leaving her and Salanne to compare babies. No chance of that, now or ever. Both Janet and I are beginning to look around to see who else might be available.

Dad puts on his overcoat, breezes out into the drizzle, heading for the Wine Pype, which he has adopted as his local now they have strippers on a Wednesday evening, at least until the licensing committee finds out. Mam's curled up on the sofa, a cushion crumpled over her head. She moans softly. I nip upstairs, grab a blanket from the bed to wrap round her. It does nothing to reduce her headache but it stops her catching her death of cold.

'Stevenson's got it all wrong,' says Harry.

'Obviously,' I say. 'What did he have? Eight boats. Every single one of them gone. Totally incompetent. I suppose he got out with a pile from selling them on to the Spanish and the Dutch. Enough to retire to the Costa Brava. Bugger all for the poor sods thrown out of their jobs.'

'Not that Stephenson. Robert Louis Stevenson. The one who wrote *Treasure Island*. All about treasure hunters, Jim Hawkins, Long John Silver and the black spot. Listen, this is what really happened.'

Harry launches into one of his stories. He's become more sophisticated. Now they come in serial form, one adventure every night leading up to an explosive final chapter. This one's about two boys who discover a treasure map, which leads them off on a voyage of discovery. Like any good suspense writer, he leaves them tonight somewhere in the Caribbean, having been captured by bloodthirsty pirates who threaten to make them walk the plank unless they turn over the treasure map to them. A load of rubbish, but far better than poring over calorific content or trying to translate 'asparagus in mayonnaise topped with coriander' into French.

'Don't go on too long,' I tell him. 'I have to pick Janet up from work in half an hour.'

'Can't understand why you bother. She's never going to let you have what you want. Why don't you try your luck on Marusia or Debbie? Mind you, Debbie might be too expensive since she's become Mam's apprentice. She may let you have a quickie as a family favour.'

I throw my French dictionary at him, which he ducks expertly. 'Just what I need,' he says. 'Trying to figure out what the natives say to the boys when they arrive in Guadeloupe. Off you go. Give Janet a kiss from me.' He dodges away upstairs, taking my dictionary with him. If I'm supposed to have difficulty finding a job, what on earth's going to happen to my dizzy little brother?

Mam and Dad aren't the only ones worrying about my job prospects. At college, Mr Berry's taking his tutor role seriously, not like some of the others. He has us into an empty classroom one by one for a 'confidential chat' followed by a filling out of forms. Those students who have relatives in the trade are in and out in a flash. They'll work in the family business until it's time to take over. I can hardly work in our family business, can I?

I explain to Mr Berry about my continuing work at Chef's and the offer I have from Abe to take over the front-of-house operations at the curry house. He's not impressed. 'You can do so much better than that, Daniel. With your expertise and enthusiasm, you could find yourself one day working in one of the big hotels in London: the Ritz, Claridge's, almost anywhere. All you need is more experience in the trade, a year or two working your way up, preparing the kind of dishes you are so fond of, not chicken masala or prawn chow mein.' He says this with a look of distaste on his face. I wonder if he's ever been in a Chinese restaurant or a curry house in his life?

'I can't leave home,' I say. 'There's my little brother to look after and Mam's not well at the moment. Besides, my girlfriend wouldn't like it. She sees little enough of me as it is.'

Mr Berry sneers. He knows how stable most teenage love affairs are. 'All very well,' he says, 'but we have to make contingency plans. Your mother will be better soon and your brother is, what, thirteen, fourteen? He will be leaving school next year himself.'

'Not our Harry,' I say. 'He's at the grammar school. Mam had to sign a paper saying he'll stay there until he's sixteen, take all his exams. We'll have the Social down on our necks if he leaves before then. They'll take him into care again.' I've no idea if it's true, but Harry's scared stiff of being back in the Home and I'm not going to do anything to frighten him further.

'Right,' says Mr Berry, not at all put out. He's used to dealing with stubborn students who don't know what's good for them. 'I've got several application forms here for various companies. Most of the information has been filled out by the girls in the secretarial class already. One of their more useful exercises. All you have to do is date and sign them, then I'll send them off with the others. Not as many as I had hoped. Your year seems to be lacking in ambition.'

'This one says I have to be eighteen,' I say, picking it out the pile.

'Don't worry about that. Purely a bureaucratic matter. I know the manager there; he'll get round it somehow. Finished?' He grabs the papers from me before I can as much as look at the names of the companies. Anyone receiving them will take one glance at my address and throw it in the bin. Best let it go and try and negotiate terms of employment with Abe. With luck I can work up to manager of the local restaurant while his brother goes off to start the one in Lincoln or Doncaster.

Abe is ecstatic. Grabs me round the shoulders, dances round the shop, knocking over packets of poppadoms as we go. 'At last we are in partnership!' he cries. 'Morley and Company, fine food for connoisseurs! When can you start?'

'Don't get too carried away,' I say. 'College isn't over until July and I've not made any firm decisions yet. Need to consult the family.'

'Good, I'll come with you.'

I shudder at the idea of Dad confronting Abe, especially when he's spent all lunch time down the pub. 'Not a good idea,' I tell him. 'Dad's out and Mam's not well. Come and see Gran instead, she's always ready to talk recipes. You must know her; she comes in here from time to time for the odd head of garlic or a jar of pickles.'

'I might do,' he says. 'A handsome woman. Mature, but still good-looking. If she's interested in cooking, I'd love to meet her.'

The image of Gran as mature and good-looking doesn't fit with the person who taught me how to make a roux whilst complaining about her arthritis. 'Come on, then,' I say. 'Trade seems slack. Close up for the day and I'll take you to meet Gran.' The thought of walking through the Chatham Estate with a full-blown Paki tickles my fancy. The neighbours may not like living next to us, what with Mam's profession and all, but parading a Paki in front of them will throw them into a dozen fits.

Abe packs up a wild collection of vegetables: aubergines, chilies, green peppers, curry leaves, a few soggy tomatoes and a jar of garlic chutney before turning the shop sign to 'closed' and locking up. 'The restaurant here is going well,' he says as we walk along. 'Not as good as I expected, but well enough. My brother's English is rather poor and the waiter he has understands none at all. The customers have to point at the menu. Then they ask what the item is and the waiter just looks blank. Many people simply walk out at that point. Having you there will be just what we need.'

I'm not too sure. Dealing with drunken trawlermen after a Thursday-night pub crawl isn't my idea of fun. I'd rather be back in the kitchen trying out new combinations, become the Elizabeth David of Pakistani cuisine. Who Abe really needs is Mrs Kirkwood; she'd put the customers right and make sure they pay the bill with a hefty tip into the bargain.

The lace curtains twitch all the way down Gran's street. One old woman walks out of her front door. Stands there with arms folded, looking thunder at me and Abe as we pass. 'Nosey cow,' I mutter, just loud enough for her to hear, quietly enough to pretend the comment is part of some other conversation.

'Tart's brat pimping coloureds now,' she says to her neighbour, not caring whether I hear or not. A candidate for some cat shit through the letter box, that one.

Gran's not at all worried by having a tall, hawk-nosed, dark-skinned man standing at her front door. 'Hello, Gran,' I say. 'This is Abe. You know, who runs the shop in town.'

'Of course I know him,' says Gran. 'I was the one who sent you down there in the first place, remember? Come on in. Harry's already here. Says he's got a new story to tell me. Do you fancy a cup of tea?'

'Not for me,' declines Abe. 'No stimulants of any kind.'

'That's a pity,' says Gran, a roguish twinkle in her eye. 'Come into the kitchen anyway. Perhaps we can lash up some supper together.'

Harry's sitting in the living room, toasting a crumpet in front of the coal fire. I notice his blazer pulls up almost to his elbows. 'I know,' he says. 'But it'll last until the summer term. We're allowed to take our blazers off in school then, so nobody will notice.'

'Your cap isn't in much better condition, either.'

'Stupid old thing. We all hate wearing them. Makes us look like cheap Billy Bunters. Look here. It's two sizes too small so it sits on top of me head like a blueberry, and the peak is hanging off one side. Good thing is, the kids at school think I do it deliberately. They all hate wearing a uniform, so now I'm a style hero, standing out against the authorities. My year has a thing about authority. You know the school has a Cadet Force? All of us in year four are expected to join. Voluntary, of course, but the teachers get real sniffy if we don't. Do you know how many of us joined up this year? One!'

Harry rocks with merriment, a sound which echoes the laughs and chuckles from the kitchen. 'This woman is wonderful,' shouts Abe. 'Look what she's cooked up out of nothing!' Gran proudly prances in bearing a bowl of rice exuding an eruption of vegetables. To be honest it looks a complete mess. Mr Berry would go hairless if I presented him with anything like this. Abe follows, expertly carrying four plates, sets of spoons and forks, three jars of pickles and four glasses. I check to see he isn't carrying a jug of water on his head.

Harry and I approach the mess with care. We look at one another and pile in with gusto. I don't believe for a moment all this is Gran's doing; she's never given us anything like it before. Boeuf bourguignon without the wine sauce is more her line, with a plain lettuce salad. I guess Gran boiled the rice and Abe did the rest.

'What were you saying about your uniform?' asks Gran between mouthfuls.

'Getting a bit small, Gran,' says Harry. 'Going to need a larger size next September.'

'Growing almost as fast as that swollen head of yours,' she says. 'Shit in your shoes, eh?'

'Talking of shoes, Gran.'

'I know, but you'll have to wait for them as well. I've only got a widow's pension, you know. Your dad should be giving you money for new shoes.'

All three of us laugh. Abe looks on, puzzled. 'Why isn't the boy's father buying him clothes?' he asks. 'In my country a father would rather walk around in rags himself than see his children starving or without clothes.'

'Because his father's a complete layabout, neither use nor ornament,' says Gran. 'Don't know why my daughter took up with him in the first place.' She looks at Harry and me, daring us to contradict her. We both shrug, pile in another spoonful of supper, fight over who gets the brinjal pickle first.

'How do you fancy making a bit of extra money on the side?' Abe asks Gran.

'We're not all on the game in this family, you know,' says Gran in her best 'I'm a respectable woman and don't you forget it' tone.

'Of course you are a respectable woman,' says Abe. 'You know I've made Danny a proposition to come and work for me when he leaves college? That won't be for another four months, so I need assistance in the meantime. Someone who has perfect English, understands the subtleties of our cuisine and can explain them to our clients. Also help the waiters from time to time and look after the cash desk.'

'Why? Can't your brother count?'

'Of course he can. He knows how much the bill is going to be before the customer has finished ordering. Except the customer can't, or he's too drunk to find the right money. My brother's English isn't good enough to convince them they have got it wrong or to pacify them. Drunks in particular don't like being ordered about by a coloured man.'

'So, a white woman would be better? Do I have to wear one of those Indian things, a sari? Or fishnet tights and a frilly blouse like the girls on *77 Sunset Strip*?'

'Not at all. Come as you are.'

'In me old frock and carpet slippers? Remember, if I go out to work I'll lose me pension.'

'You can be a friend helping out the staff with their language problems. Purely voluntary, of course.'

'And how much would this voluntary work pay me? Danny, what does Chef pay you for a Saturday?'

'A quid, Gran.'

'That sounds fair. I'll come in Saturday nights, from opening to closing for a pound a night.'

'I wasn't thinking of spending that much,' Abe objects. 'And Danny works double shifts.'

'Well, it's off the books, so no national insurance to be paid, and I'm over twenty-one so expect to be paid an adult wage, not an apprentice like Danny. What do you say?'

They continue to negotiate until Gran comes back from the kitchen with four bowls of chocolate ice cream. 'Not too much of a stimulant?' she asks Abe, who throws up his arms in surrender.

'Think of the pound as a voluntary contribution to young Harry's uniform fund,' he says.

Abe stays behind to help with the washing-up while Harry and I trundle off back home. The kitchen's full of smoke. Mam has tried to make Dad cheese on toast for his supper. For a change she's managed not to burn the toast in the first place but has left it under the grill too long so the cheese has run all over the cooker and the bare edges of the bread have caught fire. Dad has the kettle in his hand, about to pour it over the flaming toast, while Mam's running her burnt hand under the cold tap to ease the pain. 'Fucking stupid cow!' Dad shouts. 'Can't even boil water. Get out of me way while I fix this.'

'Leave it to me, Dad,' I shout. 'Give us the kettle; keep out the way.' Typically, he's happy to be absolved of all responsibility, shuffles out of the kitchen, watching my fire-fighting from the safety of the living room. I simply turn off the gas, pull out the grill pan and leave the bread to burn itself out while Harry stands at the kitchen sink looking after Mam.

'Not too serious,' he says. 'More from the hot toast than a proper burn. A bit of Savlon cream'll fix it.'

Savlon is one of the luxuries I've imported, courtesy of the job at the Chinese. 'Your kitchen is the most dangerous place you will ever be in,' they taught us at college. Any cook who says he hasn't burnt or cut himself at least a dozen times is a lying bastard. I'm not getting blood poisoning for anyone. Except Mam. And Harry. Maybe even Janet.

'What a shitty day,' says Mam. 'Me head is splitting, me arm is on fire and your father's roaring for his supper. It's too much; I'm off to bed.' She disappears at a steady plod. Harry clears up round the sink while I scrape runny cheese off as much of the cooker as I can reach, before throwing Dad's supper in the bin.

'Bread and cheese, Dad,' I shout. 'Unless you want lamb phall on toast?'

'Fucking foreign muck. Just give us some cheddar and a bit of onion to go with it. There's a bottle of Bass in the fridge.'

Harry takes him his beer, pouring it expertly into the glass so the head doesn't overflow over his hand. There's a loud noise as he comes back. 'You trumped,' I say. 'Sounds like a fucking elephant. And it stinks.'

'You wait. Don't know what Gran put in that meal but it don't half go through you. Come on, homework time.'

I might have guessed it. He doesn't want to do his homework; he wants to tell me more of his story.

The boys clung to the wrecked mast as the waves crashed over them. In the distance they could see the last of the pirates being flung from their ship as the gales blasted it against the reef. Ahead was only a rocky shore, the lights of the wreckers' fires shooting up into the coal-black sky. Bravely they allowed themselves to be carried forward with the waves towards the threatening storm and the welcoming fires. Little did they know what dangers awaited them from the greedy cannibals dancing around those fires.

'Don't look so smug,' I say. 'Why should I care what dangers they're running into?'

'You must always care about what dangers are ahead. That's the only way to avoid them.'

So my little brother's giving me lectures on life skills now. Glad to see he's learning more than Shakespeare and algebra at that school of his. Or has he started listening to Mam at last?

May

'Listen; this is simple. "*En papillotte*" means it's wrapped up. Right? In the old days people used to wrap paper round their meat to slow cook it. Now we wrap it in pastry. So, "*saumon en papillotte*" means what?'

Dave Douglas shakes his head. 'I don't get all this froggy stuff,' he says. 'Why can't we just write it in English? Even in the teaching restaurant I have to give the customers the English version because they don't understand the French. You don't write the menus at the Chinky place in Chinese, do you?'

Dave is the doziest of all the dumbos in my French group. He has pretentions of working in London but has difficulty in navigating himself out the gates of the college. We have our final French test on Thursday and I'm trying hard to push enough of the language into him by rote for him to meet the minimum grade. I suspect twenty per cent would be enough, but Dave will be lucky to make two.

'Yeah,' he says. 'Wrapping salmon in newspaper. Stupid idea. The paper will burn. What's it in French again?'

I'm rescued from my task by a dusty hand on the shoulder. A messy set of dungarees slides into a chair at our table, slops down a brimming cup of dark brown tea, the tea strong enough to stand up on its own without the support of the cup. 'How's it with you, partner?'

Jeff Parker, commonly known as 'Nosey'. Addicted to American films. Wants everyone to call him Wayne, after the actor. We all insist on calling him Nosey. 'Not seen you around for a while,' I say, glad to be finished with banging my head against the linguistic brick wall that's Dave Douglas.

'Been on my holidays,' says Nosey. 'Trip round the Caribbean, fortnight in the south of France.'

'Six months in Boston, more like,' I say. 'What was it this time? Shoplifting?'

'Found this old feller outside the Royal Oak in town. Pissed as a fart. Picked him up and sat him on a bench.' Nosey fails to continue.

'And what did you do then?' I prompt.

'Helped him on with his coat.'

'And off with his wallet,' I continue for him. 'Hope it was worth it.'

'Nearly twenty quid. I was well away when some interfering old bitch came along with a copper. Hadn't had time to get rid of the wallet.'

'So you ended up in the borstal at Boston playing rugby and fiddling with yourself.'

'No rugby; the new governor doesn't agree with it. Gardening and basic building studies. Fixed me up with an apprenticeship at Brown's and a place on the block release plastering course here. Six weeks here, then six weeks out on site. Piss-poor pay but it keeps me out of trouble. And I get to meet the lasses. Look at them two over there.'

I turn round to a table in the corner where two girls are sitting deep in conversation. One's slim and dark with perfectly straight hair which shines in the uncertain light of the student canteen. The other's more rounded and sports a dazzling white bob immaculately cut. 'Jean Harlow,' Gran would have said. 'Very nice,' I say to Nosey. 'But I'm taken. Janet wouldn't like it.'

'Are you still with Janet?' He looks genuinely surprised.

Not much is genuine about Nosey, including his name and his attraction to other people's money.

'Of course. Over a year now. What's it to you, anyway?'

'Down at the Odeon last Saturday. *El Dorado*, great new John Wayne film. You ought to see it. There was your Janet and Alex Kirkwood snogging like mad on the back row like they were going to eat one another. Can't have seen more of the programme than the newsreel and the half-time ice cream. Come on, let me introduce you to Sylvie and Nicky.' He grabs my arm, almost upsetting the dregs of his tea as he pulls me across the room.

We sit down next to the girls, both of whom are perfectly groomed. Nosey seems to know them already. 'Nicky lives at the end of our street,' he says, stroking the back of her hand with his dusty fingers. 'We've known each other for a long time, eh?'

Nicky isn't too sure she wants to own up to a long-term neighbourly relationship with Nosey. She's no better than us, stuck on the same estate. What she wants is to be up and out, somewhere smart with a man who will buy her all the clothes she wants and set her up in a new house with a big garden. Can't say I blame her.

She and Sylvie are on the hairdressing course, she explains. Four days in the salon, one day in college. Not the sort of salon what does the perms for the old ladies on a Friday night or cuts the hair of the women at the food factory so it fits under their hygiene hats; a proper salon where the girls from the grammar school have their hair washed and cut in perfectly straight lines while their mothers indulge in a gentle tint to eradicate any hint of white or grey. Estate girls they may be, but a cut above Nosey and me.

Nosey is spinning a line. 'What about Thursday?' he says. 'There's a band out at the Hog in Armour in Welsby this week. I can borrow me uncle's car. We can all go out together, have a good time.' The girls are impressed. Not only has Nosey got access to a car; he also must have a driving licence. Maybe. He hasn't asked me whether I want to go, assuming I'm not going to turn down a night out with a couple of neat, tasty lasses.

We arrange to meet at Nicky's house at seven on Thursday, which doesn't give us much time to get home and get changed. Mid-week the pubs round here close at ten, even the ones out in the country, like Welsby.

Thursday's French test is an absolute doddle. Even Dave Douglas seems confident, especially since *'saumon en papillotte'* figures prominently in the menu section. I'm looking forward to a good night out and compliments from swotty brother Harry. Instead, I walk into a huge family row. Dad's so drunk he can hardly stand up. Mam's walking round and round the living room screaming her head off. 'I can't do it!' she shouts. 'My head's splitting in half. Let me alone, let me alone the lot of you. Just fuck off and let me die. You're supposed to look after me, you drunken pig. Look at you! Any bother tonight, what use would you be?'

Dad grabs her, swings her round, bouncing her off the wall, starts flailing at her with his fists. Not doing much damage, he's so drunk, but Mam's wailing and sobbing fit to bust. Harry's in there, pushing himself between the two of them, getting buffeted round the head for his pains. Mam collapses on the floor. Dad starts kicking her where she lies. Harry grabs hold of his hair, trying to pull him back, his skinny arms knotting with the effort. 'You lazy cow!' shouts Dad. 'Get out there and get to work. Fucking headaches! Think you're the fucking queen or something, lazing about here all day.' He kicks at her again.

No-one messes with my mam. I'm not having it. My chef's bag is to hand. Hit him over the head with it? No, I put it down, grope inside. I reach for the boning knife. Ten inches long, sharp enough to cut a chicken in half, a point to tease out the smallest sliver of beef from the bone. This must be done with precision. Nothing smart, nothing subtle, just fast.

Breathe.

Bern Finnegan would be proud. A solid kick to the side of the knee of Dad's standing leg brings him down, crushed against the sofa. I grab his hair, so much more effectively than poor Harry, bend his head backwards, sticking the blade of the boning knife against his throat. Rage is bubbling inside me like the North Sea in a gale. Contain it. Think. Brain, not heart. 'Do you know what I can do with this?' I shout at Dad. 'I can bone and skin a whole cow inside fifteen minutes. I can cut you to pieces in five. You touch my mam again and I'll have your guts all over the floor for the rats and the dogs to eat. Feel this.'

I drag the knife as gently as I can across his throat. Softly enough not to do any real damage, hard enough to draw blood from every inch of the line. I am proud of my precision, disappointed not to be dealing with the problem once and for all.

He screams. 'You've cut my throat! I'm dying. You ungrateful cunt. Let me out of here. I need a doctor. I want a doctor.'

Off he goes, staggering down the street, shouting that his son's murdered him. I wipe the knife on my trousers, stow it neatly back in its case.

Breathe. My hand's shaking. Good job it didn't do that earlier. Mam's easing painfully to her feet, a cut above one eye, bruises on her arms. 'He'll bring the police on us,' she says.

'Not him. They'll think he's a drunk caught up in a street fight. More likely to arrest him for drunk and disorderly. How are you, young Harry?'

Harry straightens himself up, looks at the strands of greying hair in his hands. 'Fuck all to get hold of,' he says. 'Old man's going bald.' Harry's as white as snow, bruises beginning to form on his cheekbones. 'Were you really going to slit his throat?' he asks.

'Doesn't only happen in your pirate stories,' I tell him. 'Let's get Mam off to bed, then some food inside you. I need to be out before seven.'

'You're not going to leave us here alone,' Harry wails. 'What if he comes back? I'm no good with a kitchen knife and Mam's not in a fit state to do anything.'

'He won't be back. I'll call in to Gran's on the way out, get her to come round, stay the night. Put the bolts on both doors, lock the bugger out. A night sleeping in the garden'll do him good. Do you know where my brown jacket is?'

'Upstairs. Mam's been wearing it; says she needs something to keep her warm.'

I have to settle for a pullover instead. The one without any holes in it.

Gran's at her dining-room table tucking into a mess of lamb with something she calls 'ladies fingers', which smells of cumin. Abe's watching proudly as she demolishes half the plateful in seconds. 'Of course I'll come and look after Harry and your mam. Abe'll do the washing-up for me, won't you, love?' says Gran. Abe does not look impressed with the allocation of tasks. 'Look, here's my spare key. Lock up after yourself. Bring the key back tomorrow night. Danny, you can help me finish off the rest of the lamb.' Abe is mollified by the extra responsibility. Or is it the possession of Gran's spare keys?

Nosey's already waiting outside Nicky's house, proudly at the wheel of a huge white Ford Zephyr. 'Where'd your uncle get this?' I ask.

'He knows someone at the Ford dealers,' he says. 'Got a special discount. Hop in the back, here come the tarts.'

I'm trying to figure out what's strange about them, until I realise both are wearing trousers. Girls are not permitted to wear trousers at college and big nights out are still a battle between the traditionalists with big flouncy skirts and the modernists with skirts twelve inches above the knee. Trousers are a fashion matter to be discussed later with Mam or Salanne. Must say, they do look smart in them, showing off their pert little bums and stretched tight over flat stomachs. A couple more years of fish-and-chip suppers will soon change that.

Nicky gets into the front seat as if it's her right, while Sylvie squeezes in next to me. She doesn't need to squeeze; there's enough room for four of us back here, but I'm not going to object. I wrap both arms round her shoulders and pull her close to me, rubbing off her face powder against my pullover. Why the girls wear face powder I've never understood. Their mothers wear it to hide the slide into old age but the girls have fresh young skin and all it does is aggravate the last of their acne spots. Not that Sylvie has any. Not fresh ones, anyway.

Welsby isn't far out of town, less than ten miles or so, but far enough for us to get acquainted. 'You smell nice,' I say, nuzzling behind her ear and getting a mouthful of scent for my pains.

'Like her old man,' shouts Nosey from the front seat. 'He smells like a brewery.'

'Because he works in one,' continues Sylvie. 'Humps the barrels about all day. Gets a pint of bitter with his lunch and a couple of bottles to take home to have with his supper. Nice and steady, gives Mam his pay on the nail every Friday. He can sup as much beer as most men can lift and never turn a hair.'

'Wait till he gets on the whisky,' butts in Nicky. 'Couple of glasses of whisky inside him and he's a right pig. Put your mam in hospital a couple of times. Nearly did for you once.'

'That's when I left home,' says Sylvie to me quietly. 'Ran off to Gainsborough to live with me gran. Had to go back in the end. Gran's got no money and the pair of us nearly starved to death. Dad's been better since then. Only beer nowadays. No wine, no spirits. Still, I'm not staying when I've finished at college. Off to Birmingham. Gran's got a mate there with her own salon. All the black girls go to it, desperate to get their hair straightened like the Shirelles or Martha and the Vandellas. Then they have to do something with it. They need an expert, like me. You try cutting a bob on African hair that's been straightened! We'll make a packet.'

Childhood, Boyhood, Youth

'Good to meet someone round here with ambition,' I say. 'Me, I'm going to run a chain of restaurants all over the north of England, from Watford to Carlisle.'

'Have you heard?' says Nosey from the front seat. 'They're building a new road into town. A single carriageway coming in and a dual carriageway going out for all those who say they're leaving. I'm staying here. Make me money when the Council finishes pulling down the old terraces round the docks and builds new housing estates to replace them. Self-employed plasterer on piece rates. Good job, plastering. Always indoors, never get rained off like the brickies. Oops, here we are.'

The Hog in Armour used to be a spit and sawdust village pub. Now a brewery chain has bought it, smartened up the outside, redecorated, replaced the barrels with metal kegs and brought in new chairs and tables to replace the old benches. Out back, where we sit, is the old stables and store sheds knocked into one. During the day you can see how grim it is but at night with the lights dim and a band belting away on the stage it could be the best Mecca ballroom in town.

'Better than the Mecca,' says Nicky. 'No girls in trousers there. No stilettoes, no boots with heels, no under-eighteens.' I look round to make sure the barman isn't listening.

'Don't worry,' says Nosey. 'If they checked everybody's age they'd never have anyone in here at all.' Sure enough, some of the girls look like they're only just out of junior school and the lads hardly have a face hair between them. I'm emboldened to walk up to the bar, order a pint of bitter, two halves of cider and a lemonade. The barman looks puzzled at the lemonade, shrugs, takes the money and sidles down the counter to serve another customer, who can barely reach over the top of the bar to take his drink.

'What's in there?' asks Sylvie over the noise of the band.

'Lemonade,' I reply. 'Like your dad, I've a problem with alcohol. Even a tiny bit of it has a bad effect on me.' A complete lie, of course. I just don't like the stuff and I've seen what it does to Dad, even on his better days. It doesn't take everyone that way; there are plenty round our estate who stick to a couple of pints with no harm at all. Better to be safe than sorry is my motto. Be in control at all times.

The band belts out a string of popular numbers: 'Glad All Over', 'Wheel's on Fire', 'Baby Love', and we all dance. I don't dance well but the girls don't care. Nosey keeps them topped up with snowballs and ciders now and again. The music gets slower as the evening wears on, leaving us to lean on one another, snogging away in the middle of the dance floor. Sylvie feels like she'd collapse totally if I let go of her.

From the other room we hear the landlord calling last orders. We all moan and complain there's still ten minutes to go and stand around smooching, not making any move to the exit. The ceiling lights flash on and off. Still no-one moves. Finally, they come on in all their dirt-streaked glory, heralding the appearance of the landlord himself. We know the score. This is a village pub and the landlord's a law unto himself. Get banned from here and bang goes your social life for the next five years until you're old enough to sneak into one of the sharper pubs in town. He has his own agenda. No police are going to bother him during regular hours, but to show a light after last orders is to invite the boys in blue into his front parlour searching for a free pint for themselves and catching after-hours drinkers, particularly ones under eighteen.

We all stagger out into the car park, Nosey holding himself stiff and straight as a guardsman, the girls clinging to one another and giggling fit to burst. Nosey has trouble fitting the key into the lock, blames it on the poor light, though the moon is bright and the pub's exterior lights still flicker gently. I dive into the rear seat, Sylvie landing almost on top of me. By the time Nosey has the Zephyr moving I have my hand up her pullover, struggling to find her bra fastening.

Nosey's pushing the chunky car along too fast for this narrow country road, anxious to find a good stopping place. Finally, he pulls in down a cart track, its verges littered with discarded beer cans and condom wrappers. By this time, I have Sylvie's pullover over her head and her bra somewhere on the floor of the car. Similar disrobing noises are coming from the front seat, alongside much giggling and grunting, followed by a period of muttered negotiation. Sylvie and I have our own discussions, ending with my hand trapped firmly between her thighs. 'What's wrong with the girls I meet?' I say to myself. 'All the other lasses around are banging away like mad, yet all I ever end up with is determined virgins.' Not that it isn't fun, if a little more cramped than Sunday evenings at home with Janet.

'I need a pee,' Nicky warbles from the front seat. 'All them ciders is getting the better of me.'

'More than I am,' complains Nosey.

'Don't be greedy. A little bit more later. Come on, Sylve, wee-wee time.'

Hand in hand the girls trot off further down the lane, faint shadows in the moonlight. 'Watch this,' says Nosey, as the shadows move back towards us. He turns the headlights of the car full on, illuminating them in all their nakedness: Nicky long and slim, Sylvie solid and full-breasted. What shocks me, although it shouldn't, is the contrast between the brilliant white Jean Harlow above and the coal-black thatch of pubic hair below. Truly in the dark all cats are grey.

Sylvie instinctively folds her hands across her crotch and hurries back to the car, while Nicky indulges in a series of provocative poses she's picked up from some men's magazine from under her dad's bed. Nosey's evidently excited by her exhibition and reaches across to open the front door for her to get in. 'No, no. Change over,' cries Nicky, pushing Sylvie into the front while she climbs into the back and into my hot and eager hands. Another half hour of stroking, kissing, fumbling and general negotiation ensues; all with an unsatisfactory ending. Nosey has his hands full with Sylvie, while she has at least one hand full of him. I reflect on what his driving would be like if she'd left it all to the trip home.

Which is quiet and regretful, the girls trying to find items of clothing scattered around the wrong parts of the car, neither Nosey nor I offering any sort of assistance. 'We must do this again,' says Nosey, dropping the girls off at Nicky's house. 'Sometime next week?'

'We'll think about it,' says Nicky, sounding like the queen deciding whether or not to take on yet another corgi. 'We'll see you about college sometime.' I look up at Sylvie, who smiles at me and nods. Looks like I've passed the test and will make good boyfriend material. Despite the car, Nosey appears to have come up short.

At home the doors are locked and bolted. Dad is fast asleep on the back doorstep, a puddle of piss seeping from his trousers. No point in trying to wake the house up; they'd only think it was Dad wanting to get in again. Instead I leg it to Gran's and bang on her door until I remember she's sleeping at ours, looking after Mam and Harry. For a while I stand undecided, thinking about curling up on the cement floor outside Gran's front door. 'Like father, like son,' I mutter. To be surprised by a light turned on from inside.

'Who's there?' comes a voice.

'It's me, Danny.'

'Wait a minute.' Sounds of bolts being pushed back and the Yale lock turning.

'What are you doing out this time of night?' asks Abe.

'Couldn't get in. Gran's barricaded herself in like she's Davy Crockett at the Alamo. What are you doing here?'

'Your gran left me the key. Reckoned I had to wait for her to get back in case she hasn't got a spare. Come along. You can doss down on the sofa.' Sounds like Abe is sleeping in Gran's bed. Don't know what she'll have to say about that.

Saturday morning, I'm lazing in bed, hand wrapped around me cock in remembrance of Thursday night's excitement.

'Here, our Danny,' shouts Harry from the other bedroom. 'There's a copper at the door. What do you think he wants?'

June

'All the fault of that stupid cow Nicky.' Nosey slops his tea across the canteen table in his fury. 'Her old man heard her coming in late and gave her a right leathering, then demanded where she'd been. Couldn't keep her mouth shut, could she? Went on and on about us being out at a dance in the country, so they were late getting back. The old man was having none of it. Where was the dance? How had she got there? Who was she with? The whole twenty questions. Neither of us is good enough for his daughter, what with what your mother does and me having been away for a holiday, so he gives her another leathering and next day goes off to complain to the police.'

'Which is why they turned up at our house.'

'Exactly. Worse still, they wanted to know what car I was driving and did I have a licence. Of course I've got a licence.'

I must've looked shocked, because Nosey laughed, spluttering tea down his chin.

'Only a provisional licence, not one what lets me drive on me own. Now they have me dead to rights on driving without a licence and with no insurance. I give them all the shit about the Zephyr being my uncle's. Except they know my uncle hasn't got two pennies to rub together, never mind owning a beauty like the Ford. Next thing I know I'm down Lower Bedlam while they check on reports of stolen cars.'

'Which naturally includes an almost brand-new Ford Zephyr?'

Nosey nods his head, dislodging the plaster-covered paper helmet he's forgotten to take off after a morning in the building department's practice area. 'I thought I'd be fine,' he says. 'Put it back where I found it on the Friday morning. Can't say I stole it if I put it back, can they?'

'How did you get hold of it in the first place?' If the cops are going to come after me again I need to be prepared. Knowledge is power.

'I were doing some work off the cards for an old biddy down by the train station. I'm looking out the window when this feller, he rushes up to the station in his car, zooms out with a briefcase under his arm and dives for the London train. Leaves the car unlocked, keys in the ignition. So, I hustle out, lock it up for him, pocket the keys for safekeeping.'

'And drive it home after work, before taking me and the girls out for the night.'

'Clever, don't you think? I could have made a few bob if I'd driven it out of town, tried to sell it, but no dealer would ever believe I owned a posh car like that. So I put it back. My solicitor says I can't be done for theft; all they've got are the driving offences. Just a year's ban and a fine, he says. I don't have the money to pay a fine. I'll make an offer to pay two bob a week out of me wages. Case comes up next Wednesday. If it weren't for stupid Nicky none of this would've happened. She was the one who blabbed about you being in the car as well.'

'Can't be helped,' I say. 'No harm done.' Or at least I hope so.

'Cops are furious,' Nosey continues. 'Say there ought to be a new law to stop joy-riders. No-one's harmed, are they? The feller made his meeting and got his car back in one piece. Don't see what the fuss is about.' He slopes off, his dungarees covered in blobs of plaster like he's been dive-bombed by a set of pink seagulls. I've got an exam, a practical with one of the City and Guilds external examiners watching. Dead easy, preparing and slicing vegetables,

June

together with a bit of prep work. The examiner, a tubby man with spectacles which keep misting over in the kitchen, seems suitably impressed, as he should be.

College is over for the day by two, giving me a half-day to meself. Salanne is at home, little Robbie crawling about up and down the living room making funny noises and banging into everything in sight. To my surprise he smiles when he sees me, allows me to pick him up and throw him into the air. This is fun, I think. I could get quite used to this. ''gain,' he says over and over until my arms are tired and Salanne's beginning to complain I'll make the child sick.

'Where's Mam?' I ask at last.

'Upstairs putting on her best frock and her second-best face.'

'What on earth for? She's not going out to work of an afternoon, is she?'

'Don't be stupid. We're going to the doctor's. Mam needs a good check-up for all those headaches she's been having and I need a new prescription. Hope she hurries up; we've got a bus to catch.'

'You're not still going to old Bailey on the other side of town, are you? I never understood why you keep trekking over there.'

Sal looks at me pityingly. 'I would've thought Janet had put you right on it by now. Bailey's the only doctor in town who'll prescribe the pill to unmarried women. Half the medics round here are Catholics and won't prescribe it to anyone. The other half are scared stiff of the "moral majority" and don't want to be seen to be encouraging immorality. Anyway, even the nearest doctor's a good bus ride away. Funny the Council didn't think of providing a surgery when they built this estate. Here's our mam now.'

Mam looks a wreck. Her brash red lipstick stands out against the pallor of her face like the lips of a circus clown. She's plastered on a dark powder so thickly it's already flaking off and her green eyeshadow looks like she's put it on in the dark.

'I don't know if I can make this, our Sal,' she says. 'Feel like shit warmed up. Can't we go tomorrow?'

'Who says you'll feel any better tomorrow? Besides, I need to get some more pills or Robbie will have a little sister.'

'Doesn't matter,' says Mam. 'If you fall, you can always get rid of it.'

'Yeah? Look what it did to you. Three times in two years, with your insides so mashed up there's nothing left. The last one nearly killed you. If Gran hadn't got you into a taxi and straight off to the hospital you'd never have made it. Wonder they've never locked dirty old Mrs Thomas up, with her coat hanger and scalpels. Sooner have a house full of kids than trust meself to her.'

Mam's turned a delicate shade of green and I don't feel much better. No wonder Janet and Sylvie are so careful, hanging out for a wedding ring. 'Deferred gratification', the teacher in childcare called it. Deferred far too long as far as I'm concerned. Sal helps Mam into her coat, imprisons Robbie into his pushchair, where he proceeds to be sick all down the front of his vest, rushes the three of them off in the general direction of the bus stop.

Plenty of time for me to have a quick snack, a warm bath and get changed for a night out. Off to the pictures tonight, down at the Tower. Oldest of the three cinemas in town, the Tower is in a rundown area by the river, opposite the animal food factory, which adds an interesting smell to the half-time ice creams. Its main attraction's the balcony, encouragingly priced at two bob each, with only six rows of seats. The back two rows are double seats, ideal for snogging in the dark, if not as private as Nosey's nicked motor car.

Sylvie's a good girl, always pays for herself and understands my weekends are taken up by work at Chef's. I don't tell her about the cosy Sunday evenings tucked up in bed with Janet. Talking of whom, there she is on the back row of the stalls, cuddling up to Alex Kirkwood. I know she's seen me but pretends she hasn't, and I return the favour. Might've known: *Frankie and Johnny*, typical Elvis Presley rubbish but just the sort of crap Janet loves. Who cares? None of us, except her, is here for the film. She even stops snogging when the musical numbers come on.

I know I should be jealous, but I'm merely annoyed. Annoyed it's leg-sweep, grammar-school creep Alex she's picked on, not some older man with a flash car and plenty of money to fling around, which is what she deserves.

Nobody hangs about for the national anthem. We carefully time our exits so as not to run into one another. Alex wraps his hand round Janet's waist and heads off to her place 'over the marsh' while I take Sylvie's hand for the short walk back to our estate. One big problem with these new estates: there's no dark back alleys for a last-minute canoodle, or even more if you are lucky enough.

As a result, I'm early home, where Salanne and Robbie are saying their last goodbyes. Robbie doesn't want to let go of his grip round Mam's neck and she's not trying too hard to disengage. Gran's cleaning away the remains of a disgusting nappy to the accompaniment of banging noises from the kitchen. 'Abe washing up,' says Gran, folding a nappy liner into a neat package before going upstairs to dump it in the toilet.

'How was it?' I ask Salanne. 'What did the doctor say?'

'Useless old fart. "Nerves," he said. As if Mam has a nerve in her body. "More than that," I said, but he wouldn't listen. Spent more time looking down me cleavage than checking up on Mam.'

'I'm a lot better now, though,' says Mam. True enough, she's a lighter shade of pale green and there's a hint of sparkle in her eyes. Nevertheless, she still looks more like Gran's sister than her daughter. I take her by the arm, guide her to the sofa.

'Settle down, Mam,' says Harry, who should've been in bed long ago. 'Danny will make you a cup of tea, while I tell you a bedtime story.' From the kitchen I hear him excitedly rabbiting on about his two heroes, now crawling across the Atacama Desert, desperate to find a spring flowing down from the mountains.

'"We have survived so far," says one of them. Once we reach the mountains there is only fifty miles to go. Then we are at the coast, where we can take ship to treasure island.'

I carry in the teas, two in each hand. Mam and Gran are fast asleep; Salanne has taken Robbie, slipping out unheard and unseen.

Friday's the last serious college day of the year, the day of the final presentation to the examiners. There are six of them, each at one of the round dinner tables in the teaching restaurant. Mr Berry's one, the principal, vice-principal and head of catering superintend a table each, as does the tubby man from City and Guilds. Pride of place goes to the Lady Mayoress, glorious in twin set, blue rinse and chain of office. Each one has invited five guests: friends, relatives and those to whom they owe favours. Only Mr Berry's an exception. He's trawled through his list of trade employers, desperate to show off his new fledglings and help them take wing in the industry.

To some extent we students have divided duties among ourselves. Six will produce entrées ('starters', insists Dave Douglas); another six, of which I am one, the main course, and six the dessert ('pudding', says Dave). The rest of the class, those judged barely competent, are relegated to prep and waiting duties. We cooks are the ones in line for merits or even distinctions. The idea is each table will have sight of all six offerings, though able to taste only one, while every one of the examiners will have tasted one of the student offerings, whilst having had a clear sight of all of the others. They will confer afterwards on their experiences.

Putting together six entrées, six main courses and six desserts in one teaching kitchen is a huge challenge. People are for ever getting in one another's way, shouting and swearing, dropping plates, cutlery and ingredients all over the floor. I've brought my knives in specially, tucking them away against a wall so they can't be 'borrowed' while I'm not looking. Originally, I'd intended to use some tasty breast of cod which Dad promised to get from a mate of his. Typically, he's let me down, leaving me with three sad-looking pollock. A crappy fish, pollock. Skinny, lots of bones, little taste. If ever a fish needed jazzing up it's the humble pollock. Abe had suggested a fish curry with masses of turmeric and onions, which even the mildly adventurous Mr Berry was unlikely to tolerate.

I fillet the pollock as best I can, leaving six fillets, which I bake slowly in a sauce of asparagus, root fennel, chopped olives, garlic and a little chilli, adding a touch of fenugreek as the 'mystery ingredient'. Despite the diners taking far too long over the entrée, I get my cooking time dead right, serving up the six plates hot and elegant for the waiters to collect. 'Don't look too bad,' says Dave Douglas, balancing three plates precariously through the swing doors. I murmur a silent prayer to beg he doesn't drop them before he gets to the tables.

We main course chefs peek out at the diners from the safety of the kitchen. A good sign: all the plates have been emptied, bar one, where Patrick Burns has lived up to his name and cooked a leg of lamb to a near cinder. We congratulate one another and move on to the next task, washing up what seems to be every pan and receptacle the college catering department possesses.

Lunch drags on well into the afternoon, prolonged by the six examiners, who gather in conclave afterwards finishing off two extra bottles of Blue Nun. By the time they go we're all exhausted and sweaty, unfit for human company. Fine for the others, but I've no time to go home and change before rushing off early to the night shift at the Chinese. Tonight's a private booking, a twenty-first birthday party with thirty settings and four different set menus. We have no idea who'll choose what, so I have to prep everything thirty times over. It's not really that bad, since there are bean sprouts in all the main courses and sweetcorn comes out of litre tins, but there are still piles of peppers to be cut, aubergines to be laid out and salted, carrots and celery to be chopped. And, it being a twenty-first, the party goes on for ever, so it's well past midnight when I set off for home.

All the buses have finished; everyone except me is at home in bed. I'm glad to be walking. Chef's kitchen gets hot at the best of times, and with so many customers to be served my cubby hole began to feel like the Black Hole of Calcutta. June isn't always the hottest month here but today must've been in the mid-seventies and the walk cheers me up after a hard week. College is nearly over, Mam looks better and the summer has begun in earnest.

I'm just on the back straight, passing my old school, when a cop car pulls up. Out crawls old double-chin, shines a torch straight in my face. 'I know you,' he says. 'You're Morley's lad. Up to no good, I'll be bound. George, look who we've got here.'

The other cop gets out. Yawns, leans on the side of the car. 'I recognise him,' he says. 'He's one of them two lads what nicked that car from the station car park.'

'Not me, Officer. I never stole nothing,' I say as politely as I can after a long day.

'And what's here?' he continues, wrenching the bag from my shoulder. 'Load of dirty white underwear, looks like. And knives! A whole pack of knives! Now we've got you, my lad. Loitering with intent, going armed to commit a robbery. What have you got to say to that?'

I silently count to ten. 'My chef's knives, Officer. Only just finished work.'

'Load of crap,' says George. 'Let's have him in. A night in the cells is just what he needs. Have him up in front of the magistrate tomorrow morning.'

I consider making a run for it but know it would make me look even more guilty. Besides, a good sleep in a comfy cell's exactly what I need. 'Talk to Sergeant Finnegan when he comes in in the morning,' I say. 'He'll sort everything out.'

'*Inspector* Finnegan,' growls George. 'Don't expect he'll have anything to say to scum like you.'

June

The back seat of the squad car is incredibly comfortable, as is the bed in the cell. Not that I really notice, I'm flat out the whole night. Funny, you know. I walk through our estate in the early hours of the morning, not a light on in any of the houses, and yet here's Mam at Lower Bedlam at half past eight having been given full chapter and verse by some nosey busybody on how I've been nicked for burglary.

'You'll be the death of me,' she says. 'Out all hours, nicking cars and breaking into houses. Just wait till your dad hears about this.'

'I've not done nothing, Mam,' I shout. 'Bastards picked me up because they were bored and had nothing better to do. Took me best knives, they did.' Mam does not look impressed. A few years ago she would've been banging on the desk sergeant's window demanding to see the chief constable. Today she looks ready to burst into tears.

'Fuckin' kids,' cries Mam. 'Nothing but trouble. You can't talk your way out of this one. You've made your bed; you must lie on it.' She hesitates, looks to go out.

'Don't leave me, Mam,' I say in a whisper. 'I need you. Keep the bastards at bay. Fight back. Don't lose hope.'

Mam straightens her back but still looks around irresolutely as if unsure of exactly where she is and what she's doing here. At that moment a tall figure in brand-new uniform sweeps in 'as if he's God almighty', says Mam later.

'Sensei,' I shout. 'Sensei, tell them they've got it all wrong.'

Newly promoted Inspector Finnegan halts in his tracks, turns to look at me. 'Danny Morley,' he says, 'what have you been up to?'

I explain about the twenty-first birthday party and working late and the chef's knives in the bag with me whites. His eyes gleam. This is the chance he's been waiting for. He disappears into an inner room where George and double-chin are finishing off the paperwork prior to my court appearance. The air turns blue, the very walls shake. At this remove it's like being caught in a hurricane. God knows what it's like for double-chin and George. I grin at Mam and she smiles back, the happiest the pair of us have been in weeks.

Hurricane over, Finnegan having exerted his new-found authority, we're back home in time for a late breakfast and a quick wash ahead of the lunch serving back at the Chinese. 'That was fun,' says Mam, 'we must do it again. Good to have friends in high places, isn't it?'

July

Sunday lunch time I get away from Chef's early. Customers are few and far between in the summer heat, most diners having taken themselves off to the beach or to a pleasant country pub. Since he's going to get the benefit, Dad has at last stirred himself and found some sizable cod for supper. Free, of course. It's dumped any old how in the sink when I get home, still in the bass it came in. I'd asked for fillets but such niceties are lost on Dad. Out, then, with my trusty knives, fillet the fish into individual portions. Making the sauce is a ten-minute job, especially since I don't bother skinning the tomatoes.

Behind me the room is filling up. Owen and Salanne have arrived with Robbie and two chairs. Gran bursts in, sweeping Robbie into her arms, leaving a sweating Abe to negotiate his two chairs through the back door and into the kitchen. I told them all to come in through the front, but they never listen. Robbie still perched on her hip, Gran proffers a carrier bag full of half a dozen strange objects which look like hairy hand grenades.

'For the dessert,' she says. 'Abe says he'll see to it, and have you brought the lychees home?' Of course I have. I might forget my head but I wouldn't forget ingredients.

'Up, HaHa,' burbles Robbie at the sight of Harry, still in his pyjamas. 'Jimjams,' he says. 'Up.' On cue, Harry takes over from Gran, whirls Robbie round by one arm and a leg.

'Not in my bloody kitchen!' I shout. 'Too damn dangerous. Go outside if you want to play war games. And go and get dressed when you've finished. You're not having supper in your pyjamas.'

'Grumpy bugger,' says Harry. 'You sound like Dad with a hangover. What's so special about today, anyway?'

'It's by way of being a birthday party,' I say.

'None of us has a birthday today, or even this month,' says smartarse Harry.

'OK, it's a saint's day. Saint Jude or someone.'

'The patron saint of lost causes. Quite appropriate in this family. His day is in June, by the way, so you're a month late.'

'Better late than never. Now get out of my kitchen and get yourself dressed.'

'Grump,' says Robbie.

At least Dad's away from under my feet, wandering round the garden with a bottle of beer in his hand. He won't come anywhere near until the food's on the table, leaving me free to magic eight plates from somewhere, a portion of baked cod on each one. Then the sauce, exactly the same as I made for the college exam but with extra garlic, chilli and fenugreek. Harry's at last changed into something resembling Sunday best, a white school shirt and a pair of faded jeans Mam found at the market and I wore until they become painful round the crutch. Faded jeans are trendy nowadays, so for a change he's happy to have my cast-offs.

He gives me a hand carrying the plates through, avoiding the dangerous Robbie on the way. Salanne's planted him in the middle of the floor with a dummy in his mouth and a full bottle of milk. Gran's bought him a present, a push-along toy car which stands abandoned next to the milk. Robbie sits with an intense look on his face, carefully tearing the wrapping paper into precise one-inch strips.

July

Mam makes an entrance in a bright blue ball gown, another offering from the market; does a twirl to show off the flounces. 'What do you think?' she asks, before clutching desperately at the back of a chair. 'Whoops!' she says. 'Went all dizzy there. Better sit down for a minute.' She slides gingerly onto a chair, brushes back a strand of hair which has become disordered. 'What?' she says. 'No Janet today.'

'No, Mam,' I say. 'Said she wasn't well.'

'Off with Alex Kirkwood, I expect,' says Mam. How the hell does she get to know everything going on in the whole town? 'You should've invited that nice Sylvie Robinson. She's a steady lass. Be good for you. Janet's too flighty.'

Useless to explain to the present company that I did invite Sylvie, except her dad wouldn't let her come. Described us as 'low life'. 'Mother's a tart, father's a drunk and a pimp, grandmother's fucking a Paki. No good for a daughter of mine.'

'I thought of it, Mam, but like us their family always eat together on a Sunday dinner time.'

'Not good enough for them, I expect,' says Mam. 'As if humping beer barrels around all day is anything to be proud of. She'll come round when she's ready. This is nice, Danny. Something special you learnt at college?'

'No. This is what I did for the final practical exam. Do you like it?' They're not going to say 'no', are they? But the plates are already half-empty, washed down by half a dozen bottles of beer which Harry's smuggled in from Dad's cache in the coal hole. Dad thinks Abe's brought it. There'll be hell to pay when he finds out.

'Tremendous!' Abe enthuses. 'You must have got the prize for the best meal.'

'Afraid not,' I say, rather deflated. 'The Lady Mayoress hated it. Too much garlic, too much chilli and with some disgusting after-taste; picked out all the olive slices. She thought the fish was quite nice. Frank Evans got the prize. Crispy Yorkshire pudding, golden roast potatoes, beef done to a turn.' Dad nods approvingly.

'Don't suppose you got student of the year, either,' budges in Salanne.

She knows damn well I didn't. 'Max Todd got that,' I say. 'Distinctions in everything. Nasty swot. His parents own three bed-and-breakfasts on the sea front. He's going to do the hotel management course next year.' Mam's looking worried. 'I got distinctions in all the practical subject, merits in food hygiene and food science.'

'Because you can't read and write,' shouts Harry. I throw a handy bread crust at him, setting up a cross-table war of bread balls, much to Robbie's delight.

'Stop that, you two,' says Mam, her face wreathed in smiles. 'Stop being a pain in the arse, you Harry. Let Danny show off a bit. Six distinctions, two merits and a distinction overall.' How does she know about the overall distinction? I never told her.

Abe brings in dessert. I know he's cheated, because he told me. Each base is a cut from an oblong cake he bought from the Co-op. On top's the same size oblong cut from a bar of Wall's vanilla ice cream, topped with chocolate shavings. The side's decorated with cut lychees and slices of the hand grenades, which he calls 'kiwi fruits'. All he did was slice the fruit and put it all together. There's a lighted candle atop each one. 'To celebrate the end of Daniel's year at college,' he announces.

'Fucking wog food again,' Dad grumbles. Harry turns up his eyes, Abe grins in amusement, everyone else looks embarrassed. Dad takes not a blind bit of notice. As if in retaliation Harry sneaks off to the coal hole, reappearing with more beer.

'Great,' says Gran, pouring a pint glass for herself and some water for Abe, 'helps me relax a little.' Mam looks like she's relaxing, too. She's shrinking before my eyes, getting smaller and more vacant, her eyes turned inward, fingers playing absently with her spoon, which is mashing the dessert to a pulp.

July

Harry leans over, grabs her hand. 'Gently now, Mam,' he says, taking the spoon from her hand. As if he's feeding Robbie, he coaxes morsels of cake and pools of dripping ice cream into her mouth. Slowly she returns, only for all the colour to leave her face, replaced by the sickly green we've learned to dread.

'Don't feel well,' she says. 'Have to go to bed. Lie down for a while.' She stands. Wobbles. Holds on to the chair back, looks longingly at the stairs, willing them to come to her so she doesn't have to negotiate the dangerous passage across the room. Harry takes her hand, wraps an arm round her waist. I realise how tiny she's become, smaller even than her scrawny thirteen-year-old younger son. Harry guides her upstairs, leaving us all silent and still, interrupted only by a loud belch from Dad.

'Better be well soon. Expecting a heavy night tonight. Any beer left?'

Robbie starts to whine. He's run out of wrapping paper. Salanne props him on her lap, persuades him what he really wants is a good pull at his milk bottle. Owen starts packing up to leave while I gather the dirty plates together. Dad filches another slice of kiwi fruit from Mam's leftovers.

'We'll do the dishes, love,' says Gran. Abe sighs, caught once again into doing women's work. By six, all's done and the visitors have departed, taking babies, chairs and extra plates and cutlery with them. Mam's still in bed. She's probably asleep by now even if Harry's persisting in telling her one of his adventure stories. Dad's changed into his barman's gear: white shirt, black tie, charcoal trousers and running shoes. 'No-one sees the shoes,' he says, 'and they're comfortable if you're on your feet all night. Where's your mam got to? We have to leave in ten minutes if I'm going to be on time for work. She has appointments tonight.'

'Come on, Dad,' I say. 'She's not in any fit state to go to work tonight. You saw what she was like.'

'I'm not having her skiving. No bastard trade union round here. Work is work. Who don't work, don't eat.' He eases himself off the sofa, farting loudly as he does so. 'Mother!' he shouts. 'Get yourself down here. You can put your face on at the Yarborough. Come on! Harry, get your mother moving.'

I'm amazed. Harry and Mam edge down the stairs together, holding on to one another like two drowning sailors. 'She's not fit, Dad,' says Harry. 'She can't go out in this condition.'

'Get out my fucking way.' Dad sweeps Harry aside, grabs Mam by the hair and lifts her up. 'What sort of wife are you? Love, honour and obey, you said. So, do what you are bloody well told. Put your shoes on. Danny, fetch your mother's coat.'

I stand immobile. Dad releases Mam's hair and she subsides onto the floor as if her hair was all that held her up. 'Lazy bitch,' screams Dad. 'Sunday night. Best night of the week. I've got customers waiting. Move your scrawny arse.' He drags Mam to her feet again. The moment he lets go she begins to collapse, saved only by Harry grabbing her round the waist. Dad tears at them, trying to force them apart. I crack him across the shoulder with my trusty frying pan, still wet from the washing-up. He lets go, turns on me.

'I'll kill you, you little bastard.'

'No chance,' I snarl. 'I'll get you first. Harry, hold the fort here while I fetch me knives.' Dad stands irresolute. He'd love to have a go at me but has felt my fury twice this year already. Can he take a chance of getting past the frying pan before I reach the kitchen and the filleting knife? Or should he grab Mam and make a run for it? In the end he does neither, deciding I'm too formidable and Mam too great an encumbrance. Cursing at the top of his voice he makes a clumsy exit, leaving the three of us to pick up the emotional wreckage.

Gran's on the doorstep first thing on Monday morning. 'Daniel, get your mother dressed. We're off to the doctor's.'

'Why have you brought your umbrella, Gran?' I ask on the way to the bus stop. 'It's late July, the sun's shining, not a cloud in the sky.'

July

'English summer, boy,' says Gran. 'You never can tell.' Mam says nothing. She seems better this morning, apart from the dark bags under her eyes.

Mrs Kirkwood's the conductor on the bus, moaning on to Gran about the introduction of the new one-man schedules. 'The union's no bloody good,' she says, the first time I've ever heard her swear. 'Give it five years and all on us will be out on our ears. At least Alex will be through university by then and I won't have him to worry about. Morning, love,' she says to Mam. 'Hear your lad's doing well for himself. Took up with Sylvie Robinson, too. Nice lass, that. You don't look too grand yourself.'

'Off to the doctors,' says Mam. 'Hope he'll give me something stronger than aspirin this time.'

'Doctor Bailey? Useless old fart. About time they pensioned him off. Good luck there, love.'

We get off in top town, change to a bus which takes us almost as far as the football ground. Funny this. I've almost forgotten about football since starting work at the Chink's. With Mam being ill I've even lost track of whether Town are in the First or the Fourth Division. They might be on their tenth manager and have eleven completely new players for all I know.

Doctor Bailey's surgery's a newish square brick and tile bungalow built just after the war, set among soot-streaked terraces. We sit in chairs ranged round the waiting room. As each patient is called through we move up one chair. Movement in is faster than movement out, until the latecomers are standing crushed against the door. The room's heavy with sweat, coughs and groans. Some of those standing by the door look like they'll fall down any minute but no-one's willing to give up a seat and lose their place in the queue.

As early arrivals we don't have to wait long. Our departure causes anger among some, irritated at us having taken up three seats for one patient, and relief among three others who can at last rest their weary legs. Neither the receptionist nor the doctor look pleased at seeing us enter mob-handed. Since there are only two chairs I position myself by the door to the receptionist's mini-office, like the 'minder' in some television drama. The surgery's almost as large as the waiting room. Doctor Bailey's seated behind a hefty, brown, old-fashioned desk, neatly laid out with notebook, stethoscope, prescription pad and a cut-glass ashtray containing a pile of paper clips. A battered brown envelope with Mam's medical records spills out its contents in front of him.

'And what seems to be the trouble this time, Mrs Morley?' he asks, an insincere smile on his face.

Mam sits silent. Gran does all the talking, enumerates Mam's problems: the months of recurrent headaches, which have been getting more intense and more frequent; the attacks of dizziness and irritability; a lack of spatial awareness, banging into things because she's misjudged the distance.

'Has she been taking the pills I prescribed?' Mam nods. 'Then there is little I can do. There comes a time in a woman's life when her hormones start to change, which is very disorientating. As a mature woman yourself, you must be well aware of the difficulties such a hormone change can cause. Together with a nervous disposition and an irregular mode of life they can cause a woman to be severely indisposed for some time.'

'She's not "indisposed", as you say,' growls Gran, her voice rising. 'She's bloody laid out. Flat on her back, banging her head against the wall because she can't stand the pain, burning herself on the cooker because she falls onto it in one of her dizzy spells. This isn't the change, or nerves, or earning her living on her back; this is being bloody ill!'

Gran's voice has risen to a shriek. The receptionist peeks her head round the door, unable to push past with my body in the way.

'Nothing can be done about it, madam,' says the doctor in his most unctuous voice. 'I have made my diagnosis and that is final. I shall write a prescription, then I would thank you to leave

July

the premises and not return until you are in a more polite and cooperative frame of mind.'

'Don't you get on your high horse with me, Willie Bailey. Refer her to someone else, to the hospital. I demand a second opinion!' Gran smashes the handle of her umbrella down on the desk, sending the ashtray spinning, spilling paper clips all over the carpet. She's on her feet, leaning across the desk, almost nose to nose with the doctor. I can hear the receptionist in the next room dialling 999 and asking for the police.

For a second, I think Doctor Bailey is either going to punch Gran on the nose or burst into tears. In the end he does neither. Gently he reaches across the desk for his notepad, writing some instructions on a piece of headed notepaper, which he places in an envelope, writing a name illegibly across the front.

'Take this to the hospital,' he says. 'They will arrange an appointment. In the meantime, I will have the whole family removed from my list, which is full enough as it is. Every single one of you will need to find a new doctor. Now, good day to you.'

I must admit, I admire his courage under pressure. Gran with a loaded umbrella is a formidable force, especially when backed up by a hairy, surly teenager from the wrong end of town. We make it onto the bus and away in time to pass the police car hurtling past in the other direction. 'Gave them what-for, eh, boy!' shouts Gran, loud enough for the whole bus to hear. 'Silly old fart. Knew him when he were a kid in short pants. He was useless then and he's useless now.'

By the time we change buses Mam's almost out on her feet, falling asleep on my shoulder. Passing the Gaumont cinema my thoughts turn to arranging a date with Sylvie and to what her dad had said about us. 'Gran,' I say. 'Are you really sleeping with Abe?'

'No, of course not,' she says. 'At my age? Well, not every night. You know me, I've always liked a bit of the exotic. Even your granddad was out of the ordinary, being from Louth and all. Seemed a good idea now we are business partners. He works the shop and I look after the waiters at the restaurant, then we can share the leftover meals with his brother. Saves money and I get a little bit of fun into the bargain.' I think again of Sylvie and why the whole world seems to be getting their end away, except for me.

Sharing food expenses seems a good idea, one I keep throwing at Dad. As far as he's concerned sharing means Harry and I do all the work, I buy and cook the meals, and he eats them whenever he can be bothered to turn up. I've instituted a strict regime. Supper's at five sharp. Whoever isn't there doesn't get any. Harry's religious in attendance, making sure Mam feeds herself properly or allows him to feed her during one of her bad patches. Gran helps from time to time; Dad turns up when he feels like it.

One thing he doesn't feel like doing is paying the rent or giving Mam any housekeeping. In the end I've been forced to go down the dole office and to the Council, talk them into the rent being taken out of his dole money alongside the gas and electric. Dad's furious but there's nothing he can do. A decent solicitor would tell him it's illegal but Dad doesn't know any solicitors, decent or otherwise. Two days at Chef's isn't enough to keep the four of us, so now I'm every evening and lunch time at Abe's brother's place. The brother's getting fat, since he has nothing to do except smile at the customers and pull back the chairs for the ladies. Me and the cooks see to things in the kitchen and Gran runs the front-of-house. A much more respectable family business than our old one.

There are three letters on what would be the doormat if we possessed such a thing. I open the large format one first. 'Can you read what it says?' asks Harry.

'Course I can,' I say. 'It says that Harold Morley is an impertinent, cheeky brat who is to be locked up in solitary confinement with no books to read for the next ten years.'

'Big words!' says Harry. 'Impertinent. Glad to see some of my genius is rubbing off. What is it, really?'

July

'My City and Guilds certificate,' I say. 'General Catering, with distinction. Not bad, eh?'

I'm bewildered. Harry gives me a hug. Must be going soft in his old age. The second's addressed to Mam, but I read it anyway. The address at the top's that of the local hospital, summoning Mam to a consultation in six weeks' time. Six weeks seems an awful long way ahead, but it's progress, I suppose. Six weeks is also mentioned in the third letter. Can I come down to London for a job interview? Second-class train fares will be paid. Strange, because I haven't applied for any jobs. I detect the hidden hand of Mr Berry. At first I think about turning it down, but the thought of a free day out in London's tempting, even if it means missing a day's pay.

'Harry,' I say, 'I need you to write me a letter in your best handwriting. By the way, where's Mam?'

'I'm not sure,' says Harry. 'She said something about going round to see Gran. Next thing I know she's disappeared. Gran will bring her home, I suppose.'

Harry and I sit down to compose a nice letter saying I would be delighted to attend for an interview on the day and time indicated in their missive and thank you for your kind attention. I'm wondering if I need take my whites and knives with me, but Harry says they would've mentioned it in their letter if I were required to do any practical work.

We're disputing the matter when interrupted by a loud banging on the front door. Can't be the Social, and the Jehovah's Witnesses wouldn't make so much din. Which only leaves one alternative. And it is indeed a copper giving us the benefit of his kind attentions. 'Mr Morley?' he enquires.

'I'm sorry, Officer. My father's out at the moment. How may I help you?' I'm amazed at how much I sound like Mam with her special business voice.

'Is Mrs Morley your mother?'

I nod.

'She's in hospital. She's had a bad fall and cut her head. Concussion, the doctor says. You need to come and look after her. Normally I'd tell you to take the bus, but since I've got to go back and book her, I might as well give you a lift.'

'Book her? What for?'

'Drunk and disorderly. Pretty disgusting, I call it. In such a state and it's not even lunch time yet. Well, I suppose you must be used to it. Can't see her lasting long if she goes on like this. In you pop. Your brother will be all right on his own?'

He might be new around here and look like he's not old enough to drive, but this cop is used to silent, resentful teenagers and doesn't expect me to answer or even thank him for the lift. He parks in a 'no parking' space and leads me through accident and emergency to one of the cubicles. Apart from a huge bandage swathing her head Mam looks better than she has for weeks.

'I should do this more often,' she says. 'If I smash me head on the pavement it completely takes the headache away. Perhaps I'll come back for another dose tomorrow.'

'Glad to hear it, Mam. Could have something to do with whatever they are pumping into you down the tube in your arm.'

'Yeah, it's good stuff. Much more of it and I think I'll fly all the way home.' Although he has his notebook open the copper's looking puzzled. A nurse leads him away to one of the reception desks, where they have an animated conversation in subdued tones.

'I'll not book your mother yet,' says the copper to me. 'I have to wait until the specialist arrives. One of the big consultants. Apparently there's some disagreement about whether your mother's drunk or not. I think it's pretty obvious but I can't go against medical opinion. You wait here while I go and get a cup of tea from the canteen. Don't go without telling me.'

Used to the habits of hospital consultants, he seems to expect to spend the rest of his duty shift hanging around here. A waste of time for an ordinary drunk and disorderly but there isn't much happening in town at this time of day except for kids riding their bikes on the pavement or tenants kicking up a fuss at the Council housing department.

As if to spoil the cop's day the consultant turns up out of the blue fifteen minutes later, probably before he's managed to do as much as order his first cup of tea. The consultant is Pakistani, exactly the same colour as Abe, with the same beaked nose. There the similarity ends. Mr Hasani consists of two globes, one on top of the other. His head looks like a muddy football topped with a sprinkling of white grass, while his body's a barrel encased in the best Harris tweed. Tiny spectacles hang down on a gold chain, connecting the two globes. He's well aware of his status but also of his foreignness and the anti-immigrant sentiment being whipped up by politicians and journalists. In compensation he's more English than the English, an aristocrat looking down on the serfs below.

That said, he's perfectly polite. '*Noblesse oblige*,' I suppose Gran and Harry would say. 'Good afternoon, Mrs Morley. You have made rather a mess of yourself, haven't you? Could we please disconnect Mrs Morley's drip? Thank you, Nurse. Now, I'd like you to do a few things for me. They may seem a trifle strange, but it is all for your own good. Now, if you stand up. Close your eyes.' Mam sways gently, smiles to herself.

'Very good. Open your eyes. Now stand on one leg. Hold it!' I catch Mam before she can fall. Mr Hasani nods at me approvingly. 'Very good. Now on the other leg.' Mam lasts longer this time, to my relief.

'Close your eyes again. Touch the tip of your nose with your right forefinger.' Mam's finger lands on her right cheekbone. 'Now with your left.' Which ends on her upper lip. 'Excellent. Open your eyes for a while or you will get dizzy and I do want you paying attention. Are you feeling all right?' Mam's green tinge is seeping out from her eyes. 'Only one more exercise and Nurse will reconnect your drip for you. If you will close your eyes again. Hold your arms out wide. Bring the end of each forefinger together right in front of your nose.' Mam's arms waver alarmingly as she brings them together with all the grace she can muster. The fingers miss one another by three inches or so and again I have to catch her as she totters.

'Well done, Mrs Morley,' Hasani concludes. 'Reconnection, please, Nurse. I'm afraid we will have to keep you here for a while longer. Cases of concussion are a tricky matter. Young man, it is best you go home for now. Come back tomorrow, normal visiting hours. Nurse, find the police officer for me, if you don't mind.'

Mam's picking up under the influence of her drip. She holds my hand and smiles. 'What's news?' she asks.

'Well, you have a hospital appointment in six weeks, but it looks like you've got that under control, as usual.' Mam laughs. 'Then, I've got my City and Guilds certificate.' She smiles, squeezes my hand tighter. 'And I have a job interview.'

'Not on the boats!' she snarls. 'Tell me you're not going on the boats.'

'Mam, I promise I'm never going to set foot on a trawler for the whole of my life. Interview's in London. I'll show you the letter when you come home.' She smiles again, renews the pressure on my hand. I smile back.

Consultant, nurse and policeman are in a confab over by the telephones. The cop's put away his notebook and is nodding vigorously at whatever Mr Hasani's telling him. The three finish their consultation, stroll back to Mam's bedside. 'Nurse will have you moved to a ward in a few minutes,' says the consultant. 'I will see you again in the morning.'

'Another man making promises and moving on,' says Mam sleepily.

'And I have to get back to the station,' says the copper.

'Can I have a lift?' I ask.

'Afraid not. You'll have to take the bus this time.'

July

Sleepy Mam may be but she's still a she-lion concerned with her young. 'He's had a bit of a shock, poor lad,' she says. 'Knocked him sideways, all this. I'm sure it wouldn't hurt if you took him home. He'd be ever so grateful; put in a word with his judo instructor, Inspector Finnegan, when he sees him next.'

The cop shakes his head dubiously, then beckons me to come with him. 'It's not what you know, it's who you know,' Mam whispers softly to me behind his back.

Me and Harry are back at the hospital at eleven next morning: spot on time for visiting hour. Since we don't know what ward Mam is in it takes us a while to find her. Instead of being in bed she's sitting in a comfy chair reading a five-year-old copy of *Woman's Own*.

'Amazing the things people do to their homes,' she says by way of greeting. 'You don't fancy papering the living room, do you, Danny?'

'Lovely to see you, too, Mam. How are they treating you?'

'Very nice. Clean sheets, proper armchair. Food's not up to much. You couldn't get your gran to bring in a nice lamb curry, could you? By the way, where is she?'

'Said she'd be in soon,' says Harry. 'Left her putting on her make-up. She'll be late for work, once she's out of here.'

'No problem,' says Mam. 'If you're screwing the boss, who cares if you're late for work now and again? Give me a hand up, Danny. I need to go for a walk. Can't stand those cardboard bed pans.' Mam's accident seems to have slowed her down. She shuffles to the toilet like an old lady, gripping the end of each bed as she goes but refusing any extra help from either of us. The ward sister stares at her anxiously, a warning having been issued about allowing this patient to wander off unattended. By the time we three return from the toilet Gran's arrived and taken over the armchair. 'Never mind,' says Mam, 'after all that exercise a bit of bed rest would be welcome.'

Childhood, Boyhood, Youth

We spend the rest of the hour complaining about Dad and trying to forecast how much longer Mam will be kept in. The ward sister scurries down between the beds, hurrying all the visitors away like a sheepdog harrying a recalcitrant flock. Gran disappears in a flounce of petticoats, leaving us to trail after her, heads down and grim.

'Mr Hasani would like a word with you,' says the ward sister, more in the tone of a command than a request. Even a 'thank you' from a consultant round here counts as a royal proclamation. She leads us into a narrow room, just four chairs and a window, where we wait until Mr Hasani rolls in, wiping perspiration from the back of his neck with a purple silk handkerchief.

'I should really be talking to your father,' he says, 'but I understand he is not available. Your mother seems to think you two are old enough and reliable enough to handle matters yourselves.' I hope I don't look as frightened as Harry.

'Your mother is very ill,' Mr Hasani continues. 'Her fall yesterday was not the cause but a symptom. Her GP should have referred her on to me months ago. I will have a word with the General Medical Council about that.' His brown face takes on a reddish tinge, one I've spotted in Abe on the few occasions when he gets angry. 'Be that as it may, we need to deal with the situation. I have booked Mrs Morley for surgery tomorrow. She has already signed the consent form and named you two as her next of kin, though technically it should be her husband.

'I will be carrying out a little exploratory operation. If the matter is as I suspect, we will need to move your mother to a larger, specialist hospital which can provide better facilities than we have here.' The sneer in his voice is obvious. 'All surgery carries some risks but your mother is a young, strong, determined woman and I am a very experienced surgeon, so you have no need to fear any untoward consequences. There will be no point in visiting tomorrow morning, when we will be carrying out preliminaries. Only you, Daniel, in the evening, if you don't mind. Have you any questions?'

July

Of course we do, thousands of them, like what's actually wrong with Mam, but Mr Hasani isn't prepared to tell us any more than he's already said, so all we get is bland reassurances. Harry's in tears. I'm not much better. If Mam is young and determined, so am I. We're going to leave here in one piece. All three of us.

Next evening, I'm back in the ward. Mam's bed is empty. There's a different ward sister, a brunette in her early twenties. Only about five feet tall, she's still a commanding presence, ordering around patients and visitors alike. 'Your mother's in post-op,' she says. 'She'll be back on the ward in ten minutes or so.' Normally I'd ask her for a date despite her age and even now I have to fight down the urge to give her a big kiss.

Ten minutes can pass quickly when there's a hustle and bustle around; new visitors arriving and old ones shuffling out, glum or happy depending on the day's news. Mam's wheeled back on a trolley, her face a death mask swathed in bandages. Two attendants help the sister transfer her into bed. 'I'm thirsty,' whispers Mam. 'I need a drink.'

'What do you want, Mam?' I ask stupidly.

'A gin. No lemon, just gin.'

'Try this,' says the sister, passing me a plastic cup full of water, which I hold to Mam's lips.

'Good boy, Danny,' whispers Mam before closing her eyes and drifting off out of hearing. I sit around her bedside until the end of the visiting hour, the sister allowing me to be the last to leave.

'Come in half an hour early tomorrow,' she says as I pass the nurses' station. 'Mr Hasani will be completing his rounds then and he'll have time for a quick word.'

Our family prefers to accost doctors mob-handed. Me, Gran and Harry are there together next day waiting for Mr Hasani. He doesn't beat about the bush. 'Just as I feared,' he says, 'Mrs Morley is grievously ill. There is no more I can do for her here. We will keep her a day or two in order for her to recover from the operation, then move her on to a specialist hospital. She may be there some time.' Again, evasive answers to our pointed questions, even Gran's abrasive approach failing to disturb Mr Hasani's equanimity.

Despite the grim news I'm relieved to see how much better Mam looks this morning. There's colour in her cheeks and she's managed to scrape on a smudge or two of lipstick, which Gran rubs off and re-applies for her. Her old friend the plastic tube is back embedded in the left arm. The bandages have been re-wrapped, clean ones substituted for the blood-stained products of the operating theatre. One side of her head looks larger than the other, as if part of a rugby ball is hidden beneath the bandages. Wadding and packing around the stitches, I assume.

'Terrific man, that Hasani,' she says. 'Couple of hours fiddling about and I'm as right as rain. Not up to walking yet but I'll be back home before the week's out.'

''fraid not, Mam,' I say. 'They're shipping you out somewhere else. Seems like you're such a tough old bird they need to have another go at you. Hasani reckons you've tired him out.'

'Won't be the first time a man has made me a complaint like that. When do I go?' Mam's mood has shifted and the visit ends on a sour note, complaining yet again about Dad, informing Harry his clothes are not clean and me that I need a haircut.

Home's no better. Dad puts in an appearance once or twice, asks about Mam then swans off out again. Harry takes his books to Gran's, comes home to sleep and eat before disappearing. I'm at work every evening bar Sunday and lunch times after visiting hours. Now and then I go round Salanne's to look after Robbie while she takes her turn at the hospital. In the end it's a good week before Mam's deemed fit enough to make the eighty-mile round trip to the Royal Infirmary.

August

'I might not be here next Sunday,' says Sylvie, easing herself over across the bed so I can stroke her thighs with greater ease. Sylvie's thighs are round and plump, pitted with craters the size of a penny piece, the result, she says, of having lost so much weight living with her gran in Gainsborough. According to her, they will fill up when she gets back to her normal size, which looks to be immense if her current plumpness is anything to go by. Her weight loss has also destroyed the function of one of her ovaries completely.

'So, you only have half as much chance of getting pregnant,' I say to her.

'Don't be daft. We have two of almost everything so if one ceases to function the other one operates just as well. Losing one eye doesn't make you blind. My one ovary works perfectly well, as you can tell every month.'

It was worth the try. One day I'll find out what works on Sylvie. Problem is, she's too many cautionary tales to tell. 'You know Nicky's got herself knocked up?' she asks. 'Your mate Wayne. She'll tell him when he gets out. He got her so pissed one night she didn't know what she was doing.'

I'm not surprised; he's got not morals, Nosey. 'What's he in for this time? Cars again, I suppose?'

'Nicked an E-type Jaguar. Tried to do a ton in it on the Caistor road. More bends there than there is road, rolled the car over into a field. Broke his collar bone and three of his fingers. Good job he had the top off. He was thrown out and landed in a hedge, otherwise the steering wheel would have gone straight through him.'

'Why won't you be here next Sunday?' I ask at last, having moved my hand further up as she was talking.

'Got an appointment in Birmingham. May not come back. You never know, this might be the last time we see each other.'

'A good reason to—'

'An even better reason not to. Stuck in digs in Birmingham with a grizzling brat and no job. Don't see you moving your arse and coming to look after me. You'll be too busy running Abe's country-wide chain of curry houses.'

I don't tell her Abe seems to have cooled down on engaging me as his local manager. Gran's flavour of the month at the moment. Must say, she does an excellent job of running the one in town, freeing up his brother to start a new restaurant in Lincoln. Our gran will be prime minister before we know it. If Sylvie is moving to Birmingham, I need to find a replacement.

Except I can't be bothered and I don't have time. I'm working a fifty-hour week as well as looking after the house and worrying about Mam. Why go to all the trouble just for a quick cuddle on a Sunday night? I'd be better off washing and ironing a few shirts.

Mam's been in the Royal Infirmary for almost a fortnight and none of us have got round to visiting her yet. The hospital's eighty miles away and those eighty miles present us with a real problem. On a straight road the distance itself is difficult, but it involves forty miles due west, then another forty miles due east in order to get round the estuary. Forty's our unlucky number. It's forty years since the government promised us a new bridge over the river to cut the journey down to a meagre fifteen miles. Probably another forty before it gets built, if ever.

August

I've been studying maps and tide tables like a general embarking on a campaign. 'Next Thursday,' I say to Harry. 'Clean shirt, best trousers, polished shoes. Take a jacket just in case you need it for the ferry.'

'What about food?' he asks.

'We'll get some at the bus station.'

Big mistake. The first bus goes as far as Goole, stopping in every tiny village on the way. Two hours of misery on hard seats. Midday in Goole bus station, a chilly wind already blowing in from the north. We have an hour to wait so we head for the snack bar. Typical snack-bar rubbish. I buy a ham sandwich and cover it in mustard to give it some taste, washing it down with orangeade, more fizz than orange. Harry plays it safe with a cheese sandwich, one of those processed slices which come in catering packs, with a dollop of brown sauce on top. And a Coke. All the kids at school drink Coke. Harry loves it as much for being one of the crowd as for its taste.

Another punishing trip on a bus which might be a clone of the one we got off earlier but even slower, stopping at what look like they might be the same remote villages, taking nearly three hours on country roads.

'Even you must have heard of the wily Odysseus,' begins Harry, *'who was smuggled into Troy inside a wooden horse. But no-one except me knows about his friend Demetrios. On the night before the Greeks were due to leave Troy the goddess Athene came to him in a dream. "Odysseus will not reach home for another ten years," she said. "He has annoyed the Gods too much. He will meet all kinds of delays and setback before he finds Penelope again. Frustrating and painful for him, but worse still for his crew, none of whom will survive. They will all be drowned, shipwrecked or eaten by monsters. Because your mother has sacrificed a small lamb to me I bring you this warning so you may be on the beach at Ithaca to welcome Odysseus home."*

'Whether it was the dream or the amount of wine he had drunk the night before, by the time Demetrios got down to the shore the next

day Odysseus's ship had already sailed. "A good job, too," he thought, "if what the goddess told me is true." Despite having one leg shorter than the other, Demetrios was a great swimmer. He determined he would swim across the Hellespont to Thrace and make his way on foot through the forests of the Strandja until he finally reached Ithaca.

'For a while all went well, until Neptune awoke from a heavy sleep. Neptune, too, had eaten and drunk deeply the night before and consequently was in a bad mood. He tossed and turned, raged at his servants, ejected the mermaids from his bed and went roaring round his palace. The seas boiled and trembled with his rage, sending up huge waves and irresistible currents.

'Demetrios was swept off course. All he could do was try to keep afloat. At last a particularly huge wave dumped him on a narrow shore. All before him stood vertical cliffs, pock marked with caves and overhangs. Behind him the storm still raged. Exhausted, he crawled up the beach and into the largest of the caves, where he fell into a weary sleep.

'When he awoke he was surrounded by what seemed to be hyenas. True, they stood on two legs, had arms with fingers at the end and shouted to one another in a heavily accented Greek, but their heads were those of hyenas, with long pointed noses and dripping yellow fangs. Should he fling himself once more into the still-raging sea?

'"Come with us," growled the largest of the hyenas. "Our lord must decide what is to be done with you." Demetrios was surrounded and led away along the shore.

'The hyena lord rested on a bed of fragrant dried seaweed laid on a wave-cut shelf on a promontory by the sea. "From the remnants of your clothes and by your speech I see you are a Greek," said the lord. "And by your scars that you are a great warrior. I have need of a great warrior. You may stay here and rest for as long as you wish, but I have a task for you before you can leave. To aid you on your way I will supply you with a boat and a crew, who will row you all the way to Ithaca, be it ever so far away.

August

'"I have six beautiful daughters, all of whom wish for a husband. You cannot, of course, marry all of them, but you must choose one to become your mate. Once you have done that you will be free to return with her to your homeland."

'Demetrios bowed to the lord, thanking him for his kind offer. The lord waved his hand and six maidens trooped in from behind a nearby rock fall. Each one was tall and slender with rounded hips, sharp pointed breasts and narrow waists. But they were all hyenas! Their eyes were red and slanted, their snouts ended in black, blunt nostrils, their ears stood up in brown hairy tufts. Although he could clearly see their desirable bodies, each was still covered in coarse, black hair like that on an orchard pig. Moreover, their bodies were the colour of rotting lemons, here and there stained with the juice of stale pomegranates. Each finger and toe ended in black nails which curved over like the spikes on an iron grapnel. He had never seen anything so ugly in his life.

'That night he was taken to a cave, newly fitted with fresh, clean seaweed bedding, a jug in which to wash himself and a goatskin full of deep red wine. As he drifted off to sleep, lulled by the conversation of the guards outside and the fumes of the wine he considered how he might escape. At midnight he was awoken by the eldest of the lord's daughters. She sniffed at his body cavities before licking him all over with her rough tongue, poking at him with her cold nose, finally rubbing herself up against him until he could feel his skin trembling under the roughness of the hairs on her breasts. As dawn broke, she left him. Not before squatting at the entrance to the cave and pissing a great stream its whole width.

'Next night, the second daughter arrived and repeated the process. Then the next and the next until all six had made their visit and left their proprietorial piss at the entrance to the cave.

'"Which one of my daughters have you chosen?" demanded the lord on the seventh day.

'"My lord, they are all so beautiful and talented I am unable to make a choice. Please give me more time." Time which Demetrios

Childhood, Boyhood, Youth

wanted to use to find a method of escape. But Demetrios was a warrior and nowhere as wily as Odysseus. Besides, being licked all over and rubbed against by six beautiful bodies, however strange their heads, is easy to get used to.

'*Nine years passed and Demetrios began more and more to dream of home. His body was covered with sores from so much licking, the cave smelled of piss and he was tired of offerings of raw haunches of venison and unskinned rabbits from his enamoured harem. The girls themselves were getting older, their fangs longer and yellower, their breasts beginning to sag, the hair on their bodies, longer, thicker and coarser. He must make his escape, be there in Ithaca to welcome Odysseus when he returned from his travels.*

'*It was the dead of winter, when the nights are colder and longer. His guards had grown old and bored with their duty and lay outside, asleep, wrapped in deerskin cloaks. Demetrios had not forgotten his warrior skills. The moment night fell he crept out of his cave and strangled both of them as they slept. Silently, he made his way along the beach, following the great north star which pointed his way home. For leagues and leagues he tramped until at last the beach ended in a vertiginous outcrop thrown up by some angry giant in the years before men. No point in trying to go inland from here. He would swim, guided by the star, and so reach home.*

'*Behind he heard strange noises. Not feet. Sniffing. Snuffling. He turned. All six of the lord's daughters stared at him in the moonlight, their fangs dripping. Demetrios turned to fling himself into the sea. Immediately the women were upon him, tearing and biting his diseased flesh, gnawing away at his bones. By morning all that was left was a chewed carcass, which the lord ordered thrown into the sea.*

'*A year later the battle-scarred Odysseus landed on a beach in Ithaca, kicking aside the bones which were scattered on the shore, unaware they were those of his friend Demetrios welcoming him home.*'

An old lady in the seat across the aisle stared at us, her mouth open. She twisted a dirty lace handkerchief between her fingers.

'We change buses here,' I say. 'The local one this time. No more stories.'

Into the town bus station at last, to pile into yet another bus which takes us out to the Royal Infirmary. We're already forty minutes into the visiting hour, many of the other visitors making ready to leave, having run out of conversation.

Mam's walking about chatting to some of the other patients, ones who, like her, don't receive visitors of their own. 'You two took your time,' she says. 'Only fifteen minutes from here to home as the crow flies.'

'We're not bleeding crows, Mam,' says Harry, flinging his arms round her waist. Like everything else her waist has filled out. Rubbish hospital food, but regular and forced down her throat when she doesn't want to eat. The ward sister looks like Hattie Jacques from the *Carry On* films, built like a barn door with melons for tits. Bet even the consultants are afraid of her. Mam's head has grown as well. She no longer sports rolls of bandages but instead has a stretchy cap like the support stockings Gran has taken to wearing now she's on her feet all day. The rugby ball on the side of her head has been inflated, giving her face a lopsided appearance and half-closing one eye.

'You ought to have told me you were coming and I'd have put some make-up on. Like to be seen at me best by me boys.'

'You look lovely, Mam,' says Harry, tears streaming down his face. 'When are you coming home?'

Mam can be aggressive, violent, positive, autocratic, but she's a terrible liar. 'Only a few days,' she says. 'A couple more days, perhaps another operation, and I'll be out of here.'

We talk about inconsequential things, as people do in hospital, skirting around the important issues. Hattie Jacques comes round to throw us out even before we've sat down on Mam's bed. I lead her aside, explain it's taken over six hours to get here and how we won't be able to get back up for maybe another fortnight. 'All right,' she says. 'Another half-hour. The neurology houseman will be available then and you can have a word or two with him.'

'What's neurology?' I ask Harry.

'Brain surgeon,' he says.

'Thank God,' I say, looking at Mam. 'I thought it was cancer.'

The houseman's late arriving, which gives us an extra half-hour with Mam. She seems more worried about us and Gran than curious about her own condition. We kiss her goodbye, carefully avoiding what she calls her 'nightcap', anxious not to reveal whatever horror may lie underneath.

Doctor Roberts is old to be a houseman. I guess there's only room for one consultant at a time and he has to wait for the current one to die or retire before he can step into his shoes. A typical Yorkshireman, he's not one to mince his words.

'Your mother is very ill. We've done almost everything we can for her. Now she's in better shape physically" – he glowers at us meaningfully, as if to imply we have not been looking after her properly – "we will try surgery once more. I have to tell you, the chances are not good. Whatever happens, we will need to keep her here for a couple of weeks. Then she will be released home to recuperate. Social Services will be in touch with you so arrangements can be made. Have you any questions? Good.' He rushes off, white gown flowing behind him.

'Is that good news or bad news?' Harry asks. 'Why does no-one ever tell us what's wrong?'

'I'm not sure. Depends on the op, I suppose. At least Mam's coming home soon.'

We have to hurry to catch the bus to the docks. Ferries only run at high tide, which waits for no man. Me and Harry are the last ones on the last ferry of the day, happy to hang over the side watching the clouds roll in off the North Sea, the antiquated paddles of our steamer churning up the muddy waters of the estuary. Gulls are wheeling in with the clouds, happy to escape

August

the approaching bad weather, sliding behind the ferry in the hope of the odd discarded sandwich. Off the ferry on the other side and half an hour on the bus to home. Six hours out, ninety minutes home. The promised new bridge can't arrive soon enough.

The lights are on in the house. Can't be Gran; she'll be bossing the waiters around at Abe's. Salanne will be putting Robbie to bed. Of all people it's Debbie Marchant sitting there in our living room destroying a friend's character, talking with Lily Jeavons. Lily was in the year behind me at school. Pretty enough, but with a mouth like a sewer. Today she looks smart in a pencil skirt and light floral blouse, her face made up in what Mam would call 'respectable office girl' style. Her language seems to have moderated, too, the swear words only there 'when they slip out'. She's been coached, probably by the same person who's turned around the sluttish Debbie.

'What's going on?' I ask. 'What are you two doing here?'

'Your dad asked us to come over,' says Debbie, looking at me under eyelashes nearly an inch long. 'He's more business than he can cope with. Asked us to bring a friend to help him out.'

There's a regular thumping sound from upstairs. 'What's that?' asks Harry, who should really know better.

'Your dad's auditioning.' Lily giggles. 'Part of the job interview. If she's suitable, she can start with us on Saturday night. Big party Saturday night down at the Yarborough. Lots of work for us girls. Your dad set it up. A regular function from now on, he reckons. Perhaps even carry on here afterwards.'

I'm silent. Debbie and Lily chatter on to the background sound of Dad grinding away upstairs and Radio Caroline on Lily's transistor radio. Harry curls up into a ball on the sofa, hugging his knees, face turned to the wall. Eventually, another girl flips her way down the stairs, red in the face, lipstick awry, pulling at strands of hair which will not stay in her hastily arranged bun. She looks at us in surprise, smiles and nods at Debbie and Lily before picking up a light jacket from the back of one of the kitchen chairs.

'Straight down the pub,' sings out Lily. The three of them march out the front door, completely ignoring me and Harry, and leaving it wide open behind them. With luck the bad weather blowing in from the north will soak them well before they reach the pub.

I fetch two chairs and my box of knives from the kitchen. I lay them out on the table: the little paring knife, good for taking the eyes out of potatoes; the filleting knife, already well worn from shoals of fish; the long boning knife for extracting every last sliver of meat; the long carving knife for roast beef and chicken; the heavy-duty chopping knife which will take all but the heaviest bones in its stride; the cleaver, ready to crush marrow bones or slice a chicken into quarters. Next to them I lay an old-fashioned whetstone, looking at it with approval. To pass the time I sharpen the knives one by one.

Dad comes downstairs at last. Looks at Harry still lying on the sofa. Looks at my knives. Looks at me. 'Sit down, Dad,' I say. 'Let's have a nice chat.'

He pulls back the chair, as far from the table as it will go. Sits. Looks at me nervously.

'Me and Harry went to visit Mam today. All day, it took us. Before you ask, I can tell you she's looking well. She'll be having another operation soon and will be back home in another fortnight or so. I'm sure you'll be glad to see her.' He looks like I've just forced him to suck on a lemon. 'Now, Dad, I know you've got a business to run. We've spent a pleasant half an hour talking to two of your employees. Charming girls and I'm sure they'll do you proud.'

I pick up the boning knife. I have a certain affiliation with the boning knife. Its purpose is clear, its design obvious and to the point. Carelessly I draw a line across the table, one which will blend in with the rest after a few days but which stands out now white and sharp as a whiplash. 'Harry's a bit upset at the moment, having had a hard day and coming back to find you auditioning in Mam's bed. Like me, he doesn't find it appropriate for you to be conducting your business from the house in any shape or form. Even less so when Mam gets home. You also have to remember Harry's only thirteen. Any "untoward incident" or hints of this house being an unsafe environment for him and Social Services will drag him off to a home first and ask questions afterwards. He wouldn't like that. I would be very angry and couldn't answer for my actions in the event of such a calamity.' I gouge a hole in the tabletop, draw five short lines spreading out from it like a wooden sun at the end of the universe.

'Since I left college I keep my knives here at home with me, ready to be used for anything which needs carving. They're very sharp and I'm very skilful.' A vision of Mr Hasani pops momentarily into my head. 'You're always welcome here,' I say. 'After all, it is your home and you pay the rent. But if your business or any of your employees come anywhere near this house my knives will find some extra work besides filleting fish or carving up a leg of lamb.' I look pointedly at his leg, his arm, his neck.

Dad's turned a strange colour, a chalk white with an undertone of magenta. His eyes seem to have changed from their normal dark brown to a bilious green. 'You vicious little brat. I'll get you yet. Make sure you lock your bedroom door at night. I'll have your bollocks off for this. Got no use for them anyway, bloody nancy boy.'

He makes a theatrical exit, making as much noise and fuss as possible, slamming the front door in an attempt to smash the glass in his temper.

'Nice one,' says Harry. 'Pity he's not gone for good.'

Two weeks later and Mam's back from the Royal Infirmary. Gran's made up the sofa in the living room into what she calls a 'day bed'. We all know Mam will not move far from it, day or night. Owen's rigged up an old workers' toilet outside the coal hole so Mam doesn't have to trail upstairs or use the cardboard bed pans the ambulance crew have left behind. I have her pills stashed in the kitchen cupboard, especially the pale yellow ones, to be administered religiously every four hours. Mam gets twitchy around the end of the third hour, anxious in case the 'yellow perils' are forgotten. Harry washes her hands and face every morning and evening. Only Gran's permitted to wash the rest of her, including her head, a duty from which Gran emerges showing every part of her fifty-eight years.

'I have a job interview tomorrow, Mam,' I tell her. 'Down in London. I'll be back by bedtime.'

'A good job? Not on the boats?'

'I've told you, Mam. I'm never going to set foot on a trawler if I live to be a thousand.'

'I know, don't keep on about it. Good luck with the interview. You're a good lad, Danny, even if a little too handy with those knives of yourn. Come back, though, won't you? You won't abandon me?'

As if I would do any such thing.

To my surprise, the interview's great fun. The building on the Thames is very impressive; less so Mr Saunders, who I recognise as one of Mr Berry's coterie at the college lunch. Only just, because Mr Saunders is totally insignificant, a small grey man in a small grey suit, the sort of man who could be at a gathering of four and five and who you will have totally forgotten he'd been there ten minutes later. What he lacks in appearance he makes up for in jollity. We spend the first few minutes rubbishing Fanny Cradock, the next few in mutual praise of Elizabeth David. 'Why did you use pollock for your meal instead of a nice bit of cod? Whose idea was it to add the sliced olives? Who told you about fenugreek?'

I explain pollock was all there was to be had from the docks that morning, then tell him all about Chef and Abe, how I watch what goes on in their restaurants then use it to experiment on the family. 'You work long hours?' he asks.

August

'About fifty a week, I suppose, now college is finished. I'll have to cut down to look after Mam when Harry goes back to school.'

'Could be a problem there,' says Mr Saunders. 'Never mind, we'll work something out somehow. Anyway, all very impressive, Daniel. I cannot add anything for now. I have to discuss matters with the personnel director, but you will be receiving a letter in a week or so's time. Remember, any position we offer you will be no higher on the ladder than the one you have at the Chinese restaurant or the curry house, but a smart lad like you will easily work his way up to better things. Whatever happens, you have a good career in the industry ahead of you. Keep clear of the police and don't do anything stupid.' He shakes my hand and escorts me to the door, smiles me on my way. By the time I reach Buckingham Palace I've totally forgotten what he looks like.

There's plenty of time before my train for me to take in Piccadilly, Oxford Street and Trafalgar Square. Wouldn't want to work here: too busy, too crowded. One last visit. The Houses of Parliament or the Tower? Has to be the Tower, chopped heads far more interesting than chopped words. Where I go next in life is a far more difficult problem.

Mam's still awake when I get home, only fifteen minutes into one of her yellow perils. 'How did it go, then?' she asks. 'Did you get the job? Are you going to take it?'

'I won't know for some time. Perhaps ages yet. I'm not sure I want it if they give it me. It may mean having to leave you, Mam, and I don't want to do that.'

'Don't you worry about me. I'm old enough to look after meself. Here, help me to the bog, will you?'

Who does she think she's kidding? 'Look after herself' when she can't even get to the toilet on her own. She's getting forgetful as well, surprised one day to find Salanne's around when she thought she was still in Care, trying to send Harry off to school on a Sunday in the middle of the school holidays. 'Weekends and holidays mean nothing to me nowadays,' she says. 'Every day's the same. Here, Harry, come and tell me a story.'

Friends and neighbours come and go. The ladies from the church, a church none of us has ever set foot in, turn up with a large basket of fruit. Maisie Kirkwood arrives still in conductor's uniform to complain how Alex has turned wild, started drinking and staying out late with his mates. 'At least he isn't smoking,' says Mrs K, who always stinks of cigarette smoke herself. Didi Moffatt has all the gossip and Sylvie's mam comes to ask when I'm going to marry her daughter and prevent her swanning off to the flesh pots of Birmingham.

Mam's delighted to be the centre of attention, perks up with every visitor like a young girl being courted by the most handsome young men in town. Each one tires her visibly, the conversations become progressively shorter. Me and Harry have come to an agreement and the yellow perils are now administered every three and a half hours.

My letter arrives at last. 'We are pleased to offer you... We would be obliged if you were to respond to this offer within the next fourteen days.'

'What's up with you?' demands Mam. 'You look like you've lost a pound and found a penny.'

'It's this job, Mam. They say I have to accept it by the week after next and I don't know what to do. I can't go away and leave you on your own.'

'I won't be on my own. Your dad's here, and Gran. Harry's around to tell me stories after school. Salanne and Owen and Robbie. A proper little band of carers all to myself.'

It's not enough and we both know it. Our arrangement only works because I'm here at the centre, making sure Mam has her pills at regular intervals, seeing she always has someone to take her to the toilet. Stopping Dad from dragging his tarts home. I go in search of Harry. He needs to write me a nice letter saying I'm flattered by the offer of the position but that family circumstances mean I must decline. But please keep my details on file for such time as my circumstances change. I'm certain the company won't.

Saturday morning, I'm wiped out. The lads from the grammar school got their A-level results yesterday. To celebrate they booked four tables at Chef's, eating vast amounts and trying to drink the place dry. I didn't get away until gone two, arriving home in time to take Mam to the toilet and make sure she has taken her midnight pill. Harry leaves out two pills and two glasses of water on her bedside table, one we picked up cheap from a junk shop, on which to keep her midnight and four in the morning pills.

Nearly nine by the time I'm up, Harry still curled round his pillow next door snoring his head off. Downstairs, Mam's sitting up on the sofa, fast asleep. Somehow she's got up during the night, dragged herself into the kitchen and pulled out all her pills from the kitchen cabinet. They're carefully laid out in front of her: the blue ones to keep her regular, the white ones in case she has a fit, the dark red one full of essential vitamins and the four bottles containing the yellow perils. The bottles for the yellow perils are empty, all four of them. I'm sure I brought the prescription from the chemist only on Thursday. Both glasses of water are empty, one of them lying on its side on the floor.

I ease Mam back into her bed before she can catch cold. She slumps back, rigid. She is not asleep.

Breathe.

I sit down beside her, hold her ice-cold hand until Harry comes down around midday. He goes off to fetch Gran.

I make us lunch.

The funeral's at the crematorium, wedged between Harry's school and the railway line. There must be a hundred people here. Few of them are respectable: Mrs Kirkwood, with Alex and Janet in tow; Sylvie with her mam, but not her dad; the publican from the Victoria; Inspector Finnegan, to my surprise. Perhaps he'd been

Childhood, Boyhood, Youth

one of her regulars? And the rest, ladies who don't look their best in the cold light of day, now in flat shoes and plastic macs against the drizzling rain.

We've supplied the vicar with a couple of paragraphs about what a wonderful mother and grandmother Mam was, which he reads almost word for word, making it obvious he never knew the deceased and can't believe such a paragon of domestic virtue ever existed. There is much annoyed muttering among the less respectable parts of the congregation. Few sing along with the hymns, knowing neither words nor melody. Only 'Abide with Me' raises any semblance of enthusiasm.

Dad goes home in the funeral car. 'Got to get me money's worth,' he says. Not his money: mine and Gran's and Salanne's. Sylvie walks home with me. 'I really am off this time,' she says. 'All fixed up, sharing a flat in Smethwick with another girl from the salon. She's black, but I don't care as long as she's clean and doesn't smoke in the house. I'll miss you, Danny, but you'll be off yourself soon.' I'll miss her, too. Not got so many friends I can afford to lose yet another one.

I still have the job letter sitting under my vests at home. Four days yet before the fortnight expires. Mam's gone but Harry still remains to be taken care of. Time enough yet to come to a decision.

Gran's arranged the wake at home, moving the kitchen table into the living room and laying it with an assortment of cakes and sandwiches. Abe's supplied triangular pastries full of curried vegetables, which go down a treat. Even Dad's chipped in, a crate of Hewitt's best bitter, available for all who wish to fill themselves with gas and alcohol. Me and Harry stick to Coke, Abe to water and Gran to a bottle of what I can only assume is gin. Owen's a beer man. He takes me aside while Dad talks in a loud voice about how wonderful Mam was.

'Salanne and I are moving,' he says. 'Now your mam's gone, she's given in at last. Off to Coventry. There is a new Kawasaki dealership opening there and they want mechanics. Twice what I'm making here and maybe a part-time secretarial job for Sal as well, if she doesn't decide she wants another little 'un.' He smiles at the thought. Naturally, I congratulate him. Good to see at least one member of the family bettering himself. How soon before my pool of friends empties completely? Salanne sees us together and wanders over, leaving Robbie to jump up and down on Harry's stomach as they roll on the floor together. She gives me a hug and leads Owen away to Harry's rescue.

Thursday afternoon and I'm home for a rest between shifts at the curry house. The house has a strangely familiar air to it, which confuses me. Lying down on the sofa in the living room, now cleared from Mam's bedding, I'm drifting off to sleep when I pick up on the background sound of our old radio gently crackling away, un-tuned to any of the usual channels. Harry must have left it on after trying to find Radio Luxembourg or Radio Caroline.

'You're the culprit,' I say to him as he comes in the door, laden with parcels. 'Left the radio on again in a hurry to dive out to the shops and spend money we don't have.'

'Not me, your lordship. I'm innocent. Never touched the radio. Look what I've got. New blazer for next term, new school tie, proper regulation trousers and, best of all, brand-new shoes. Not ones which have had your sweaty feet in them for the last two years.'

'Where'd you get the money for that lot?'

'From Gran.' Harry looks sheepish. 'Hope you don't mind. Gran pulled out all Mam's old clothes, sold them to a feller she knows down the market. He was proper tight, but you know Gran, not to be outdone by no-one.'

'Anybody,' I say. 'Get you back to school soon and sort out your English. No point in having Mam's old clothes hanging about. What would we do with them? Knowing Dad, he'd just throw them in the bin.'

Talk of the devil, here's Dad now, carrying a small suitcase, Debbie Marchant in tow. 'Deborah's moving in with me,' he says. 'It's my house, I say who lives here. Any shit from you, Danny, and I'll have the police round in an instant and Harry carted off by the Social at the same time.'

My knives are locked away upstairs and Dad for all his fat is still three stone heavier than me. Harry's no good in a fight, a fly against an elephant.

Breathe.

Count to ten.

Consider.

All Dad has to do is phone up Social Services and tell them that, with his wife dead, he can no longer look after his children. Can they come and take them away?

Debbie plonks her suitcase down at the foot of the stairs. Turns round, tunes the radio. 'Dock gates open sixteen hundred. Arrival times required for those wishing to book berths.' The fleet's on its way.

'Don't do anything stupid,' Harry says to me. 'I've gone to pack.'

'Take your time,' I say to him. 'I need you to write me a letter.'

On the way round to Gran's I tear up the old letter and shove it into a waste-paper bin at the bus stop on top of the fag ends and green spittle. We stop off at Kirkwood's newsagents for me to buy a stamp before posting the new letter in the box on the corner.

'What are you going to do?' I ask Harry.

'Nothing much. Move in with Gran and Abe. They've got a spare room and Abe can help me with my maths.'

'So, what do we tell Social Services?'

'Bugger all. As far as they're concerned I'm still living at home but I'm very attached to my old gran, so I spend a lot of time looking after her.'

'And Abe?'

'He's her lodger. Which makes me a kind of chaperone. When will you be back?'

'No idea. Three weeks, maybe four. I ship out on Sunday.'

As it is, I only get a reply from P&O on Monday, so it's not until Tuesday that I find myself in a smelly two-carriage diesel train crawling over the Pennines on the way to Liverpool. Kitchen assistant on a cruise liner. Hardly the Ritz, is it? 'But not a trawler, Mam,' I say under my breath. 'Not a trawler; not in a thousand years.' Abe's rescued my best kitchen equipment and set me up in his flat over the shop for my return. The train's slow and hot, the steady clickety-clack of the wheels on the rails soporific.

Is it a dream or a memory? Harry is sitting on the floor next to Mam's bed finishing off his story.

'The boys pulled themselves up the beach, soaking wet. They lay resting a while, allowing the rising sun to dry them off.

'"Do you have the map?"

'"Of course I have the map. Here it is." He pulled out the map, wrapped in its deerskin cover, from the waist band of his trousers. "Assuming we have landed on the right island for a change, the treasure should be over there, buried beneath those three trees."

'"There should be four trees."

'"Never mind. Look, here is a tree stump. One of them must have been blown down in a storm. Help me dig."

'The boys scrabbled away with their hands, easily turning over the light sandy soil.

'"I see it! Look, here it is!"

'Together they eased the sand away from the old wooden chest, even larger than they had hoped. It was difficult to move but they hauled and pulled at it until it stood in all its glory under the trees. It was locked!

'"We don't have a key. How do we get into it?"

'They pulled at the metal lock, trying to force it open. For nearly an hour they tugged and tugged, to no avail. Both of the boys were in tears when one last concerted effort failed to tear the lock apart but instead detached it completely from the rotting wood of the chest.

'Delighted, they lifted the heavy lid, thrust their arms inside in search of the treasure they had fought so long to find. What was in it? Nothing but old pots and pans, rusting through and useless. "Rubbish!" they cried. "Nothing but rubbish! After all our effort and suffering. Just useless rubbish."'